THE BEOWULF MURDERS

A Warne and Elias Adventure

Will Adams

ISBN: 9798327729957

Cover design by Victoria Barbera

*To my friend Clive Pearson, who – even more than
is usually the case – gave me the idea for this
story and helped me with the research.*

Then fashioned for him the folk of Geats
firm on the earth a funeral-pile,
and hung it with helmets and harness of war
and breastplates bright, as the boon he asked;
and they laid amid it the mighty chieftain,
heroes mourning their master dear.
Then on the hill that hugest of balefires
the warriors wakened. Wood-smoke rose
black over blaze, and blent was the roar
of flame with weeping (the wind was still),
till the fire had broken the frame of bones,
hot at the heart. In heavy mood
their misery moaned they, their master's death.

BEOWULF,
TRANSLATION BY FRANCIS B GUMMERE

PROLOGUE

The River Idle, Nottinghamshire

Autumn, 616 AD

T he day before they'd set off north, Oswine had waited all afternoon for lovely tawny-haired Eormenhild to return home from market. When finally he'd seen her coming, he'd stepped out onto the path in front of her to make her stop. 'I'm off with the others in the morning,' he'd told her.

'Oh,' she'd said, holding her wicker basket of fine fabrics up across her chest, as though she needed some kind of protection from him. 'And what's that to me?'

The haughty way she'd lifted her chin had got beneath his skin, as it always did. It had made him want her so crazily, he could think of nothing else. 'I'm going to win gold in the battle,' he'd told her. 'A gold ring at the very least. The king himself is going to give it to me when he appoints me to his guard.'

'So?'

'So no-one will ever dare call me bastard again. Not you, not your father, not anyone. Then I'll be coming for you, to have you for my wife.'

The look on her face had kept him warm these past two days and nights, despite the incessant cold rain. Affront and shock and scorn yes, of course, but a touch of fear too. Not fear that he'd hurt her – she knew him too well for that – but rather fear that his force of will would prove stronger than her own; and, even worse, that – despite his lowly status, the certain disapproval of her family and the mockery of her friends – deep down inside her, it was what she wanted too.

He'd nodded at her and walked off, and had been fifty paces up the track before she'd found her voice and a typically salty riposte. But he hadn't paused or looked around. He'd said what he'd come to say.

Two full days of marching since then. He'd never thought to be this far from home, or that his feet could be so sore. Now the river their scouts had chosen ran slow and grey across the valley floor beneath. It was called the Yddla, they said, for all the corn that grew along its banks. But there was no corn here at its ford, only mud and trampled grass from the woods to his left all the way up to the top of the ridge away to his right.

They made their way down to a stone's toss from its bank before a horn sounded the halt. The water was shallow and so clear that, even from this distance, Oswine could make out the pale flat stones that littered its bed like half-baked loaves, and the silver flicker of little fishes darting in between.

Kings didn't hand out gold rings to everyone who lined up for them in battle. Nor did they appoint them to their guard. Ambitious young men like Oswine had to work to get themselves noticed. That was why he'd volunteered not just for this contingent but its front rank too, where the danger and the glory would both be greatest. His offer had been gladly accepted. Though he was just sixteen summers old, he was already as tall and strong as most other men, and bearded like one too. Yet now that they were forming up along the bank, his heart began to pound like a marching drum. Promises were cheap. Making good on them was what cost. And brides were of little value to a dead man, no matter how beautiful.

Their young lord prince sent a party of mounted scouts across the river, their horses kicking up mud to turn the water brown. They spread out as they cantered up the far side of the valley, looking for any sign of the northern army. They'd barely reached the summit before they turned as one and came back at a gallop, shouting warnings and hunched low over their mounts. It took only a few moments more for Oswine to see the reason why, as the first of the northerners crested the hill behind them, a ragged cavalry perhaps three dozen strong, followed by a horde of Bernicians, Deirans and other northern savages who now poured over the crest like mead slopping from a barrel until the top half of the facing hillside was covered by them. They came to a ragged stop some hundred paces on the Yddla's far side, shouting insults and waving their banners back and forth to make the dragons on them fly, what with the stillness of the day.

There were so many of them, it hit Oswine like an almost physical blow. At least twice their own number. Their faces and bodies were painted lurid colours, and even from this distance they looked so *big*. It seemed unfair to him, how big they looked, as if they'd gone recruiting from some ancient race of giants. Suddenly he remembered the stories they told about the man they'd be facing that day: not just how he'd never lost a battle, but the horrors he'd inflicted on any and all who'd dared oppose him, his inventiveness with torture and how he'd put twelve hundred monks to death just for praying for the wrong side.

Old Ælfgar, standing to Oswine's right, noticed his sudden attack of trembles. 'They'll be shitting it as much as we are,' he said, with a friendly nudge of his elbow. Oswine wanted to say something funny in return, about how he hoped not, or they'd all be knee-deep in the stuff, but he couldn't even open his mouth, so tightly clamped were his teeth. He nodded instead, and grinned, praying that he wouldn't disgrace himself and let his comrades down; but also in the hope that it would stir some fellow-feeling in Ælfgar so that he'd look out for him when the time came.

A double horn blast from behind. They shuffled sideways to let their young lord prince pass through their lines on his dappled grey stallion. Up and down their front rank he grandly rode, handsome, slender, tall and kingly in his gleaming mail and helmet, exhorting them all to valour. Glorious deeds would be done this day, he shouted, such that their bards would have to outdo themselves to capture the moment, should they live or should they die.

'Shut up, you bloody tart,' muttered Ælfgar.

'He's trying to give us courage,' said Oswine.

'He's trying to get us killed,' retorted Ælfgar. 'Dangling himself like an apple for those bastards across the river to pluck. Only he'll scuttle off behind us before the fighting starts. You watch.' It didn't take long either. His speech finished, he raised an arm to win some ragged cheers, then trotted rearward again, back between their lines, which closed once more behind him. 'See,' growled Ælfgar.

'As long as God is with us,' said Oswine. 'That's what matters.

'Keep your damn God. Give me good commanders any day.'

'And are our commanders good?'

'We'll find that out soon enough, won't we?'

Oswine didn't reply. Not for the first time, however, he wondered what they were doing here, so far from home. Word was that their king had been ordered to give up his friend Edwin or else. With his honour so at stake, he'd chosen the 'or else'. But others said that that was merely cover for his and his queen's ambition. Not that it much mattered to Oswine. He was an Angle. He knew his side. Defeat this day would leave their land exposed, his mother and two half-sisters, and sweet Eormenhild too – all of them too pretty and too tender to be left alone. Those tattooed monsters across the river would rape them for sure, and steal them for their beds. The thought made Oswine sick – though every so often he'd picture the young northern women who victory this day would leave without their husbands, fathers or brothers to protect them, and he'd feel a strange sweet stirring in his loins.

There was a lull, with neither side showing much appetite to attack across the river. But something had to give. A burly Bernician warrior with plaited dark hair danced forward to hurl his spear. It landed well short of them, provoking only jeers. But now his comrade ran right up to the Yddla's far bank, a little way into it indeed, water splashing around his ankles. His spear flew high and straight and true before it arced, plummeting to earth close enough to Oswine that a man two to his left had to step sideways to avoid it, only for its point to catch in the mud and its shaft to twist around so that it clattered into his ankle, provoking a roar of indignation that made the others laugh.

The speed of it as it had come down unnerved Oswine. The speed and weight and sharpness of it. He'd always been cursed with too vivid an imagination, so that he could picture all too clearly the way it would pierce deep into his flesh, the damage it would do, the pain and blood and gore. He yelled out an oath and banged his spear upon his shield, setting off a cascade that turned into a rhythmic beat to which his own pulse now pumped, bringing that strange taste of iron to his mouth, giving him courage and a restless hankering to start the fight right now. But then the drumming died away and his courage went with it.

The northerners finally began their advance. They must have counted numbers and decided to press home their advantage before reinforcements could arrive. Horns blared on every side. It was happening. Old Ælfgar raised high his shield against further missiles from the sky, so Oswine did too, and all the others around them, rippling out along rank and file, creating a solid carapace above their heads. Another long blast of horn and they themselves began to move forwards. He shuffled only reluctantly himself, until the man behind cursed him and punched him in his back. Time seemed to slow down to nothing, yet, almost before he knew it, spears, arrows and stones began clattering against their shields, until the safest place, perversely, was closer to the enemy. The northerners must have sensed this too, for their front ranks now broke into a run, yelling their incomprehensible war-cries as they plunged into the river.

'Only up to your knees,' said Old Ælfgar, shouting to make himself heard above the din. 'Let them be the ones to wade.'

'I know,' said Oswine.

'The moment we meet, throw your weight behind your shield. All of it. Even big lads like you get taken by surprise.'

'I know,' said Oswine.

'And don't be the one to break. That's the only rule that truly matters. If our wall must breach, let it be someone else.'

'I know,' said Oswine, for a third time.

'Then good luck to you,' muttered Ælfgar grimly, as they stepped into the water. 'And may your damned God not let us down.'

Oswine took firmer grip of his spear. 'Nor your commanders neither,' he replied.

ONE

A Friday afternoon in August

Woodbridge, Suffolk

It was in an unexpectedly buoyant mood that Ben Elias turned off the A12 at the Woodbridge roundabout. Yes, it was a bore having to work over the August bank holiday, but the forecast was glorious, he'd be staying at one of Suffolk's stateliest private homes, and his duties would be ultra light – or so, at least, he'd been assured. Best of all, though, he'd be seeing Anna Warne again, for the first time in months, since their night out together to celebrate him leaving Lincolnshire police for his new job as a London security consultant.

Elton John came on the radio. *Rocket Man.* Elias sang along for a few bars while playing piano on his steering wheel. Everyone had some kind of artistic talent, they said. It was just that Elias hadn't discovered his yet. He reached his turn, drove up a short steep hill then took a sharp left along a winding, narrow, country lane studded with expensive homes set well back behind large front lawns, and afforded extra privacy by their high hedges and fences. But then the houses gave way to thick old woodland, while a series of signs beside the lane advised him that he was entering the Dragon Stone Hill Estate, that it was Private Property, and he should Keep Out.

He pulled up by an automated steel gate set in a drystone wall. It had more of the same forbidding signs upon it, along with an entry-pad system by the driver window. He found a smile for the camera as he tapped in the passcode his host had sent him. Nothing happened. He thought maybe he'd got it wrong, and was reaching for his phone to double check when he heard a click and the gate began to trundle open. He drove on for fifty yards or so to a narrow bridge over a railway cutting that had been sliced through this hill the best part of two centuries ago, to spare every train since the effort of labouring up and over. Its tracks were flanked by a pair of almost sheer embankments built from massive concrete slabs and topped by narrow strips of yellow gorse and purple heather, and by bushes of bracken and other ferns whose fronds fell like unruly bangs over their edges.

He reached another stretch of woodland on the far side. He passed, to his left, the gatehouse cottage where Anna would be staying. He could see no sign of her, however, only of a navy blue Land Rover Defender parked out front. He continued onwards for another few hundred yards until the woods parted like a magician's hands to reveal Dragon Stone Manor itself, a half-timbered Tudor mansion of twisting chimneys and herringbone brickwork with a more modern extension on its far side, set in a slight dip in the terrain and looking out over neatly-mown front lawns and a narrow strip of marshy ground to the River Deben beyond. And, in this cloudless sunshine, it looked even more of a picture than its pictures had.

Eight vehicles were parked on its gravel forecourt, including three vans in the blue and gold livery of a high-end catering firm. Elias added his Nissan Leaf to their number, got out and stretched his legs. He popped his boot for his overnight bag only for the crunch of footsteps on gravel to make him turn. A stockily-built man in his mid forties came marching around the last of the vans, hands clasped behind his back. He had thinning wild red hair and an unkempt beard, both lightly flecked with grey, and – despite his military bearing and obvious air of command – he seemed to care little for clothes, for his red poloshirt and baggy blue jeans were both spattered with white paint, while his old army combat boots were caked with dried mud, as though they hadn't been scrubbed in weeks. His teeth were a little crooked and discoloured, but his eyes were green and uncommonly bright. His forehead was red and peeling, as if he'd spent much of the summer outdoors, and he had a noticeable indentation above his left temple, where the hair no longer grew, along with livid scarring that ran all the way from there down across his cheek and throat to such of his shoulder that Elias could see through his open collar.

'You must be Detective Elias,' he said, holding out his hand, only to notice too late the lemon-yellow golfing glove Elias had taken to wearing on his right hand, in part to protect it after his latest round of reconstructive surgery, but mostly to alert people to his injuries, so that they wouldn't be offended by his refusal to shake.

'I would be, if I were still a detective,' Elias told him, clasping the man's still outstretched hand awkwardly with his left. 'And you must be Major Brook.'

'I gave up being a major long before you stopped being a detective,' said Brook. 'Call me Hector.'

'Thank you. And you can call me Ben, if we're doing first names. But everyone else calls me Elias.'

'Then I shall too. And, before I forget, may I say again how grateful I am that you could make it here today. I know what bank holidays mean to a family man.'

'No worries. The kids are in Spain with their mum. And her new man.'

'Ah. I'm sorry.'

'Forget it. I'm curious, though, about what you expect from me. Like I told you over the phone, after-dinner talks are hardly my thing. And I know nothing whatsoever about archaeology.'

'You had a front-row seat to the greatest discovery of the last eighty years,' said Brook. 'That alone would be worth your fee. But yes, you're right, there's more to it than that.' He gazed Elias up and down, as though inspecting some new recruit to his unit, to see how much whipping into shape they'd need. He seemed pleased enough with what he saw, save for a slight furrow of his brow.

'You'll never guess,' said Elias, well used both to the puzzlement and to the reticence about asking. 'Grandparents from Sweden, Jamaica, Wales and the Philippines, would you believe? All mushed together by my years in the ring.'

'You were a boxer?'

'Less so than the people I went up against.'

Brook gave a smile that was ninety-nine percent politeness to one percent amusement. Then he glanced around, as if expecting someone to be at his shoulder, only to be irritated when they weren't. He touched Elias on his elbow to steer him through the Manor's front door into a tall and gloomy hallway furnished with a hat-rack, an umbrella stand and a loudly ticking grandfather clock. 'I promised my sister I'd let her know when you arrived,' he said. 'She thinks I'm stark staring mad, and therefore that you need to be warned about me.'

'That's good to know.'

'Quite. Greta!' he boomed. 'Greta! Where *are* you?'

Several seconds passed. They heard footsteps and then a gangling, middle-aged woman arrived along a passage. She had a friendly rather than a beautiful face, with her brown hair up in a neat bun, and wearing a red and white polka-dot cotton apron over a bright yellow summer dress and some sensible brown shoes. 'Forgive me,' she said, holding up her hands, covered in a crust of wholemeal flour. 'You did ask me to do the bread for tonight.'

'Yes, yes,' said Brook impatiently. 'This is Detective Elias. Elias, my sister Greta.' They nodded politely at one another, neither in a position to shake hands. Brook frowned briefly as he pondered what next, then brightened again when he realised the solution. 'With me,' he said, turning on his heel and striding back outside, leaving Elias torn between hurrying to catch up and waiting for Greta, who threw off her apron onto a chair, then vigorously rubbed her hands together as she crossed the forecourt, so that flakes of pale brown flour fell in a little snowstorm to the gravel.

A footpath of Indian sandstone had been laid through the front lawn, running parallel with the River Deben to their right. Brook marched all the way along it to the latched gate at its far end. Then he stopped and turned to wait. 'You're right,' he said, when Elias joined him. 'I *am* a lucky man.'

'I didn't say anything.'

'You didn't have to. It's what everyone thinks. And they're perfectly correct. But at least I'm aware of my good fortune. We both are, aren't we, Greta?'

'We've been blessed,' agreed Greta, panting a little as she caught up with them.

'It wasn't always like this for us, you see,' said Brook. 'A little background is in order, I think. You'll need it for the weekend. So, then. Our mother was a well-meaning woman, or so I choose to believe. Unfortunately, however, she was also addicted to heroin and whatever other drugs she could lay her hands on, as were the various men who moved in and out of our tower block apartment over the years. Both our fathers were gone by the time we were born. We never had a clue as to who they were. I'm not convinced our mother did either. Her memory wasn't the best. Then one day, when Greta was about ten, and I was seven, a man came to visit. He claimed to be a private detective, and he offered our mother ten brand new twenty pound notes in exchange for swabs from both our cheeks. She couldn't believe her luck. I can still remember the way she held them up to her nose and inhaled them as though they were a bouquet of red roses from some aspiring lover. We thought nothing more of it for a month or two. Then the same man returned, only this time with momentous news, which no doubt a skilled detective like you will already have guessed. For it turned out that one of the junkies who'd passed through our home many years before was the only child of the man who owned this place. And he'd managed to impregnate my mother while he was there. His father had disowned him by then, for stealing too many

11

heirlooms to feed his habit. But, after the heroin killed him…
well, I won't say that grandfather was overcome by remorse. He
wasn't the kind to do remorse. Let's just say he had a strong sense
of familial duty. His son had talked of children sometimes when
he'd come begging for money, so he'd felt obliged to make sure.
Hence the private detective. Hence the swabs.'

'And you were indeed his grandchildren?'

'I was. Not Greta. Her father remains unknown, sadly. But,
anyway, grandfather saw it as incumbent upon him to improve
our lives and form some kind of relationship with us. Never a
very warm one, it has to be said. But at least he made the effort.
He paid for rehab for my mother, though frankly it was too late
for her by then, and it wasn't long before she took the same
path out that my father had. After which grandfather brought us
both here to live.'

'He wanted to take only Hector,' said Greta. 'But Hector
refused point blank unless I came too.'

'Yes, well,' said Brook. 'The man terrified me. Greta was my
champion.'

'He always says that. It's not true.' She threw him a fond look.
'Grandfather put him under incredible pressure. He stood up to
it all. And he was still only nine years old at the time.'

'Yes, well,' he said again, uncomfortable with her gratitude.
'Anyway, grandfather soon realised that he didn't much like
having a pair of uncouth brats beneath his feet. Money was
no issue to him, so he sent us both off to expensive schools
to have our tower block ways tormented out of us by the
cruelty of our peers. Greta was the bright one. She went on to
Cambridge. I, being a dolt, barely scraped into Sandhurst. The
years passed. I did tours in Iraq and Afghanistan, where I was
caught by an IED.' He touched the left side of his face, somewhat
unnecessarily. 'I was still in hospital when grandfather called.
He'd been diagnosed several weeks earlier with a particularly
virulent form of liver cancer, and only now that the end was
upon him did he think it time to share. For all his emotion,
he might have been telling me that the roof had sprung a leak.

He was in a coma by the time I made it back here, and gone within two more days. Suddenly I owned all this, along with the responsibilities that went with it. My career was already effectively over by then, thanks to the PTSD and the epilepsy that the IED had left me with, so I resigned my commission and came here instead, to take charge of this estate and the rest of my grandfather's interests, including three very substantial farms, a pair of fine vineyards, several dozen holiday cottages and two hotels. Managing them is more work than you'd think, but my god! When I look back on where I came from, I can't believe how lucky I've been.'

'How lucky we've both been,' amended Greta.

'Which has what to do with my being here?' asked Elias.

Brook laughed. 'A fair question. A fair question indeed.' Yet instead of answering it, he led them through the gate then up the slope along the winding path that had been mown through a curated meadow of tall grasses dotted with colourful wild flowers, then into a small apple orchard beaded with hard young fruit. To their right, as they climbed, an escarpment fell away so sharply to the Deben beneath that someone had thought it necessary to put in a timber rail fence – and fairly recently, too, to judge from the pale freshness of the wood.

They continued onwards and upwards however, cutting away from the escarpment fence towards the summit of the hill, upon which stood a single-storey building with a pitched tile roof and a front mostly given over to huge panes of smoked glass that had to offer a spectacular view over the river to the woods on its far bank. It clearly wasn't yet finished, however, for not only was it unpainted, but a cement mixer, some lengths of piping and a septic tank of toughened green plastic were being stored down its side, imperfectly covered by a pair of weathered blue tarpaulins.

'I built this with my own bare hands,' said Brook, stopping in front of it and turning to Elias. 'A labour of love. I'd hoped to have it finished long before this weekend, but I came to realise, while I was working on it, that this was where I was happiest, much more so than at the Manor, for all its comforts. So I kept adding to my plans here and there, making alterations and improvements, until it turned from a simple one-room summerhouse into a modest dwelling instead, somewhere I could spend the night, or even longer. But that of course meant plumbing and electricity and all the rest, which involved teaching myself whole new skills. And so I rather lost my way. I could have brought people in to do it for me, of course, but – as I say – this was a labour of love, and you can't exactly pay other people to do those for you, can you?'

Elias had once renovated a derelict cottage all by himself, largely as a way to show his wife and children how much they meant to him. 'No,' he said.

'And it will do for the moment,' nodded Brook. 'It will have to. Because we're dedicating it on Sunday evening, as the climax to our weekend. I built it in honour of a very close friend of mine called Charlotte Ash, you see. This hilltop was her favourite place in all the world. I loved her very much. We were engaged to be married, briefly, after she fell pregnant with our first child. But then, five years ago, come Sunday night, she fell over the edge of the escarpment you see beneath us, and tumbled head first down onto the concrete dock beneath, from which she slipped unconscious into the river and then drowned. And the real reason I invited you here this weekend is to help me work out which one of your fellow guests it was that pushed her.'

TWO

It was only fifteen minutes by train from Ipswich to Woodbridge, yet that was plenty enough to make Anna Warne feel more cheerful about the weekend ahead, for the track ran for a short while alongside the Deben, one of the estuarial rivers that veined and nourished this stretch of Suffolk coast, and which had made it such a tempting target for seaborne invaders over the centuries, in particular for the Angles who – from what she'd gleaned from her email exchanges with her host Hector Brook – were likely to form the theme of the next few days. This was their ancient heartland, after all, and home to Sutton Hoo, the greatest archaeological discovery of England's last hundred years. Yet while she'd had a mental image of it as mist-covered and vaguely ominous, it could hardly have looked more delightful on this sparkling late summer afternoon, with the pleasure boats out in force and countless people out walking their dogs or sunbathing on its banks.

The train slowed to a halt as they arrived at Woodbridge station. It was clearly a popular stop, for half her carriage got to their feet and made for the doors, carrying footballs, kites and picnic baskets. Some set off for the town centre, while others headed over the footbridge towards the river. Anna followed this latter group, thinking it a nice afternoon for a walk, only to catch a glimpse of what, even from this distance, she recognised as Dragon Stone Manor, nestled in a dip beyond a bend in the river a good forty minutes walk away. And suddenly she realised just how warm the afternoon was, after the air-conditioned cool of the carriage, and how heavy her bags were too. So she turned, a little guiltily, and made her way back down the steps and over to the station's taxi rank instead.

Her driver looked to be at least seventy years old, yet lean, fit and neatly groomed, dressed in an open-necked white silk shirt and a lightweight pearl-grey suit. A retired businessman, if Anna had to guess, looking for something to do with his time as much as for the extra income. He raised an eyebrow when she told him the address, but he stashed her bags in his boot before she could change her mind. 'They don't get so many visitors up there these days,' he said, as they got in, phrasing it more like a question than an observation. 'Not since the young lady died.'

'I don't know anything about that,' said Anna, fastening her seatbelt. 'I'm only here to give a talk.'

'A talk?' He squinted sideways at her. 'Aren't you a bit young to be giving talks?'

'No,' said Anna.

His lips puckered into a smile, perhaps thinking of how to turn it into a story for the good lady wife. He thought better of saying anything, though, which was probably wise. His silence didn't last beyond the car park exit, however. 'Charlotte,' he said. 'That was her name. Charlotte Ash. Gorgeous blonde young thing. Bit like you, if only you were blonde.' He slid her another sly glance, to see how his compliment had gone across. She gave a sigh in the hope that he'd shut up. No such luck. 'A Melton girl, as I recall,' he continued, undeterred, as he waited for the lights to change. 'She and her little sister used to come into town a fair bit. Gawky little kid, with a mouth full of metal braces and wearing these huge tortoiseshell glasses that kept slipping off her nose. You'd never have looked twice at her. Then she turns up one summer with her teeth fixed and her contacts in, and suddenly all our local lads are walking into lampposts. Not that she gave a hoot for any of them. Already had her eyes set on higher things. Your man Hector Brook, for one. Won't be getting many calls from Hollywood, I don't suppose, not after what those bastard Taliban did to his face; but then it helps when you own half the county. Only they'd barely got engaged before she fell off the escarpment and drowned. That's what the inquest said, at least, though there's many round here reckon they only said that to spare his feelings. I'd have flung myself off the edge too, facing life with that tough old bastard.'

'You were wise to turn him down, then.'

'Not his type, love. You're the one needs to watch out.'

Anna turned to gaze at him. 'What are you saying? Is there something I should know?'

'No, no, no,' he said hurriedly, before he landed himself in trouble. 'Sorry. That was unfair of me. No one's ever accused him of anything like that, not as far as I know, and certainly not with her. He adored her. I only meant that he clearly has a good eye for the ladies. But how about I leave you my card? Call me any time of day or night. I'll be straight over.'

'Thanks. I'm sure I'll be fine.'

'Your funeral.'

'Nice,' she said, turning away, grateful for the excuse not to talk to him any more. He took the hint and fell silent, though she could see from the way he worked his hands on the steering wheel that there was more he wanted to say. They passed out of the centre of Woodbridge, turned left and left again along a pleasant wooded lane to an automated gate with CCTV and an entry-pad. She gave him the code. He tapped it in. They crossed a narrow railway bridge and found Gatehouse Cottage to their left on its far side. She'd been disappointed when Brook had told her that all the Manor's bedrooms were spoken for, and that this was therefore to be her base for the weekend, but she took to it at once, with its sturdy charm, built from large blocks of sparkling granite and topped by a steeply pitched slate roof, with honeysuckle and clematis climbing its front like unruly children, and a pair of lavender bushes throwing their sweet perfume into the afternoon air. A small lawn to the right was bordered by rose bushes and beds of colourful flowers. There was a sprinkler on a length of hose and a wooden table flanked by a pair of benches, with a tattered yellow sunshade leaning at a louche angle through its central hole. Another bench sat in the shade of an ancient oak, from whose lowest branch hung a child's swing of orange plastic on some frayed brown rope.

A blue Land Rover Defender was parked out front, yet there was no one home. Instead, a cream envelope with Anna's name handwritten on it in beautiful Gothic script had been taped to the cottage door. It contained a card from Greta Brook, her hostess for the weekend, apologising for not being there in person, but explaining that her brother had summoned her up to the Manor to help prepare tonight's feast, and urging her to make herself at home until she got back – which would be by six o'clock at the absolute latest – plenty of time for them to get ready for the welcome drinks that would kick off the weekend.

Her driver popped his boot to take out her bags. 'So what's your talk on?' he asked.

'I made a discovery last year,' she told him. 'It caused a bit of a stir.' An understatement, that. She'd found the crown jewels King John had supposedly lost in the Wash, only they hadn't been in the Wash at all, but rather in the heart of Lincolnshire, in an underground network of passages and chambers beneath an old Templar preceptory. She'd become famous for a while, with the disconcerting experience of seeing her face splashed across newspapers and the TV. But the story had soon enough been ousted by fresher news, and her moment had passed – which had suited her just fine, allowing her some peace and quiet to finish off her thesis, and then to convert it into the book she'd foolishly promised a particularly persistent publisher.

'A discovery, you say,' said her driver. 'An *archaeological* discovery, would that be?'

'Yes. Why do you ask?'

'They love their archaeology up here. That Charlotte Ash I mentioned, she was an archaeologist too. She had a whole crew digging here that summer. The summer she died, I mean.'

'She did?' asked Anna, interested for the first time. 'What were they looking for?'

'Anglo-Saxon burials. They found them too, on the back lawns. Only they'd already been plundered, from what I understand, likely back when it was all levelled for the lawns. Though...'

'Though?'

The man hesitated. But not for long. 'There've been whispers around town, these past few weeks. That they've gone and found something proper, I mean.'

'Really?'

'You don't want to pay attention to these things,' he told her, perhaps worried he'd said too much. 'Place like this, there are always whispers.'

'Even so,' she said. 'What are they saying?'

'Another ship burial, is what I heard. Just like the one across the river at Sutton Hoo.' He slammed shut his boot and turned to her with a mischievous twinkling of the eyes. 'Only bigger.'

THREE

A bird was singing its heart out in the woods behind the summerhouse. Down on the river below, someone was hauling at an outboard motor, struggling to make it catch. But otherwise there was an almost perfect silence. Elias gazed coolly at Brook, trying to figure out how serious he was, and how sane. 'You want me to find out who murdered your fiancée five years ago?' he said finally. 'Isn't that a job for the police?'

'You *are* the police, or as close as I can get. Our Suffolk lot have given up. In truth, they never even started. They were convinced from the first that there was nothing to investigate. I had to twist their arms to get them here at all. But it was no real use. They'd already reached their conclusion. Either her death was an accident, or perhaps she did it to herself. And so naturally the coroner agreed.'

'But you don't?'

'Of course not. Suicide is absurd. Charlotte was happy. She'd just discovered that she was pregnant with our child. It gave her the jitters at first, I admit. She was young and ambitious and she feared what motherhood would mean for her career. She loved working at the British Museum, you see, and didn't want to risk losing her place there. But I vowed to her that she'd have all the money and support she could wish for, should she decide to see her pregnancy through – whether she stayed with me or not, and wherever she chose to live. She knew I meant it, too.

I'd never have put a child of mine through what Greta and I endured. And then she did decide to marry me, and something changed inside her. Or maybe something changed first, and that led to her decision. I don't know which. But she became... *settled.* She was ready. At peace. She actually started looking forward to it, visiting websites and chatrooms for pregnant mums, ordering books, browsing wedding dresses. She became expectant in every way. Excited. Radiant. There's no way she would have killed herself, let alone her child, which she'd already come to dote on. As for it being an accident, it was a brightly moonlit night, and she wasn't reckless enough to go that close to the edge, not in her condition. If there'd been any trace of her slipping, or of the escarpment giving way beneath her, then perhaps I could have accepted it. But there was nothing.'

'You wouldn't necessarily expect there to be. Not if she simply lost her footing.'

'It's not just that,' scowled Brook. 'Her phone vanished too. I had the river dredged for it. It wasn't there. No. Someone killed her that night and took away her phone out of fear there might be something incriminating on it. I suspected it at the time, but I was too shattered to fight as I should have done, either then or at the inquest.'

'You still think the same?'

'More so than ever.'

'May I ask why?'

'Of course. I'll tell you everything. But first...' He crooked his finger to invite Elias and Greta to accompany him a little way down the slope towards the river, before stopping by a huge grey boulder the size of a minivan, so deeply embedded into the grassy hillside that it might have been crushed there by an industrial steamroller. 'We don't get much natural rock in Suffolk,' he said, putting his foot upon it. 'All we have are a few sarsens like this: great blocks of stone that used to form a kind of crust over the earth, but which were broken up and then pushed hither and yon by glaciation, before being left behind by the melt. This is the largest in the county, I'm told. What's more, if you stand in the right place when the shadows are just so, and let your imagination run a little free, you can just about make out a dragon lashing its tail and with its wings swept out.'

'Ah,' said Elias. 'The dragon stone of Dragon Stone Manor, I presume?'

'I can see my fee won't be wasted on you, Detective,' said Brook dryly. 'Yes. The dragon stone of Dragon Stone Manor. It wouldn't have been here originally, so I'm assured, but would instead have been brought in specially from some other region, much like the menhirs at Stonehenge. It was almost certainly the work of the Angles, yet no one's quite sure why they went to such effort, although it does seem to serve as a kind of marker or beacon for arriving ships – which, as I understand it, qualifies it as a megalith. You can actually see it when you're sailing up the Deben from the sea, thanks to the way the hill slopes. And it would have been even easier to see back then, for it would have sat upon the ground rather than being half swallowed up by it, as has happened over the centuries since. It's even sunk a few more inches since Greta and I first came here.'

'A lot of work to go to,' observed Elias, 'just for a marker.'

'Well, quite. Which is why some people think it served another purpose too. Maybe this is where the Angles first landed on their arrival from Scandinavia, and the stone was put here to commemorate that. The area is certainly inviting enough. Far enough inland to be safe from tides and storms, and with all these flat riverbanks for beaching your boats on, even should the existing inhabitants greet you more warmly than you'd like. But there's a snippet of local folklore that tells a different story. It says this is the site of another royal burial – an even greater one than Edith Pretty's.'

Elias shook his head. 'Should I know who that is?'

'Forgive me, Detective. I'm too used to talking to locals and archaeologists.' He pointed upstream and across the river. 'Back in the late 1930s, a Mrs Edith Pretty lived in that big cream house you can just about see through those trees. There were some intriguing mounds upon her land, so she commissioned an amateur archaeologist called Basil Brown to excavate them.'

'Ah,' said Elias. 'Sutton Hoo.'

'Yes, indeed. Sutton Hoo. Mrs Pretty was under no obligation to give her finds to the nation, did you know? And yet she did, along with her house and whole estate. A remarkable woman. An inspiration to us all. But though Sutton Hoo is exceptional, it's not unique. Other ship burials have been found at Snape and Ashby. Then you have Iken and Ipswich and Ufford and countless other such centres of East Angle life.' He pointed upstream, past the sailboats and pleasure craft moored off Woodbridge's waterfront. 'The most important of which is Rendlesham, just four or five miles in that direction, where they recently found the remains of an entire royal compound, including a magnificent great hall. So you can see why people think this stone might mark something truly special. The local archaeological society used to pester my grandfather to let them run a survey. He grew so annoyed that he took to greeting them with a shotgun under his arm. After I inherited the place, they tried it on with me instead. I said no too. I'm a very private man, and frankly I didn't want the disturbance. But then, one afternoon, there came a knock upon my door, and it changed my world forever.'

FOUR

Anna left her bags by the foot of the stairs in order to take a quick tour of the ground floor. There was another note for her on the kitchen door, asking her to keep it closed so that the cats couldn't escape into the main part of the house. There was one in there when she went through, slurping water from a large white plastic bowl. It glowered at her then slipped out through a flap in the back door.

The room was spotless and well equipped, with a set of Ruffini cookware on the open shelves, a high-end espresso maker and a Neff air-fryer on the marble worktop, none of which looked as though they'd ever had much use. The pine table was laid for four with immaculate precision, and a pair of scented candles stood either side of a vase of fresh white roses. There was a modestly stocked pantry, and a utility room equipped with a deep-freeze, a washing machine and a dryer.

She retraced her steps past the staircase to a dining room with French windows covered by lacy white net curtains. A set of charming Victorian watercolours of countryside scenes decorated the dark green walls. The walnut dining table had six high-backed chairs around it, upholstered in red leather. And while it and the matching walnut sideboard were both polished to a gleam, they were also covered by a thin layer of dust that suggested they didn't see a great deal of entertaining.

The sitting room was maroon with a deep-pile cream carpet. A vast bowl of dried flowers filled the blocked-up fireplace, whose chimney breast was flanked by fitted shelves crammed to bursting with books. A set of brown leather armchairs and a sofa were angled to face a pedestal TV on a low coffee table. It was hooked up to a compact DVD player half hidden away on a low shelf, along with a modest collection of classic movies and romcoms, and an elaborate music system with a much larger collection of classical and jazz CDs in a pair of spiral racks. White roses in bubbled glass vases stood on either end of both windowsills, and there were numerous framed class photographs on the walls of girls and boys from what Anna took to be the local primary school, smartly dressed as they were in silver and mauve uniforms. A tall, thin, angular woman with a chestnut bun and anxious hands appeared in several of these, sometimes smiling for the camera but mostly beaming at her pupils with such obvious fond pride that Anna took to her at once. Surely Greta Brook, her hostess for the weekend. There were some press-cuttings too, of former students made good: an actress who'd played Desdemona in an RSC production of Othello; a footballer who'd scored on his debut for Colchester Town; another who'd appeared on University Challenge.

Anna took her bags upstairs. Her name was written in the same Gothic script on a white card taped to a bedroom door. The room was small, sweet and very feminine, almost cloyingly so, with framed photographs of flower arrangements against the pink and yellow striped wallpaper, a large hanging cupboard and a queen size bed fitted with sheets of Egyptian cotton and a bright white duvet on which a gorgeous silk dress of bright scarlet with royal blue trim had been laid out, along with a cream headscarf and a pair of fawn lace-up boots of the softest and most supple leather imaginable – clearly her costume for tonight's Anglo-Saxon feast, for whose measurements Hector Brook had emailed her a month or so ago.

She took the dress over to the mirror, held it up in front of herself. It dismayed her a little, and left her feeling obscurely tricked. She'd lost her appetite for glamour many years before, watching in helpless horror as her mother had fallen increasingly sick and then died, forcing her to leave her Manchester home and friends for her Uncle Dunstan's Lincolnshire farm instead. Grief had left her largely indifferent to her looks, while Uncle Dunstan had refused to waste what little spare money he had on pretty clothes that wouldn't survive first contact with farmyard muck. The boys at her new school had mocked her for this when gathered together as a gang, only to paw at her whenever they'd got her alone, so it had been with some relief that she'd left Lincolnshire behind to go read history and archaeology at university. Her relief had been short-lived, however. Not only had she soon found herself the target of a stalker there, she'd been attacked while returning home from an evening shift, bundled into the boot of a car, then driven off to be raped and murdered.

Her abductor was no longer a threat. Anna had taken care of that herself. But the ghost of that awful night haunted her still. She'd done what she could to prevent further interest from men, buying a cheap paste ring for her engagement finger, letting her shoulder-length brown hair become dull and matted, going without makeup and scouring charity shops for clothes that would make her as drab and shapeless as possible. She'd had to smarten up somewhat over these past few months, when giving interviews and talks, but even then she'd worn the most severely professional outfits she could find, without hint of colour or flattery. But there was nothing remotely drab, severe or professional about this dress, with its expensive materials, flamboyant colours and daring cut. It was designed to catch the eye, and it must have cost Brook a small fortune, despite only being meant for a single night.

What a ridiculous world the ultra-rich lived in.

It was still far too early to get ready, so she went back down for a cup of tea that she took outside with her laptop to the bench beneath the oak tree. She worked for a while on the talk she was giving tomorrow evening, for while she'd given essentially the same one several times already, she tried her best to throw in some local colour and to personalise the jokes.

The tabby cat came to glare at her. She patted the bench to invite it up. It hissed and arched its back before stalking off. Crows heckled her from the tree-tops. A huge wasp, or maybe even a hornet, took a disconcerting interest in the back of her neck. A dozen or so copper and white butterflies fluttered like autumn leaves in a shaft of sunlight. She set down her laptop to watch them dance. A car arrived over the railway bridge. She looked up in hopes of seeing Elias's red Leaf, but it was a navy blue Audi A5 instead, presumably another of the weekend guests.

Elias had been a detective inspector with Lincolnshire's Major Crime Unit when they'd first met. He'd been leading the investigation into her uncle's murder – a harrowing episode that had somehow ended with her discovery of King John's crown jewels. They'd got off to a wretched start when he'd virtually accused her of killing her uncle herself, but that initial animosity had quickly turned to friendship and respect. He'd twice risked his life to save hers, after all, first by jumping up onto the wing of a light aircraft as it had set off down the runway, then suffering a shattered collarbone and a crushed right hand while defending her from a true monster. No surprise, then, that she'd come to trust him utterly.

But it wasn't just trust.

Elias was older than Anna, both in years and in stage of life. His face was battered from the ring and his heart was still broken from the death of his eldest son and the subsequent collapse of his marriage. Yet he was also the one she thought of first whenever she was feeling low, or had an amusing story to share. Even a day or two without some kind of contact and she'd begin to fret. She'd pull up a photo or a clip of him on her phone or laptop and instantly feel better. Or she'd invent some feeble excuse to call him, just to hear his voice. He always knew what she needed from him too, whether sympathy, encouragement or a laugh. And he had feelings for her too, she was sure of it, though less from what he said than from the silences that sometimes fell between them, content to listen to each other as they breathed.

She gave herself a shake. He lived in Essex and she in York. Their work ruled out anything more, even had they both so wished, which she wasn't remotely sure they did. They were friends, that was all. Good friends. Best friends. It was just a shame they saw each other so rarely. But at least they had this weekend together. She meant to make the most of it.

FIVE

Elias waited patiently for Hector Brook to say something further about how his world had changed forever, but the man was lost in some distant brown study. When finally he looked up again, he had such sadness in his eyes that Elias knew he'd been thinking of Charlotte Ash, of the life they might have had together, which made what he said next all the more of a surprise. 'Do you know much about how the Angles came to Suffolk and Norfolk?' he asked.

Elias shrugged. 'Nothing at all.'

The sadness vanished. He found a smile. 'An honest answer,' he said. 'I commend you for it. Then let me give you a very potted history. You'll be grateful for it over the weekend, believe me, unless you enjoy being sneered at by pompous historians. So then. It's the fourth century after Christ. The Huns are invading Europe from the east, driving a series of Germanic tribes before them. A cascade of sorts takes place, with vast numbers of Goths, Franks, Alans and the rest fleeing across the Rhine into the Roman Empire. The Romans assimilated huge numbers of them, but it caused turmoil and fracture all the same, prompting nervous emperors and ambitious generals alike to summon their most loyal legions back from distant provinces to further their respective causes. That, of course, created a power vacuum here in Britain at the exact same time as all these displaced tribes were searching for new homes. The Saxons arrived first. They hailed from Germany and settled mostly in Essex and along the south coast. Then came the Angles, from modern-day Denmark and Sweden, ultimately giving their name not just to East Anglia but to all England. They weren't exactly an invading army, as best we can tell. They simply wanted somewhere new to live. That was bad news for the previous inhabitants, even so, though it's hard to know for sure whether they found some way to accommodate one another, or more likely that they drove off the indigenous people, who no doubt lingered resentfully nearby, hoping to regain their land and taking such opportunities for revenge as came their way. I mention that specifically, because it's sure to come up again over the weekend.'

'Understood.'

'Angle language and culture soon came to dominate, however. We know that much for sure. It was the mix that gave us the epic poem *Beowulf*, ostensibly set in Scandinavia, yet almost certainly composed right here in Suffolk. Are you familiar with it?'

'I've seen the movie.'

'A strange poem, to modern tastes. But then it was written to be performed rather than simply read, and over three nights too, which explains its peculiar structure. Three separate battles against three different monsters, and not much else. Grendel was first, of course – an ogre who'd been terrorising the land, visiting the great hall at night to slaughter anyone he found there. Then Beowulf arrived, keen to make his name. They fought a furious battle until Beowulf ripped Grendel's arm clean off his shoulder.'

'I remember.'

'Grendel made it back to the mere in which his mother lived before he died. She was so enraged that she visited the great hall herself that night to take her vengeance. But Beowulf fought her off too, then followed her back home for his second great battle, eventually cutting off her head with a sword he was fortunate enough to find lying about. And the third monster was the dragon, of course.'

'Of course.'

'This was many years later, with Beowulf now a king in his own right. A foolish servant stole a goblet from the dragon's hoard, provoking it into ravaging the land. When no-one else dared take it on, Beowulf himself went into its lair, dealing it a mortal wound while taking one himself.'

'Fascinating,' said Elias.

Brook laughed. 'Very well. I won't bore you any further. Just remember that the poem is one of our best windows onto the Angles. The later Angles, at least. The ones who first settled here were very different, as best we can tell. A surprisingly egalitarian bunch, their dwellings modest and communal, their burials poorly furnished. But then a series of volcanic eruptions in Iceland during the second half of the 530s threw a heavy blanket of ash into the sky, covering not just Britain but much of continental Europe as well, leading to a decade of wretched harvests, famine and disease. Please bear this in mind as well, for it too will come up again.'

'Resentful outcasts and Icelandic volcanoes. Got it.'

'A brutal time to be alive, but a fine opportunity for skilful and ambitious warriors to make their bones. If your own stores of food wouldn't see you through the winter, what choice did you have but to go visit the next settlement along, and take theirs? And what choice did *they* have, when obviously outmanned, but to throw themselves upon your mercy and add their strength to your own? A series of power-centres thus sprang up, each led by a local warlord. And suddenly instead of all these separate egalitarian farmstead villages, you had hierarchies, you had armies, you had *kings*.'

'Like the one buried at Sutton Hoo.'

'Not just *like* the one buried at Sutton Hoo. *The* one buried at Sutton Hoo. His name was Rædwald. We know precious little about him, thanks in part to the Viking destruction of our monastic records, but he seems to have inherited the kingdom of East Anglia in around 600 AD from his father Tytila and his grandfather Wuffa, about whom we know even less, except that Wuffa gave his name to the dynasty, known as the Wuffingas. But it was Rædwald who took the firm national. It happened almost by accident. A man called Edwin sought refuge in his court, hiding from his brother-in-law Æthelfrith, king of Northumbria and the most powerful man in the land. Æthelfrith ordered Rædwald to surrender Edwin or else. Rædwald said no. So war it was. The two sides met at the River Idle in Nottinghamshire. We have only the sketchiest details of what happened, but we do know that the Angle army separated into three, led respectively by Rædwald, Edwin and Rædwald's eldest son Rægenhere. Looking at it through my military historian spectacles, I strongly suspect that Rædwald set a classic trap for Æthelfrith, showing him only Rægenhere and his small detachment to entice him on.'

'He offered his son as bait?'

'Exactly, yes. Æthelfrith charged across the river, thinking he'd have an easy victory, only for Rædwald and Edwin to spring the ambush from either side. But they messed up their timing, arriving too late to save Rægenhere and his men, who were massacred. In furious revenge, the Angles put Æthelfrith and much of his army to the sword. The river ran red with blood, we're told, as such rivers always did. Victory was Rædwald's. Victory and all England from Northumbria down to Kent, effectively making him *Bretwalda* and our nation's first true king, with the prestige and gold to match.'

'And it's definitely him at Sutton Hoo? I heard there was some doubt.'

'About as sure as we can be without having his name on a headstone. It's not just the extraordinary richness of the grave-goods, which marks him out as a king; it's the mix of pagan and Christian artefacts found among them. He was one of the first Anglo-Saxon converts, you see, yet he remained somewhat loyal to the old gods too. Then there are the coins found buried with him, every one of which was minted in the decade or so before his death, which of course rules out any of his predecessors; while his successor converted so wholeheartedly to Christianity that a ship burial and pagan grave goods would have been anathema.'

'If you say so.'

'Good. Thank you. And that was pretty much that for the Wuffingas. Which was another reason to refuse those annoying petitions from our local archaeological society. Because folklore spoke of a great royal ship burial here – the greatest of them all. Yet no other king could hold a candle to Rædwald, and he'd already been found. So I set my face against them. I refused to give them so much as a hearing. Until the afternoon I mentioned when my world was changed forever, thanks to the shabby trick they pulled on me. A very shabby trick indeed.'

'Which was?'

Brook gave another of his melancholic smiles. 'They sent Charlotte Ash to see me.'

SIX

When Philip Smallbone had still been a young boy, ITV had broadcast a celebrated eleven-part adaptation of Evelyn Waugh's Brideshead Revisited. His parents had so loved it that they'd brought the entire series on videocassette, and had made the whole family sit through it again and again on Sunday afternoons, even though it had made Philip squirm with boredom, thinking it mannered, absurd, and of no possible personal relevance. Then he'd not given it another thought until he'd arrived at Dragon Stone Manor five years ago to excavate its back lawns.

He tapped in the code for the automated gate, then rumbled over the railway bridge, past Greta Brook's gatehouse cottage and through the winding ancient woodlands that opened up exactly as he remembered to reveal the house itself. And, just like that, he was Charles Ryder in his army uniform, back in Arcadia once more. For this place had become for a while his own true Brideshead – a glimpse of a different and more magical life, one of glamour and youth and beauty, of the kind of golden sunshine that simply wasn't meant for the likes of him. Not just in terms of wealth and class, but in character too, for he'd always been a man of modest ambition and mild temperament, happy with his lot, blessed to have a job he enjoyed, three children he adored and a wife he was still devoted to, despite her lost figure and homely looks. He was no catwalk model himself, after all, and what mattered was how well they'd still got on together after nearly twenty years of marriage. They'd been glad partners on life's great journey, and so he'd proudly held her hand when they'd walked along the Marbella seafront on their annual holiday, and he'd bought her flowers religiously once a fortnight, and presents he could scarcely afford for her birthday and anniversary. He'd considered himself among the luckiest of men.

Then he'd come here and met Charlotte Ash.

She'd had a very particular smile, had Charlotte. Her eyes had been the startling pale blue of Caribbean shallows; and, from time to time, when she'd looked at him, they'd had an intimate sunlight twinkle to them, as if only he and she alone could properly appreciate the humour or significance of some situation, as if he'd been special to her in some way. The first time she'd smiled at him like that, he'd assumed it had been meant for someone else, as when some stranger waves at you on the street, and you're already starting to raise your hand in reply when you realise it's actually meant for the person behind. It had given him a thrill all the same. It had set his heart pounding like a near miss on the motorway. Then she'd done it again, and there'd been no question this time that it was meant for him, for they'd been out in the woods together, and quite alone. And then a third time, holding his gaze for a full four seconds before finally looking away.

As on-site representative of Suffolk's Archaeological Service, Smallbone had had the power to insist on certain conditions being met; even – in extreme circumstances – to shut the excavation down. It had been prudent, therefore, for Charlotte to stay on his good side. But this had gone far beyond that. There'd been no reason for it that he could see, other than that she felt something for him, implausible though that had seemed. Wild thoughts had come to him at night – thoughts that he'd known were absurd, at least until the next time she smiled at him that way. Because maybe she'd seen past his modest exterior to the man within, triggered by their shared passion for Suffolk and Anglo-Saxon history. It had been an open secret, even at the start of that summer, that she'd been sleeping with Hector Brook, despite his age and ravaged face. So maybe youth and beauty weren't what she looked for in a man. Maybe it was something else.

Driving home each evening, he'd lose himself in fanciful daydreams about their coming together – an accidental brush of hands leading to an uncontrolled embrace; a consoling arm around her shoulder after her break-up with Brook, stroking her hair, letting her sob against his chest; making some wild discovery together, their hug of jubilation turning to one of passion. Then he'd arrive home to be greeted by the chalkboard screeching of little Emily and Gordon's teenage sulking, while his wife would be red-faced and sweaty from the pasta she was boiling, weary from her own long day. And it had become harder and harder not to weigh the fantasy against the reality, and to find the latter wanting.

He'd grown colder and colder to his wife. He'd forgotten to buy her flowers. On the evening he'd arrived home empty handed for their anniversary, she'd finally called him on it, and so it had all come out in a full and frank exchange of crockery that had ended with him being booted from their home and his children siding with their mother, turning their backs on him. He hadn't cared. All he could think about, instead, was that he was free, and how to break the news to Charlotte.

That had been when he'd overheard what she'd truly thought of him.

He arrived outside the Manor, turned off his engine. But he wasn't ready to get out just yet. He sat there for a minute or two longer, giving his anger a chance to pass, along with his bitterness at the miserable, lonely and impoverished bedsit life he'd been reduced to. And only once he'd composed himself again, and had found an expression of mild yet cheerful anticipation for the weekend ahead, did he get out to fetch his bag and go inside.

SEVEN

Hector Brook took his foot off the dragon stone and beckoned for Elias and Greta to follow him down the slope to the timber rail fence that ran along the top of the escarpment. Elias gave it a good shake to check that it was sturdy. Satisfied, he leaned right out over it to look down. The Deben was a broad slow river, meandering where it willed. Unfortunately, one of the places it had willed over the centuries was deep into the soft earth out of which this hill was formed; so deep, indeed, that it had turned the face beneath him almost into a cliff, threatening to undermine the ground he was standing on, and eventually even the dragon stone itself.

Someone – the Environment Agency, perhaps, or the local council, or even a previous owner of this estate – had clearly decided enough was enough. They'd laid a long concrete berm along the foot of the escarpment both to prevent further erosion and to serve as a riverside footpath. They'd added a small dock while they were at it, or at least a flight of steps down into the water, along with a wooden post to which a rowing boat was tied, presumably for getting out to the speedboat and the sloop in matching liveries that were moored well out into the river, tugged taut on their cables by the current. They'd further shored up the escarpment face by laying a row of creosoted wooden timbers against its base, then covering the rest of its exposed face with thick black mesh secured by steel pegs, preventing landslips and creating a cliff some thirty feet high, enough to make Elias's toes tingle like a nice glass of chilled frizzante.

'Is this where…?' he asked.

'Yes,' said Brook. 'Though this fence wasn't here then, obviously. My proverbial stable door. But all that comes much later. I was telling you how Charlotte came to see me. Wisely, she didn't write in advance or use the entry system on the gate. She simply climbed over it instead, then marched up the drive to my front door. I made a point of ignoring people who did that. But she knocked again and kept on knocking, until finally, in exasperation, I went to answer. I stood there as she told me how she'd spent the summer excavating at Rendlesham, but that that was coming to a close now, at least for a while, and so she wanted something new. And because she'd been brought up in the village of Melton, which is just the other side of Woodbridge from here, she'd heard all about the dragon stone, and how it marked the burial of some great Anglo-Saxon king. In fact, as it later turned out, her granddad Tony had been the source of much of that talk, having heard it from his grandfather, who'd heard it from his, and so on all the way back.'

'There's a reason they don't allow hearsay in court,' observed Elias.

'Quite. That was my thought too. I didn't say it though. I couldn't, not to Charlotte. It was already too late. I admit it freely. I admit it proudly. I toppled like a Canadian redwood before her axe. We spoke for no more than half an hour that first time. By the end of it, I'd have agreed to anything to get her back here. It wasn't only her beauty, though that was remarkable. It was her spirit. Her enthusiasm. Her joy. She was infectious, and I caught her bad. So we came up here together a week later with a camera-drone and a metal detector, and we took some soil samples too. Sadly, they came back negative. But Charlotte wasn't the kind to give up easily. Nor did I want her to. We took more aerial photographs of other parts of the estate and eventually found a number of circles in the grass on my back lawn, each a few feet across and arranged in a gentle arc from the house into the woods. We ran remote-sensing equipment over them, and took more soil samples too. And we found enough interesting traces in them to be confident that they had indeed once been Anglo-Saxon burial mounds.'

'So you agreed to allow the excavation.'

'To allow it, to fund it, to make a significant donation to her museum. With only one condition: That Charlotte herself was to run it, using my house as her base.'

'Ah.'

'Yes. Quite. Though don't get me wrong. All that was her idea. Frankly, I'd never have had the nerve to suggest it myself. But she loved excavating more than anything, and didn't want to be elbowed out by her bosses, which she feared might happen unless her role was written into our agreement. I was thrilled, of course. I'd never been in love before. Not like that. I'd had the usual adventures you'd expect of a healthy, wealthy young army officer. But none that had ever consumed me. Then suddenly we'd found ourselves at war, and I'd had all these young men in my charge under constant threat of death. That took up my full attention for a while, until of course...' He touched the side of his face again, to indicate his injuries. 'I suffered afterwards not just from migraines and chronic pain but from fits and blackouts too. And when I looked at myself in the mirror, all I could see was scarring. No. That's not quite true. I could also see the faces of the men – *my* men – the ones who didn't make it back. I saw their mothers, and their grief, and all the ways in which I'd let them down. So I came to think of myself as unbearably hideous and worthless, inside and out. I *loathed* what I'd become. I shut myself off from everyone except Greta. It's the one drawback of being rich, you see, that it enables you to indulge your own worst weaknesses. Frankly, I'd gladly never have left home again. Until Charlotte came knocking. Within that first half hour, I felt alive again. I felt excitement. Value. Hope. She was my lifeline. I'd have done anything for her.'

'I understand. I do.'

'Good. Anyway, the excavation began at the start of the following summer. Teams of local volunteers and university students came in each day to do the actual digging, supervised by Charlotte with advice and support from various visiting archaeologists who stayed in the Manor when they needed beds for the night. And so the summer passed. The happiest time of my life. Followed by the darkest.'

'And your guests this weekend are the same as were here the night Charlotte fell?'

'Yes. Them and only them.'

'Aside from you and Greta, you mean?'

'Sadly no. I wish to god we had been here. Perhaps one or other of us might have noticed something, and prevented it. But Charlotte had her monthly progress review that evening, so Greta and I slipped off for a few rubbers of bridge with some friends we'd been neglecting on the other side of Ipswich. We didn't get back here until an hour and five minutes after she'd already fallen.'

'An hour and five minutes? How can you be so precise?'

'Charlotte's watch had a basic GPS tracker on it, for when she went jogging. She left the Manor at ten past ten, arrived here at twenty-one minutes past, then fell ten minutes later, and didn't move again. Greta and I didn't return from our bridge night until eleven thirty-six.'

'And you know that how?'

Brook looked a little sourly at him, unaccustomed to having his word challenged. 'The Manor had just the two security cameras back then, though I've put in more since. I call them security cameras, but really they were there to help me get rid of callers I didn't want to deal with in person. There was the one on the gate by the railway bridge, which you'll have seen yourself. We passed that at eleven thirty-three. The second was on my front door. It shows Greta dropping me off, as I say, at eleven thirty-six. The lights were all out by then. Everyone was in bed.'

'And you didn't notice that Charlotte was missing?'

'No. She hated people thinking that she'd only got the job because we were sleeping together, so she insisted on her own bedroom. She used it too, particularly when her colleagues from the museum were visiting. It was the one next to mine – the one I've given you for the weekend, as it happens – which allowed her to slip in to see me when the mood took her. I knocked on it as I went by, to let her know I was back. But I got no answer, nor did I expect one, so I had no reason to think anything was wrong. Not until the following morning. She was usually up first, you see, excited by the prospect of another day's digging. It was only when the volunteers started arriving, and she still hadn't appeared, that I grew anxious. Her bed hadn't been slept in, and no one had seen her since just after her meeting had broken up, when she'd popped into the kitchen for a torch before setting off on her walk. She liked the odd cigarette, sad to say, particularly last thing at night. Not even pregnancy could stop her. But she was ashamed of it too, so she wouldn't do it around other people, which is why she'd come up here. And because she loved this spot too, of course. She could spend hours sitting upon the dragon stone itself, or on the pair of benches we had up here then, painting her watercolours or simply gazing out at Sutton Hoo, dreaming of what we might find.'

'So any of the other guests could have followed her up here?'

'Except they didn't,' said Greta, whose presence Elias had almost forgotten. 'The front door camera caught Charlotte heading off across the front lawn. But no one else.'

'The camera was hardly a secret,' scowled Brook. 'Everyone knew it was there. It would have been easy to avoid by using one of the other doors. Which, as it so happens, is exactly what one of them did.'

'What?' asked Greta, startled. 'You never told me that.'

'I only recently found out.' He turned to Elias. 'I told you I was surer now than ever that Charlotte was murdered. This is the principal reason why. One of my guests that night slipped out of the boot-room door just two minutes after her.'

'Who?' asked Greta.

'That I don't know, sadly.' He gave himself a moment to think how to explain. 'Charlotte was determined to capture the moment of any great discovery for posterity. We'd therefore set up cameras on all the excavation trenches. On one of them, for a second or two, you can clearly see light coming out of the boot-room door. It's faint, I admit, which is how we missed it before. That and because no one ever used that door, which was kept pretty much permanently locked and bolted. So why bother going out that way unless for some dark purpose?'

'This light?' asked Elias. 'Did it come on just once?'

'Yes,' admitted Brook grudgingly. 'Though if they'd turned the light off as they went out, you wouldn't see anything on their return. Or maybe they used a different door.' He must have realised how thin this sounded, for he hurried quickly on. 'Anyway, back to that terrible morning. I panicked when I found Charlotte's room empty. She'd last been seen setting off up here, so I feared the worst. I came running up here with two of my guests, Raoul and Cameron. There's a metal staircase just a little further on that zigzags down the escarpment to the footpath below. I'll show you in the morning, when we have more time. We hurried down it to check. There was blood on the concrete by the dock, so I looked over the edge, and there she was, lying on her front upon those steps you can see, face down in the water.'

'I'm sorry,' said Elias.

'Thank you.' Brook gave himself a moment. 'I was... I was *broken* by her death. Especially with her being pregnant with our child. I'd had all these wonderful visions about how our lives together might...' He broke off and shook his head.

'Forgive me,' murmured Elias, 'but the child was definitely yours?'

He gave another scowl. But the question was legitimate. 'Yes. They did a test.'

'At your request?'

'There were rumours going around. I wanted them quashed.'

'What kind of rumours?'

He took a deep breath. 'Charlotte's younger sister Imogen was engaged at the time to the man she's since married. A man called Raoul Flood.'

Elias raised his eyebrows. 'The rugby player?'

'Yes.'

'And these rumours were about him and Charlotte, I presume? Was there anything to them?'

Brook nodded several times, though less in affirmation than to think through his response. 'Have you ever lost a loved one, detective?' he asked finally.

'My oldest boy, yes. Around the same time you lost Charlotte.'

'Ah. I'm so sorry. Forgive me. How awful. I wasn't trying to play one-up, I assure you. It's just that it's hard to explain how grief changes over time, how it doesn't go away or even diminish all that much, but that it does somehow lose its sharpness of bite. For me, at least. My memories of Charlotte are still painful, yet now they bring a certain consolation with them, a kind of cotton-wool cocoon in which I can curl up and even temporarily forget that she's gone while I relive the good times that we had. I mentioned how she had cameras set up on all the trenches, because she wanted to make a documentary if we found anything good. She also had me hire a film-maker called Cameron Wolfe she knew from London, to do interviews and take more lively footage. You'll meet him tonight. So, anyway, about a year ago now, I was looking through some boxes in my cellar when I came across the drives with all the footage from that summer. I mean I'd always known they were there; I'd just not had the heart to look at them before. I took them upstairs and spent the next few days going through them. Incidentally, that's when I spotted the light outside the boot-room door. But mostly I was looking for Charlotte. And it was wonderful. Seeing her again, so happy and dynamic and full of life, and in situations that I hadn't even been present for the first time around, so that they came to me completely fresh. It was almost like having her back again.'

'I can imagine.'

'Not all of the clips were like that, though. Some of them were...' he took a deep breath. '...*difficult*. Even *upsetting*. For one thing, she could be unexpectedly cutting about people behind their backs.' His eyes went a little distant, suggesting that he himself had been an occasional target. 'She was also very good at getting what she wanted, whether by pulling rank, by flattery, or by flirtation.'

'Including with Raoul, I assume. Who else?'

'You'll see for yourself. I've put some clips together into a kind of... well, a tribute, I suppose you'd call it. A celebration of Charlotte that summer that I plan to show everyone after lunch tomorrow. And it is a tribute too, though it carries a sting in its tail. A sting that should make each of my guests this weekend feel at least a little bit uncomfortable, and with luck maybe even provoke them into rashness. Because that was the most startling thing I learned from watching all that footage. It wasn't that one or other of my guests had a reason for wanting Charlotte dead. It was that *every single one of them* did.'

EIGHT

The main body of Dragon Stone Manor dated back to the late sixteenth century, when rugby had not yet been invented as a game, when there'd been no such thing as a back-row forward, and anyone weighing nineteen stone and standing six foot six in their bare feet would have been considered some kind of freak. 'I hate this bloody house,' grumbled Raoul Flood, rubbing the top of his head ruefully after banging it against yet another of the low lintels, as he'd done so very many times before, yet still without learning. 'What in the name of Christ possessed us to come?'

'It's for my sister,' said Imogen. 'Where else would we be?'

'Sure, if it really was about that.' He lugged his overnight bag and her suitcase up onto the double bed. His wife was hardly the fussiest of dressers, so it always amazed him how much she could pack for a single weekend. 'But it's not. You know it's not. Our bastard host is up to his old tricks.'

'And what tricks would those be?'

'Come on, Immy,' sighed Raoul. 'You know he's never been able to let Charlotte's death go. That's all this weekend is about.'

'He loved her. He truly did.' She went to the mirror to hold up against herself the dress that Hector Brook had left on the bed for her to wear at tonight's feast, the bright candyfloss pink of a Disney princess. If it was his effort to discomfort her, it was destined to fail. Life as a hospice nurse had taught her what was worth caring about, and what was not. 'It'll be five years since she died. Of course he wants to mark it.'

'With the exact same guests? One of whom he still clearly believes pushed her?'

'So what? He obviously doesn't suspect you, or he'd never have hired you as his financial advisor.'

'You're wrong. That's precisely why he hired me – so that I couldn't refuse to speak to his detectives or turn down invitations like this. You didn't hear him on the phone, all about it being time to review our relationship and make new plans. He couldn't have made it plainer that his account was at stake. Anyway, it's not just me he insisted on being here.'

Imogen turned to gaze at him. 'What are you suggesting?'

'Nothing. Nothing. I just want you to be careful, that's all.'

'Careful?' said Imogen indignantly. 'She was my *sister*. I *loved* her.'

'*Everyone* loved her,' retorted Raoul. 'That was the problem.'

'Yes, but I wasn't fucking her, was I?'

'Nor was I. I swear to god.'

'Not for lack of trying.'

Raoul took a deep breath. There was something poisonous about this house. Five minutes here, and already at each others' throats. 'I screwed up,' he admitted. 'But you know what your sister was like. You warned me, remember?'

'And look what good that did.'

'I wanted to get away. It was you who insisted on staying.'

'So it's my fault now, is it?'

They glowered at each other for a few moments. A marriage without love, desire or children; without even the memory of friendship and respect. Was there anything worse? But this was hardly the time or place. Raised voices travelled ludicrous distances in this old house. There were whispering galleries everywhere. You'd be gazing out a window when suddenly you'd hear snatches of intimate conversation being held in a completely different room.

Thankfully, Imogen chose to let it go, perhaps because he was right. She *had* warned him against Charlotte, as much for her competitiveness as for her beauty – the way she'd used men like him as a scratching post, to test the sharpness of her claws. Yet Imogen had spent so long in her sister's shadow that she hadn't been able to resist bringing him here that summer to show him off after he'd won the first of his England caps, despite knowing what her sister was like. Inevitably, Charlotte had reacted badly to being upstaged. Consciously or unconsciously, she'd set herself out to enchant him. And, by the time she'd realised what she'd done, it had been too late.

For them all.

NINE

To Elias's eye, Greta and Hector Brook looked very much the same age – yet there was undeniably something of the elder sister in the way she looked at him now. 'Every single one of them!' she scoffed, gazing at him with a mix of scorn and exasperation before turning to Elias. 'I've seen this famous tribute film of his,' she told him. 'There's nothing on it that comes within fifty miles of a motive for murder, I promise you.'

Elias gave a shrug. 'One of my first cases in Major Crimes, a man glassed the poor sod standing next to him at the bar, because he thought he'd nicked his two quid in change from a round of drinks. Only he then found it in his own pocket while his victim was bleeding out on the floor.'

'You see,' said Brook. 'And it's not just that each of them had a motive. It's that they lied to the police about it too. All of them claimed good relations with Charlotte. My film proves something very different.'

'People lying to the police,' said Elias dryly. 'Whatever next? I'll need to see this film, though, before you show it tomorrow. So I know who to watch.'

Brook nodded. 'I've put it on DVD, to make sure it doesn't get out prematurely by accident. I've left a copy on your bed, along with a box-folder of witness statements and other materials. Not a word to my other guests, though. I don't want them prepared.' He checked his watch again, gave a theatrical lift of his eyebrows. 'Take a look through it. Let me know if you have any questions. But right now I must excuse myself. So much still to do for tonight. Speaking of which, you'll find your costume on your bed.'

'My costume?' said Elias bleakly. 'You never said anything about a costume.'

'I feared you'd find an excuse not to come until tomorrow morning if I did,' said Brook with a thin smile. 'But it's nothing to fret about, I assure you. An Anglo-Saxon feast is all. Charlotte loved them. She claimed they were great for team building, but the truth is that she simply liked dressing up in beautiful clothes. Oh, and no phones or watches or anything like that. We wouldn't want to spoil the illusion, would we?'

'Heavens, no.'

'That's the spirit.' He nodded at them both, then turned and headed back down the hill towards the house, waving his hand in farewell.

Elias waited till he was out of sight then turned to Greta. She sighed and shook her head. 'I've been begging him to call this madness off,' she said. 'And not just because it's so disrespectful to all our guests, suggesting they might be murderers. It's that he's just begging for trouble. I mean, I don't believe for a moment that Charlotte was pushed that night. But what if she was? What if one of them really did it? He'd be playing with fire.'

'And this film of his?'

'It's nonsense, as you'll see. At least, you need to appreciate the context. As Hector just told you, Charlotte hoped to make a documentary about the summer, so she had cameras and microphones put up everywhere. She also had my brother hire Cameron Wolfe – or Cameron the Cameraman as we all obviously called him. He was here that whole summer, sneaking around behind people's backs, filming them without their knowledge. He claimed they acted more naturally that way, but it's pretty obvious in retrospect that he was trying to catch them in unguarded moments, to gain some kind of hold over them. Add it all together and you're talking about thousands of hours of footage, much of which was taken without people knowing they were on camera. Yet my brother only managed to stitch together a handful of banal incidents from it all, of exactly the kind you're bound to get with so many people working shoulder to shoulder on a project. An argument or two. Some flirtations and tantrums and mean things being said. We're only human, for god's sake. And honestly, you'd have to be a psycho to kill over such trivia. And our guests aren't psychos, believe me. They're good people. By and large.'

'By and large?'

Greta gave a grimace, annoyed with herself. 'Cameron the Cameraman arrived here with a decent reputation for making good low-budget documentaries. But the way he sneaked around made us all a little uneasy. Then, a year or two ago, it came out that he'd been offering free photographic sessions to attractive teenage girls, promising to send their portfolios to his contacts at model agencies. Except that he didn't have any such contacts, and he used the sessions instead to gain power over these poor creatures, bullying them into ever more abusive and degrading acts on camera until... Well, I'm sure you can guess the rest. But that was long after his time here. And it hardly makes him a killer. Especially as there's a far more plausible explanation for what happened that night.'

'Which is?'

'Maybe the balance of Charlotte's mind really was affected, or whatever that dreadful phrase is. I could just about believe it. Pregnancy can play havoc with ones hormones. And it came out at the inquest that she'd been quite a troubled teenager. Self-harm, bulimia, all of that. Her golden summer had been coming to a close, she hadn't found what she'd hoped to find, and she was engaged to a man she was fond of, but who, in all candour, she didn't love anything like as fiercely as he loved her. Put it all together and you can see how it might have become too much. But I honestly don't buy it. She was confident, ambitious and tough-minded – and I mean each of those as sincere compliments. They're the exact qualities I try to instil in the young girls at my school. Her first season here had been a little disappointing, sure, but archaeology is like that. This is a big estate, and she was already looking forward not just to next year, but to the ones after that. Better to travel than to arrive, as they say. She was in great spirits that whole day, including when we set off for our night of bridge. She was settled. She was happy. She was doing what she loved, and she was excited about motherhood and being mistress of this place. So I honestly wouldn't look any further than that it was a dark night and the grass was dewy and she was wearing a pair of soft-soled shoes without enough grip on them. She always stood a little too close to the edge for my comfort – far closer than I'd ever have dared myself, even now that the fence is up. It gave her a thrill, I think, though she did it to tease too. I'm terrible with heights myself, you see. I squeaked like a mouse whenever she went too close. My toes would clench up like fists. It's a horrible feeling, vertigo, even when its vicarious. It renders one so powerless. I'd beg her to come back, but of course that only ever made her go closer.'

'And her missing phone?'

'It's a deep, wide and muddy river, prone to unpredictable estuarine currents. Honestly, it could have been out in the North Sea by the time my brother had it dredged. One of her shoes had come off too. They never found that either. So unless her killer was some kind of weird fetishist…'

'Yes,' said Elias, for that was how he saw it too. But Brook was paying him top dollar for the weekend, so a weekend's worth of investigation was what he was going to get.

TEN

For some three hundred and forty-five days each year, Cameron Wolfe hated his Porsche 911 with a passion. He'd been seduced by its showroom gleam six years before, all black and waxed and sexy as hell. He'd just won his first major award, his rise had seemed unstoppable, it had fitted his image of himself. But it had soon proved a nightmare, leaky in the rain and forever in the shop, costing him a fortune he didn't have. Even so, he'd thought it had given him a certain panache until he'd overheard the cow he'd been going out with at the time mocking it as his comb over. His comb over, for fuck's sake, like he was going bald – which he wasn't, he absolutely wasn't, he just had a high forehead, that was all.

But then there were days like this, with cloudless skies and baking temperatures, burning over the Orwell bridge with the roof down and that thrilling Porsche roar – and the old euphoria would blaze through him again, that sense of being special, that anything was possible. And maybe it still was. *Two grand a day!* That was what Hector Brook was paying him for the weekend. *Two grand a day, plus expenses! And Friday and Monday counting as full days too!*

God, but he needed it.

He slowed by Suffolk Police's Martlesham HQ. No point asking for trouble, not with the contraband in his bag. Then he put his foot down once more, blasting by a series of container lorries as though they were stuck in treacle, tooting the feebs out of his way, getting his tyres to screech as he left the last roundabout onto the Woodbridge road, where the single lane and the thickening bank holiday traffic finally forced him to slow back down to mortal speeds.

Brook's initial offer had been two grand for the whole weekend. Cameron had told him to fuck off. There was no way the man was inviting him for the pleasure of his company, which meant he needed him here. And the man was so rich that money meant nothing to him. The negotiations had duly started. Cameron might have held out for even more, but he'd needed the cash too badly, and frankly he'd lost his nerve. Besides, a weekend in a stately home like Dragon Stone Manor wasn't exactly a hardship. There'd be plenty who'd pay through the nose for it – though admittedly they wouldn't typically have their host trying to nail them for murder. But then Brook hadn't managed it five years ago, and he wouldn't manage it now.

He reached the automated gate, crossed the railway bridge, roared up the drive before slewing to a stop outside the front door, spraying gravel against a catering van. He shouldered his bag and swaggered inside, letting the door swing back in the face of a red-headed woman struggling with two trays of cellophane-wrapped canapés. There'd been a time when he'd have held the door open for her, maybe even have offered to carry one of her trays for her; but the one advantage of being written off as irredeemable scum was that it freed you from all that bullshit. Up the main staircase and along the landing to his old room. He dumped his bag on the sofa, looked around. Still no *en suite*, which was a bore, though its sink came in handy for the wee hours, so to speak.

Eighteen months ago now, the country's nastiest and most hypocritical tabloid had done a hatchet job on Cameron, putting the worst possible spin on some fashion shoots he'd done to finance his next documentary. His main backers had promptly pulled out. His landlord had triggered a morality clause to boot him from his studio. None of his other contacts had even taken his calls. He'd simply become too toxic. With the writing so clearly on the wall, he'd even tried to move abroad. But getting a visa had proved impossible.

The room was stuffy and hot thanks to the afternoon sunshine pouring through the heavily latticed windows. He opened them all as wide as they would go, creating something of a breeze. Then he lit and smoked a joint while leaning out and gazing over the front lawn. Almost against his will, his eyes were drawn to the hilltop from which Charlotte had fallen that terrible night. And suddenly he saw her face – not as the beautiful young woman that he'd photographed and filmed so often, the one he'd fallen so hard for, but rather as the broken, pale and bloody corpse that had started haunting his dreams again, ever since Brook had invited him here for the weekend. And maybe eight grand wasn't the deal he'd thought it. Maybe it was Brook who'd got the better end of it after all.

ELEVEN

E lias was so surprised when he saw his bedroom that his first thought was that Greta must have directed him to the wrong one, for it was surely far larger and grander than was warranted for a humble hired hand like himself. It had its own private bathroom, a canopied king-sized bed, a walnut desk, a pair of reclining armchairs facing a huge wall-mounted TV, and some well-stocked bookshelves. A pair of doors even opened out onto a small stone balcony with a spectacular view of the River Deben, whose pewter surface was burning orange in the late afternoon sunlight. But then he remembered that Brook believed he had a murderer in the house this weekend, and so was no doubt comforted to have his own man next door. Which, now that he thought of it, perhaps also explained why Brook had packed Anna off to Gatehouse Cottage, even though there had to be bedrooms here to spare. He simply didn't want to expose her to unnecessary danger. Elias had already taken warmly to his host, but his liking for him now ticked up another notch.

His costume was waiting for him on the bed, as Brook had warned. So too was a mottled grey box-folder. He opened it up. A DVD in a plain white sleeve was sitting on top. He set it aside for later to get at the documents beneath, then settled with them into one of the armchairs. It began with dry biographies of each of his fellow guests written by some unknown hand, spiced up by acerbic comments added in red ink by Brook himself. The first three were archaeologists, all here for the monthly meeting:

Dr Lucius Hyde-Smith, Head of Early Medieval European Collections at the British Museum, and Charlotte's ultimate boss; Dr Bryony Mackay, Charlotte's former line manager at the Museum, who'd since left for English Heritage; and Philip Smallbone, representative of Suffolk's Archaeological Service. Also staying had been Charlotte Ash's younger sister Imogen with her then fiancé, now husband, Raoul Flood. And finally Cameron the Cameraman Wolfe.

The coroner's report came next, followed by an architect's plan of the Manor and a surveyor's map of the Dragon Stone Hill estate that Elias unfolded on the carpet in front of him. It was roughly oval in shape, bounded between the East Suffolk railway line and the River Deben, further protected by virtually impenetrable thickets of heather and gorse on the railway side, and by marshland and the escarpment alongside the river, so that the only two real points of access were the railway bridge and the staircase down from Dragon Stone Hill to the footpath beneath that Brook had promised to show him in the morning. Within this larger oval, the Manor, Gatehouse Cottage and the hilltop summerhouse formed the three points of an approximately equilateral triangle, each some ten minutes walk from the other two.

Elias resumed going through the folder. Brook had been so dissatisfied with the original police investigation that he'd hired a firm of private investigators to check their work. Their lead agent had done much as Elias himself would have, visiting the key sites, speaking to the attending officers and the investigating team as well as to each of the guests who'd been here that night, testing their stories and alibis. His report made it clear that he believed the police had done a good and thorough job, and had come to the correct conclusion.

Yet Brook still hadn't been convinced. He'd given a second firm of private investigators a wider brief, exploring Charlotte's schooldays, her time at university and in London. They'd interviewed former colleagues, friends and boyfriends, then had checked the whereabouts of anyone with the slightest motive for wishing Charlotte ill. They too had found nothing new.

A folder of photographs next. It saddened Elias to see Charlotte, young and every bit as beautiful as Brook had said, with fluffy blonde hair, mischievous eyes and an enchanting smile, which made the pictures of her corpse all the more dismaying, lying on her back on the dock after being dragged from the river, her face pale and blotchy, her hair matted and reddened by watery blood.

Last of all came the statements the guests had given to the police. Elias laid them side by side on the bed, both to get a composite picture of the night, and to check them against each other. They'd waved Hector and Greta Brook off for their night of bridge at around seven thirty, after which Charlotte Ash, Lucius Hyde-Smith, Bryony Mackay and Philip Smallbone had held their monthly meeting over a cold supper in the dining room. These were typically wrapped up by about nine, but this had been the last one of the summer, meaning that – in addition to the usual personnel, budgeting and reporting issues – there'd been the small matter of closing up the site for the winter as well as discussion of plans for the following year. Philip Smallbone had lobbied for excavating in the woods, and Bryony Mackay had argued strongly for the front lawns while Lucius Hyde-Smith had grumbled about having a second season at all, despite Hector Brook's offer of finance and another substantial donation.

The conversation had grown heated. Apparently, Hyde-Smith had been in a particularly prickly mood. According to his own account, the meeting had been tedious and he'd had such a vicious migraine from excavating out in the sun all afternoon that he'd excused himself at around nine thirty, taken a fistful of aspirin and gone straight to bed. But Philip Smallbone and Bryony Mackay had told a different story. Both agreed that he'd had far too much to drink, and had become belligerent and rude, dismissing the excavation as a rich man's plaything and a complete waste of all their time. Exasperated, Charlotte had taken the whisky bottle away from him when he'd gone for a refill, and had told him that he'd had enough. But this had only set him off, jabbing his finger in her face and yelling that he was her boss and she'd better treat him with respect or else. Then he'd stormed off upstairs, chuntering angrily to himself, and hadn't been seen again until breakfast the following morning, when he'd appeared looking appropriately pale and fragile.

The meeting had continued without him until ten p.m., when a kind of unofficial curfew kicked in, after which making noise of any kind was heavily discouraged. Charlotte had declared herself off for her nightly walk. Philip Smallbone had offered to keep her company, but Charlotte had told him no. Curiously, Smallbone hadn't mentioned this in his original statement to the police, though he'd admitted it when they'd come back to him after speaking to Bryony Mackay, while also brushing it off as mere concern for a young woman out alone on a dark night.

Imogen and Cameron the Cameraman had meanwhile spent the evening streaming a movie in the kitchen. They'd been the last to see Charlotte alive, when she'd popped in for a torch. Their movie had ended shortly afterwards. They'd bid each other goodnight and had gone upstairs to their respective rooms. Finally, there was Raoul Flood. He'd had a spat with Imogen earlier that evening, after which he'd set off across the railway bridge for a sports pub on the Woodbridge Road. He was a famous enough face to have been recognised in such a place, and the landlord and several regulars confirmed he'd spent the whole evening there, dining on steak and chips and watching some day-night cricket before setting off back to the Manor at a little after ten, passing the camera on the automated gate at ten seventeen. According to his own account, he'd headed straight up the drive to the Manor, arriving to find the lights off and everyone already in bed. Still hungry despite his steak dinner, he'd gone in the back way and through to the kitchen, which was why he hadn't been caught on the front door camera. He'd toasted himself a couple of cheese and ham sandwiches that he'd taken upstairs to his room, where he'd found Imogen reading her paperback in bed. According to them both, that had been at around ten forty, give or take a few minutes.

There was, however, a footpath through the woods from just behind Gatehouse Cottage up to the top of Dragon Stone Hill. If Flood had taken that after crossing the railway bridge, he could have got there several minutes before Charlotte fell. Yet, even allowing for a little slippage in the timings, it was hard to imagine him pushing her then making it back to his bedroom by ten forty, let alone having stopped along the way to toast himself a couple of sandwiches.

Murder, then, was impossible to rule out. But an accident seemed overwhelmingly more likely. Indeed, the larger puzzle that Elias was left with, was why Brook had always been so convinced otherwise.

TWELVE

The sun sank beneath the treetops, taking much of the afternoon's heat with it, yet leaving behind a pleasant warmth. There was still no sign of Greta, but Anna decided to get ready anyway. She typically wore her hair as the bird's nest intended by nature, but it would be an ungracious insult to her host to leave it that way after he'd spent such a ridiculous amount on her costume, so she washed it thoroughly in the shower then combed it as it dried, tugging out the tangles until her eyes watered.

Her eyebrows needed plucking, and her legs and armpits could each do with a shave, but she doubted that Anglo-Saxon women had been too scrupulous about such grooming, so she commended herself for authenticity instead, and left them as they were.

Her dress fitted her like a glove. Unfortunately, though, that glove was a good half-size too small, so tight around her waist that it made her cleavage pop. When she sat down on the side of the bed to pull on her sandals, it was a struggle even to reach her feet. A dab or two of perfume, a rare touch of makeup, then working out how to pin her headscarf in place, and she was done.

She went to stand in front of the full-length mirror, turning this way and that, letting the skirts of her dress swish scarlet around her legs while trying her very hardest to revive her earlier indignation at being tricked into such a costume. But it was hopeless. To her intense dismay, she couldn't help but like what she saw.

Six thirty arrived, but still not her hostess. Anna began to fret. Parties with total strangers were ordeal enough without arriving late and alone. She was about to set off for the Manor anyway when a sky blue Hyundai i10 came roaring up the drive to screech to a stop alongside the Land Rover in front of the cottage, and the woman from the photos clambered out, in a mild panic at how late she was. 'You must be Anna!' she cried, as they met at the door. 'At least I hope to god you are, or there's some explaining to do. I'm Greta, Greta Brook, as I'm sure you must have guessed, or it would be me having to do the explaining, wouldn't it?' She gave a slightly hysterical laugh, then paused to look Anna up and down. 'Dear god!' she said. 'That dress! You're going to set off riots!'

'It is quite something,' said Anna. 'Is it you I should thank?'

'Heavens, no,' said Greta. 'It's all my brother's doing. Though he did ask me to tell you that it's yours to take away and keep.'

'But it must have cost a fortune.'

'Yes, but it's not much use to him, is it? Not unless he's living some kind of double life I'm unaware of. Anyway, I love the boy to death, but he has far more money than sense, that's the truth. Make the most of it while you can, that's my advice.' She checked her watch and gave her hands a flutter. 'Oh dear, oh dear,' she wailed. 'Where does the time go? You couldn't give me five minutes, could you? Five minutes and not a millisecond longer, my word of honour. And then it's only thirty seconds in the car.'

'Take as long as you need,' Anna assured her. 'I'm in no hurry.'

She waited downstairs in the sitting room, browsing the bookshelves, as she liked to do in other people's homes. There were teaching guides on physics, mathematics, chemistry, biology, computer studies, modern languages and other such subjects, suggesting strongly that Greta was stand-in of choice when any of her colleagues fell ill. There were heavyweight works on ancient history, philosophy and the scientific revolution. More touchingly, she found a number of well-thumbed books on IVF, surrogacy and adoption pushed back almost out of sight on a top shelf, which made her realise what was missing from the cottage – any sign of children of Greta's own, or even of a partner. As for the rest, they were an odd mix of highbrow fiction and bodice rippers. She plucked down one of the latter for fun, only to find herself enthralled.

Ten minutes ticked by, once, twice and almost for a third time before Greta finally came hurrying breathlessly downstairs, her cheeks flushed beneath her make-up, fragrant with perfume and sheathed in a stunning ankle-length silk dress of shimmering dark blue flecked with silver, and with a translucent silk headdress that glittered as if tiny diamonds had been sprinkled over her chestnut hair, which she'd released from the prison of its bun. She'd put on sapphire and ruby earrings too, along with a matching choker. 'But you look beautiful,' blurted out Anna, before realising she probably shouldn't have sounded quite so surprised.

'It's these fabrics,' said Greta, ignoring the surprise and glowing instead at Anna's obvious sincerity. 'Say what else you like about them, the Anglo-Saxons did know their colours.'

THIRTEEN

Elias took a leisurely shower, washing off his long day. His right hand quickly began to ache when he asked too much of it, so he'd learned how to brush his teeth, wash and dry himself with his left instead, awkward though it still felt. He went to the bed for his costume. There were no instructions for what bit went where, or in which order, so he gave it some study before pulling on a white cotton shift like a hospital gown, then adding a leather breastplate, some leggings, sandals and a sword-belt, all finished off with a dark green woollen robe secured by a silver buckle in the shape of an eagle. He took off his yellow glove then, after a few moments thought, put it back on again. Anachronistic, maybe, but better than tedious explanations or giving offence.

He was gazing rather morosely at himself in the mirror when Hector Brook knocked upon his door and came marching in. He was dressed in a belted white gown and a robe of regal purple clasped by a dragon brooch of polished gold. They gazed at each other for a moment or two, sizing each other up as men in costume will. Brook noticed his glove but let it go, nodding instead with satisfaction at his overall appearance. 'I knew you'd make me a fine warrior,' he said.

'My lord,' said Elias, bowing slightly from the waist.

Brook laughed and clapped him on the shoulder. 'It'll be fun, believe me. Come on down, I'll introduce you to the others.'

They made their way down a set of narrow back stairs

and through a kitchen packed with chefs and catering staff all shouting at one another, out into a utility room with covered platters on a sideboard and a large silver bowl of spiced dark liquid that Elias judged to be mead, both from the smell it exuded, and from the drinking horns that lay curled up around it like so many swaddled infants.

The rear of the Manor was very different from its front, functional rather than stately, with a huge green heating oil tank and a padlocked cellar hatch for deliveries of winter logs. The back lawn was in a poorer state too, uneven and a little sickly, save for a few lusher strips that Elias took to be excavation trenches that had since been reseeded or relaid. A bonfire was blazing lustily at a prudent distance from the buildings and trees, throwing off smoke that drifted this way and that in the light breeze, making Elias's eyes water. A piglet was being spit-roasted on a firepit nearby, a woman in a sepia robe giving the handle a quarter turn every minute or so, and pouring some kind of marinade onto its glistening skin with a long-handled ladle, to dribble down its flanks and spit out in tiny shooting stars.

A row of outbuildings was set at a slight angle to the house. Furthest to their left stood a tall creosoted barn with double doors and a gabled roof of terracotta tiles. Then came a row of low brick buildings with scroll doors that had the look of converted stables. Several men and women in Anglo-Saxon costumes – presumably Elias's fellow weekend guests – were clustered in front of these, attended by a pair of serving staff also in period clothes, though their knee-length brown tunics, leggings and flat sandals were conspicuously drabber. But no sign of either Anna or Greta.

Their approach was noticed. The guests turned in unison, like meerkats at a predator. Brook threw out his arms in sham delight to see them all, then shook them each vigorously by the hand, asked them how they'd been, then introduced them to Elias as the co-discoverer of King John's lost crown jewels, here to give what he assured them would be a fascinating talk. Not by a flicker did he signal his belief that one of them had murdered the love of his life, or that he meant to expose them and make them pay. To the contrary, he could hardly have appeared in better spirits, teasing them about their costumes, which he'd evidently put some real thought into, precisely to have his fun with them.

A serving woman came by with drinks. Elias took an apple juice, wanting to keep his head clear. It was thick as soup and perfectly chilled, with a mix of sweetness and spice that was so unexpectedly delicious that he drained it straight back and took another. Then he stood there quietly, taking stock of his fellow guests as they chatted amongst themselves.

Immediately to his left was the British Museum's Dr Lucius Hyde-Smith, one of the world's leading authorities on the Anglo-Saxons – or so it was claimed on the blurb of his latest book. Elias would have taken him for an academic even without having read up on him. He simply had that look: narrow shouldered, stooped, grey-haired and querulous, a pair of half moon glasses dangling unevenly from a string around his neck. He was well into his seventies and independently wealthy, so presumably it was the work itself, or the status that came with it, that kept him from retiring. He was dressed in the belted plain white robe of a counsellor, if not a particularly valued one. Every so often, when he thought no-one was looking, he'd glance at Brook with his lips sourly pursed, as though he'd been bullied into coming, and resented it. And while it was hard to imagine him making his way up Dragon Stone Hill that night if he'd been even half as drunk as reported, he might have been shamming it to give himself a kind of alibi. Interestingly, he was on the apple juice too, perhaps wary of making a fool of himself again, or of incriminating himself with a slip of the tongue.

Standing on Hyde-Smith's other side was Imogen Flood, Charlotte Ash's younger sister. She was a little above average height, though perhaps made to look a little taller by her extreme thinness, with bony long arms, handsome dark eyes and no-nonsense short brown hair. She held herself proudly too, with set lips and a fighter's chin, as if to warn people that, while she might not be the kind to throw the first punch, by god she'd throw the second. The kind of woman you'd want on your side if it came to a scrap with authority. No makeup to speak of, and seemingly indifferent to Brook having dressed her up like a teen princess. But she flinched as though with toothache whenever her sister was mentioned, and looked sadly away.

Her husband Raoul Flood stood on her other side, instantly identifiable from his height and bulk, and from a face more battered even than Elias's own. He'd put on weight and lost some hair since retiring early from rugby, courtesy of a series of knee and hip injuries too complex, painful and persistent for even modern medicine to fix, and which had left him with a slight limp and a career in financial services. He too was dressed as a warrior, though as a king's champion rather than Elias's war-weary captain. His eyes were guarded and he looked distinctly unhappy to be here, perhaps aware of the weekend's true purpose. One thing was for sure: he'd have had no difficulty whatsoever in hurling Charlotte over the escarpment edge. And if he were the jealous type, or prone to bursts of anger…

Beyond him stood Bryony Mackay, Charlotte's former manager at the British Museum, now at English Heritage. Mid to late forties, plump, red-headed and kindly, with an attractive splash of pale freckles across her nose and cheeks, as though one of her three children had flicked a wet watercolour brush at her. She seemed rather troubled by hay fever, dabbing at her reddened eyes with a tissue, turning away every few minutes to squirt some kind of decongestant spray up her nose. Brook had dressed her in a frumpy, honey-coloured woollen robe with a knotted dark brown sash – the royal wet-nurse, perhaps, or some unusually favoured housekeeper – though in truth it made her look as if she'd been taking a bath when disturbed by an unexpected doorbell. It was hard to imagine her hating anyone enough to kill, especially with her young family to consider; yet presumably there was something.

Cameron Wolfe next, with distinctly more space around

him than anyone else, rendered toxic by his notoriety. Brook introduced him to Elias as Cameron the Cameraman, provoking an unmistakeable flicker of contempt. Mid thirties and tall, though a good couple of inches shorter than Raoul, and barely half the breadth. A high-jumper rather than a back-row forward. Militantly good-looking, his scalp shaven to disguise his widow's peak, prominent cheekbones, a well-trimmed goatee and eyebrows too thin to be natural, all of which effect was heightened by Brook having dressed him as the malevolent noble from a Shakespeare tragedy. He grabbed a fresh beaker of ale every time a tray came within reach, but his head must have been made of oak, for it had little effect on his speech or manner, other than he gradually took less trouble to hide his sneer.

Completing the circle was Philip Smallbone of Suffolk's Archaeological Service. He was in his early fifties, stumpy, overweight and dressed by Brook as a wealthy merchant of some kind; yet despite the richness of his red robe and golden buckle, he had the cheap haircut and hangdog look of a divorced dad. He came across as somehow both prickly and diffident, and what little he said was rendered mostly unintelligible by his mumbled Suffolk burr.

Brook touched Elias on his arm, nodded back across the lawn. He turned to see Anna and Greta arriving through the silvery mist of bonfire smoke, shimmering in dresses of scarlet and sapphire. It had been months since Elias had last seen Anna; he wasn't quite sure how they stood. But she beamed with such obvious delight to see him, and spread her arms so wide, that he couldn't help hurrying across to meet her, taking her in a hug and lifting her off her feet, then holding her for a beat too long, so that he felt rather foolish as he set her back down. 'You look amazing,' he told her.

'It's the dress,' she said.

'Sure,' he said. 'I'd look like that too, if I put it on.'

'You look good yourself,' she told him, taking him by his arm. 'Warrior chic clearly suits you. Or perhaps it's your new job?'

'Twice the money for half the stress. What's not to like?

You'll find this hard to believe, I know, but I haven't been stabbed in months. Or thrown from a plane.'

'What?' asked Anna, shocked. 'Not even once?'

'It's like the nation's criminals have given up.' He leaned over to murmur in her ear. 'Though who knows what the weekend will bring?'

She took half a step back in surprise. 'How do you mean?'

'In the morning, okay? I'll tell you everything.' Then he put his hand on the small of her back and led her across to introduce her to the others.

FOURTEEN

The suckling pig took longer to cook through than expected, as suckling pigs will. They milled around as they waited, snacking on crab, oysters and other treats, returning to the house for the loos, dividing into smaller groups that broke up and reformed. Cameron the Cameraman kept trying to get Anna off by herself, which set her internal alarms jangling so loudly that she turned each time to whoever else was nearest, and talked to them instead. In this way, she found herself with Bryony Mackay, a stout red-headed woman in matronly robes and open-toed sandals, so that Anna could see the blister plasters around each of her big toes. 'Of course I know who you are,' she said irritably, when Anna tried to explain herself. 'I could barely pick up a journal last year without your face upon its cover.'

'Sorry about that. They kept ambushing me.'

'How wonderful it must be! To have your career already made, and still only in your twenties!'

'Oh, come on. These things have a short shelf-life.'

'Not in our world, they don't,' said Mackay, throwing a resentful glare at Lucius Hyde-Smith, her former boss. 'And didn't I read that you have publishers bidding crazy amounts for your story?'

'I had a couple of offers, yes. But not for anything like what got reported. Anyway, I said no.' She'd actually sat down at her laptop one weekend, to see if she was up to it; but she'd quickly realised that she couldn't tell the story the publishers wanted without bringing up episodes from her past that were still too raw for her to share. Then there were the two men she'd killed. She felt not the slightest remorse for either one. On the contrary, she was proud of herself for what she'd done. But she was proud because she'd done it to save a friend, which made the prospect of profiting from their deaths feel unutterably grubby. Then an enterprising journalist had rushed out a paperback he'd cobbled together from police sources and the interviews she and Elias had given, and it had done so poorly that the moment had rather passed. Instead, for a negligible advance, she'd agreed to rework her thesis into a new biography of William Marshal, one of the more remarkable figures of English history, using it as a vehicle to recount those parts of the King John affair she felt comfortable sharing.

A little later, she found herself talking to Philip Smallbone of Suffolk's Archaeological Service. 'So you're the King John woman,' he said, striving to sound jocular, but falling short. 'We don't have much time for the man here, I'll tell you that. Tore down half our castles.'

'I'll let him know, next time I see him.'

'A bad king. A bad, bad king.'

'I only found his baggage train. I didn't crown the guy.' But she didn't want to start the weekend by antagonising her fellow guests, so she shaped her mouth into a smile and asked: 'Were you excavating here that summer too? I'm dying to know what you found.'

'Not much,' he said, nodding at the lawn behind her. 'The usual shards of pottery. Some coins and brooches. A nice clay figurine. The best was probably a pair of post-holes from what we think was likely an old gallows, to judge from all the sand bodies nearby.' His eyes glinted in the hope of discomforting her. 'You know what sand bodies are?'

'Yes.'

'They're the crusty stains that get left behind when a body decomposes. Like at Pompeii, only preserved by soil rather than by lava.'

'I know what a sand body is.'

'That's why we think it was a gallows. They used to leave them hanging by their necks until their heads popped off, you see. Then they'd toss both bits higgledy-piggledy into a pit so that you'd find their heads in all kinds of odd places. Behind their backs. Beneath their feet.'

'I know what a sand body is,' sighed Anna. She turned to look at the house. 'So you stayed here, then, did you? How lovely.'

'Not really, no. I went home whenever I could. But sometimes we worked so late that I'd have had to turn round about the moment I got there.'

'You're not from around here, then?'

'No getting past you, is there? Mr Brook obviously chose his detectives well.'

Anna gazed at him in bemusement. 'His detectives? What are you talking about?'

'It's why you're here, isn't it? You and your friend. To find out which one of us killed poor Charlotte.'

'Don't be ridiculous,' said Anna. 'I'm here to give a talk on King John.'

'Sure! Stick to the story. Just don't expect any of us to believe it.' He nodded curtly at her and stalked off, though not to talk to anyone else, but rather to stand by the bonfire and glower at the flames, as though they too had disappointed him.

'That looked like fun,' murmured Elias, coming to join her.

'He thinks Brook invited us here to find out who murdered his old fiancée.'

Elias raised an eyebrow. 'Then he's sharper than he looks.'

'Bloody hell. Tell me more.'

'Like I said. In the morning.' He was about to add something further when Brook called for everyone's attention. He waited until he had it, then announced it was time to eat and urged them towards the barn, even as its double doors were opened by a pair of strapping young men in brown tunics.

A minstrel was perched on a tall stool to their left as

they went inside, plucking music from his lyre while crooning some medieval ballad. To their right there was an easel bearing a poster-sized head and shoulders photograph of a stunning young fair-haired woman with bright blue eyes and a dazzling smile, evidently taken on an Anglo-Saxon evening just like this, for she was wearing a gorgeous silk dress of silver and gold, while her hair was lightly covered by a lacy headdress. Charlotte Ash, obviously, as confirmed by the legend beneath, which gave her dates as well as her name. Anna's heart gave a twist. Her beauty was expected, from everything she'd already heard, but not how fun she looked, how cheerful and full of life, so that Anna couldn't help but feel a sharp pang of loss, though she'd never even heard of her before that afternoon.

The others took the barn's interior for granted, no doubt having attended such feasts before, but it was all new to Anna and Elias, so they stepped out of the stream to give themselves a moment to drink it in. The place had been converted into an Anglo-Saxon great hall for the night, its walls decked with shields, swords and tapestries, while rush matting had been spread across its worn brick floor, and three casks of ale or wine had been lined up against its back wall – all subtly lit by a set of candle-bulb chandeliers hanging from the rafters.

Three long wooden tables had been set up in a kind of horseshoe in the centre of the barn, with all the place settings on the outside, leaving a hollow aisle inside, presumably to make it easier for the staff to serve out food and drink. There were four settings on the near side, but only three on the far, with another three at the top end. Those on either side had padded wooden benches to sit on; but, at the top end, there was a huge gilt throne in the centre, flanked by more modest high-backed chairs on either side.

The tables themselves were covered by starched white cotton cloths with delicate floral arrangements upon them, and fat red candles on bronze holders, their flames dancing this way and that from the swirl of air allowed in by the open doors and shutters. Hector Brook went directly to the throne at the head of the horseshoe, while each of his guests searched the name cards for their assigned place. Anna was surprised to find herself on one of the high-backed chairs at the end table, with Hector Brook to her right and Greta on his other side, with Elias beyond her and then Imogen Flood and Philip Smallbone. As for the other side, Anna had Lucius Hyde-Smith immediately to her left, followed by Raoul Flood, Bryony Mackay and finally Cameron Wolfe.

'I trust your dress fits okay,' murmured Brook, as she arrived beside him.

'It's perfect,' she told him. 'It's beautiful.'

'The scarlet was Greta's suggestion. Not a comment upon your morality, I assure you, but rather on your complexion. Not that I understand these things.'

'She said I was to keep it. That's incredibly generous.'

'Not at all. Worth it just to see you wear it.' Yet he appeared completely indifferent as to how she looked, and smiled politely to declare the matter closed.

Everyone took their seats. Only Brook remained standing. No doubt he'd have tapped a glass had he had one, but he rapped the tabletop instead. 'Let me start by thanking you all for coming,' he began, once he had their attention. 'I know how precious bank holidays can be. But I promise you this weekend will be one for the ages. As you all know, it's the fifth anniversary of the loss of our beloved friend Charlotte Ash, which I couldn't let pass without tribute. Yet she herself was the most fun-loving of people, and the thought of marking it with some melancholic dirge would have made her furious. I therefore intend this weekend to be a celebration of her life, of the joy and love and happiness she brought to all who knew her, the way she inspired people.'

'Hear, hear,' muttered Lucius Hyde-Smith.

'So! Our feast tonight is just the start. We'll be doing all her favourite things at one point or another. We'll go sailing on the Deben and we'll pig out on Orford oysters. We'll hear a wonderful talk from our special guests Anna Warne and Ben

Elias, who I hope you've all had a chance to say hello to, because they recently made exactly the kind of discovery we'd hoped to make ourselves five years ago – a discovery that I now believe more strongly than ever we will make here, and sooner than any of you might imagine. We'll have other special guests too, though I intend to keep those as surprises. I'll also be sharing with you a tribute to Charlotte I made, and plenty else besides. But I don't want to give too much away in advance. So, for the moment, please just enjoy your dinner and the opportunity to catch up with old friends.'

He sat down to a light smattering of applause, upon which Hyde-Smith made to rise, clearly believing it incumbent upon himself, as the most senior of the guests, to make some kind of reply. Fortunately for them all, a pair of serving women appeared at the doors before he could get started, pushing a silver soup tureen on a wheeled wooden trolley into the aisle between the tables. Mouthwatering aromas filled the barn as they took off its lid to reveal a rich seafood broth swimming with clams, mussels, oysters and fat chunks of fish and lobster that they ladled into wooden bowls and then passed out, along with crusty wholemeal rolls still toasty from the oven, and individual little pots of salted butter.

'Charlotte's favourite dish,' confided Hector Brook, as Anna began in on it. 'She liked to cook it herself. I once suggested it could do with a pinch of nutmeg. She almost took my head off. Apparently nutmeg didn't arrive in England until much later.'

'No,' agreed Anna.

'Still. Garlic, coriander, bay leaves and sea salt. Can't complain, eh?'

'It's delicious,' she assured him, underlining the sincerity of her words by wolfing down her portion before looking up hopefully for more, only to find the trolley and the tureen already gone. She tore her bread roll into chunks instead, and buttered it, the better to wipe clean the sides of—

'Hwæt!' roared a man.

She looked up, startled, as a tall, grizzled and bare-chested warrior came swaggering in through the barn's open doors. His shaven torso and his long limbs all gleamed with oil, and he was holding a helmet in his left hand while his right rested on the pommel of a long sword hanging from his leather belt. 'Hwæt!' he bellowed again, even more loudly, in case they hadn't caught it the first time, or had failed to recognise the famous opening word of the epic Anglo-Saxon poem *Beowulf*.

Their attention gained, he allowed silence to return. He stood there for a good ten seconds before finally advancing towards them with a braggart's cockiness, making his way into the gap between the tables, so that Anna belatedly realised it wasn't there merely to help serve them with food, but also as a makeshift stage for the night's performance, whatever that was to be. Now he crouched a little, darting his eyes this way and that, a conspirator wary of being overheard. 'Listen.'

He stood tall once more, set his helmet down on the table between Anna and Hector Brook. It was, she saw, a perfect replica of the one from Sutton Hoo, with its panels of dancing warriors and its nose-piece in the shape of a dragon whose slender outspread wings formed the eyebrows on either side. And now the lyrist, whose presence Anna had almost forgotten, began a rhythmic soft strumming, while the warrior made slow laps of the tables, declaiming in his growling deep voice passages from Beowulf's famous battles against Grendel, Grendel's mother and finally the dragon, stopping every line or two to supply the translation, while Brook and a few of the other guests got fully into the spirit of it, stomping their feet, shouting approval and toasting him with their mugs of ale.

He was still at it when their main course arrived, already served out onto large wooden platters. Fatty slices of spit-roast pork that came with crackling, cabbage, parsnips, carrots, onions and a mushed-up pea omelette. The pork was salty and perfectly cooked, perfumed as much as flavoured with spring onion, garlic and another fragrant herb that Anna recognised but couldn't quite identify. And the crackling was a dark gold except where it had been charred black by the firepit, crisp yet deliciously juicy as she crunched it between her teeth.

Dessert next – a medley of fruits and chilled cream that Anna had little room left for, followed by the return of the wooden trolley, only this time bearing a large silver bowl of mead, along with a jewelled silver goblet and a number of drinking horns lying on their sides, jolting back and forth as the trolley bumped over the uneven matting. The *Beowulf* actor strode so emphatically out of the barn that Anna assumed his part in the entertainment was fully played. But he returned half a minute later wearing a welder's mitt and carrying a long sword whose tip was glowing orange from the firepit. He thrust this into the bowl of mead, making it hiss and fizz and spit, filling the barn with pungent aromas. Then he and the two serving women left once more, and the barn doors closed behind them.

The chandeliers began to dim and then went out, leaving only the red candles fluttering upon the tables. A pair of spotlights, hidden in the rafters, now came slowly on instead, throwing bright yellow ovals onto the barn's double doors. Anna and the other guests caught and held their breath. Half a minute passed. Anticipation turned to restlessness. Then finally the doors began to open once more, slowly and grandly, creaking on their hinges. But there was no-one there. Anna turned to Brook with a puzzled frown only for the spotlights suddenly to go out altogether, plunging them into darkness. It was only for a second or two, not long enough for their eyes to adjust; and, when they came back on, a young woman had appeared as if from nowhere, magicked up as with smoke and mirrors. She was dressed in a silver and gold silk dress and had a sheeny silk headscarf resting lightly upon her fluffy blonde hair, provoking startled and even angry murmurs from all around, for she looked so exactly like the portrait photograph of Charlotte Ash that it couldn't be coincidence. She even had the same mischievous, cheerful expression. It must have taken Brook hours poring over casting photos to find someone so perfect, yet he himself wasn't looking at her, but rather at his guests, his green eyes sharp and fierce as they flickered from face to face.

The woman stood motionless for several seconds, stretching the tension out as taut as it could reasonably go. Then she advanced with graceful, dancing steps into the aisle between the tables and to the trolley with its bowl of mead and drinking horns, all while being tracked by the spotlights and followed by the *Beowulf* actor, declaiming and then translating more lines from the great poem.

> *"Wealhtheow now entered,*
> *Hrothgar's queen, the night's hostess*
> *Adorned in silver and gold, she welcomed*
> *The guests into the Hall, offering mead to all.*

The woman ladled mead into a drinking horn then handed it to Philip Smallbone with a gesture not to drink just yet. Then she filled and passed out the remaining horns to each of the other guests in turn. Their design meant that they couldn't be set down until they'd been emptied, so they each held them as they waited for her to finish. Only the jewelled silver goblet now remained. She ladled mead into it, as before, then bore it as reverently as a chalice to where Brook was seated in his gilded throne, presenting it to him with a fractional curtsey. The spotlights had followed her closely all this while, but now they expanded to embrace Brook too, leaving the rest of the barn in virtual darkness, while the actor continued his recital.

> *"Now it was Beowulf's turn to take a goblet from her hand.*
> *Greeting him with warm words,*
> *She thanked the heavens for his arrival*
> *A hero that finally she could believe in*
> *To set right those ancient wrongs."*

Brook rose to his feet to accept the goblet, then gestured for all the other guests to rise and hold aloft their horns. Cloth rustled and bench legs scraped across the matting. Then Brook declaimed the next few lines himself, turning it into a toast:

> *"We vowed, my companions and I,*
> *Before undertaking this campaign*
> *That we would bring the monster down,*
> *or perish in the act.*
> *To this I here commit once more.*
> *This Hall sees justice soon.*
> *Or it sees death."*

He put his goblet to his mouth and drank it all down, trickles of mead spilling down his cheek and chin, staining his robe. And though it seemed an ugly toast, Anna drank too, as did Elias and everyone else, as if sealing some kind of morbid pact. The spotlights faded but the chandeliers came partially back on, relieving the wider darkness. They set down their empty horns and retook their seats. All but Raoul Flood, that was, who stayed upon his feet, flushed and swaying slightly from too much drink. His wife threw him a pleading look, but he chose to ignore it, except with a strange admonitory expression, warning her to stay out of it. 'This hall sees justice, is it?' he said, as the actress bowed from her waist and withdrew. 'This hall sees justice or it sees *death*?'

'It's a toast,' said Brook calmly. 'From a poem.'

'Bollocks,' said Flood. 'How stupid do you think we are? It's about Charlotte, isn't it? This whole weekend, it's about Charlotte. About you still thinking one of us pushed her. Why can't you get it into your bloody head? None of us pushed her. We loved her. She was special. She slipped, that's all. She liked to stand too close to that damned edge. It set her heart pounding and it made her feel alive. Only it was a bit dewier than usual that night, so she slipped and fell. That's all that happened. That's all it ever was.'

'It was dewier than usual, was it?' asked Brook, feigning a frown. 'How would you know that?'

'Because it's bloody obvious, is how,' snapped Flood. 'She

wouldn't have slipped otherwise, would she?' He should have left it there, but he was too stirred. 'Unless of course part of her wanted it to happen. Unless she suddenly realised what marriage to you would mean. Beauty and the Beast makes for a fine fairytale, but it loses its charm a bit when the frog stays a frog even after being kissed.' He frowned at that, vaguely aware of his confused imagery, but then pressed on anyway. 'I mean, come on. Even you must have realised that it was only ever this place she really wanted. This place and all your money. You just happened to come with it.'

'Maybe,' said Brook. 'Or maybe she was pushed by a man who couldn't bear it that she'd chosen someone else.'

'Fuck you,' said Flood.

'Or maybe it was a different kind of jealousy,' said Brook, unperturbed. 'Or maybe it was fear of exposure, of mockery, of rivalry, of disgrace. Who can say?' But his eyes slid from face to face with each suggested charge.

'I beg your pardon?' said Lucius Hyde-Smith angrily, when Brook's gaze settled finally on him. 'What are you implying?'

'Me,' said Brook. 'Nothing. Why?'

'Staring at me like that when you talk about disgrace. Impugning me like that.' But his indignation was unconvincing. Maybe he sensed it too, for he threw down his napkin and rose to his feet. 'I'll not stay to be insulted, I'll tell you that.'

'As you wish,' said Brook. 'May I take it, then, that you're withdrawing the British Museum from consideration in the new excavation season I'm planning to fund, and in the six-figure donation that will go with it?'

'We already wasted one whole season here,' scowled Hyde-Smith. 'There's nothing to find.'

'What about that gift I sent you?'

'A piece of rusted iron. It could have been anything.'

'Except it wasn't, was it? It was a rivet from an Anglo-Saxon ship burial, just like the ones they found at Sutton Hoo.'

'One rivet does not a ship make.'

'*Three* rivets. One each for you, Philip and Bryony.'

'Three whole rivets!' scoffed Hyde-Smith. 'They found hundreds at Snape and Ashby and across the river. For all we know, these could have come from one of those. They could have come from anywhere. You could even have forged them yourself.'

'Except that's not true, is it? You had them tested, didn't you? Don't bother denying it. I know it for a fact. I have a copy of the results, supplied for a small fee by an underpaid technician at the lab you used. As for there being just three of them...' He left the table and walked over to the row of wooden casks that Anna had noticed earlier, standing against the barn's rear wall. He grabbed the first of them by its lip and hauled it off its base so that it tipped forwards, its lid spilling off and its contents clattering noisily out over the rush matting. Not ale, as Anna had supposed. Nor wine nor water neither. But rather rusted iron rivets, dozens of them, all showing clear signs of having been scorched in some great conflagration.

Everyone got to their feet and gazed in disbelief. Everyone save Brook himself, who instead hauled over the second cask, and then the third, equal numbers of the charred rivets spilling out from each. Even Hyde-Smith couldn't help himself. He made his way unsteadily around the table to crouch and pick one up. Anna could see the bobble in his throat as he swallowed away his astonishment and excitement, though pride wouldn't yet allow him to admit it. 'Rivets are one thing,' he said. 'Treasure hunters had no use for them. Proper grave goods are a different matter.'

'Yes, they are,' agreed Brook. He stooped for a polished wooden casket that Anna hadn't noticed before, half hidden behind the barrels as it had been. He opened its lid and tipped it up a little way to show Hyde-Smith, before returning to the tables for the rest of them to see. And there, lying on a bed of purple velvet, was a large golden buckle shaped like a dragon with outspread wings, with twin emeralds for its eyes, and breathing rubies of flame from its open mouth.

FIFTEEN

Anna left her place along with everyone else to gather round Brook for a closer look at his dragon brooch. It was breathtaking – not just for its size and beauty, or for the cunning of its design, but also for its condition – for it looked almost pristine, as though it had come straight from the workshop where it had been made, so that she couldn't help but think it a replica of some kind. Even the great treasures from Sutton Hoo, after all, had mostly not been found in the condition familiar from the exhibitions and photographs. They'd been reconstructed instead from fragments that had survived being crushed beneath mounds of earth and centuries of exposure to the slow corrosion of the soil.

But *this* hadn't been crushed. *This* hadn't been corroded. If it was authentic – a huge if, admittedly – then it had clearly been protected in some way, presumably in some kind of container or chamber that had survived the centuries intact. And how rare was that? The iron rivets strongly suggested an Anglo-Saxon ship burial – yet the interment chambers for those had typically been made of timbers covered by massive mounds of earth, meaning that they soon rotted and then collapsed, and couldn't even come close to protecting an artefact this well for so long. Indeed, they weren't really intended to. The nearest analogue Anna could think of was in a town called Prittlewell near Southend-on-Sea, where a road-widening scheme back at the turn of the century had uncovered the burial of another prominent Anglo-Saxon – most likely a man called Sæxa, brother of Sæberht, king of Essex. Whoever he'd been, he'd been laid to rest in a large and lavishly-furnished timber-walled chamber that clearly had been meant to last, though of course its wooden walls and ceiling had ultimately given way as well, so that the excavating archaeologists had had to deduce its existence from its scant remains. But no wooden burial chamber, however sturdy, could have survived this long. It would therefore have had to have been made of stone instead; and this part of Suffolk was so short of stone that they'd had to bring it in from elsewhere, sometimes even from abroad, meaning that it had been used only in the most important works. And who on earth could possibly have warranted such effort and expense?

Anna wasn't the only one to recognise the significance of its condition, of course. Bryony Mackay and Lucius Hyde-Smith both threw sharp questions at Brook, torn between scepticism and the longing for it to be true. But Brook didn't answer, except to snap closed the box's lid. 'Tomorrow,' he promised. 'I'll tell you all more tomorrow.' Then he pushed between them and set off for the house without so much as a glance around, despite surely being aware of the gazes burning into his back.

It was Greta who broke the silence. 'Well!' she said. 'What a night! What a crazy, crazy night! But that's enough excitement for us all, I think. And we need to give our poor caterers and entertainers a chance to get home at some kind of civilised hour. How about some appreciation for their efforts? Haven't they been wonderful?'

The muted round of applause that followed seemed to break the spell. The lights were turned all the way up and the candles blown out. People knocked back the last of their drinks then set off for the house, yawning as they went, as much from the release of tension as from tiredness. Anna was walking with Elias when Greta came to join them. 'My bloody brother!' she said in a low yet furious voice. 'I had no idea he had all that planned. I'd never have gone along with it if I had.'

'I expect that's why he didn't tell you,' murmured Elias.

'Those rivets! That dragon buckle! Dear god! I thought we shared everything.'

They arrived in the kitchen to find Brook waiting for them, though without his casket. Greta shook her head at him. 'What were you thinking?' she fumed, struggling to keep her voice down. 'Couldn't you at least have waited for the caterers and actors to leave? You've just sent out an embossed invitation to every burglar in the county.'

'Relax. It's in the safe.'

'And how do *they* know that? Who knows what intruders might not get up to, wandering blindly around the house hunting for it?'

'You worry too much. I'll lock up before I turn in. As always.'

'As always!' scoffed Greta. 'Do it now. I mean it.'

He grunted with amusement, but gave in anyway, perhaps aware she had a point. They made a round of the ground floor together, with Brook checking that all the windows and doors were properly secured from the inside, and Greta giving the cellar door a good rattle to make sure it was both locked and bolted. 'Satisfied?' asked Brook, as they arrived at the front door, their tour complete.

'It was still unbelievably stupid,' Greta told him.

'You're right,' he said. 'I'm sorry.' But his smile rather undermined his show of contrition. 'You'll come for breakfast, yes?'

She gave a long sigh, to let her anger go. 'What time?'

'Seven, as usual,' he told her. 'Though feel free to lie in yourself, if you like.'

'Seven it is,' retorted Greta. 'I'll see you then.' She was about to add something further, only to be silenced by a huge yawn that began with a trembling of her chin as she fought valiantly to hold it back, but which ultimately proved too powerful for her, triggering Elias, Brook and Anna into yawns of their own, making them all laugh at themselves, releasing the last of the tension.

They bid each other goodnight then Anna and Greta went

out to the Hyundai and set off up the drive back to Gatehouse Cottage, the intruder lights on the Manor's roof blazing down on the gravelled forecourt for another sixty seconds after they'd gone before falling back to darkness.

SIXTEEN

L ast night's feast had left Anna too drained even to have closed her curtains properly, an oversight she paid for when an early shaft of morning sunshine slid through the gap between them to fall upon her cheek. She opened her eyes with a reluctant groan. Her mouth was tacky and she had a soft but insistent headache, despite having been careful about what she'd drunk. For all its honeyed sweetness, that mead had packed a punch.

She reached for her phone to check the time. Nearly six thirty. She couldn't hear Greta but assumed she was up already, in order to make her date for breakfast at the Manor. She got up herself, showered, dressed and went down. Greta wasn't there. She went back upstairs and stood by her bedroom door, from the other side of which she could hear the soft yet unmistakable sound of snoring. She elected to let her sleep on and went back downstairs for a cup of tea while she read the news on her laptop. Seven o'clock arrived, but still not Greta, making Anna concerned enough to return upstairs and knock, earning a cry of dismay when Greta woke and saw the time for herself. She came to the door, still wrapping herself in a mauve woollen bathrobe. 'I haven't overslept like this in months,' she wailed. 'You couldn't give me five minutes, could you? Not a nanosecond longer, I promise.'

She did better than last night, arriving downstairs just ten minutes later, dressed but still visibly frazzled. She waved off

Anna's offer of tea and insisted on setting off at once, speeding up to the main house in her Hyundai only to find the front door locked. They went around the side and then the back, but all the other doors were locked too, and there was not a sign of life inside when they peered in through the kitchen window.

'I guess we all overdid it,' said Anna.

'Yes,' said Greta. But she looked uneasy. She took out her mobile to try her brother, then called the Manor's landline instead. They could hear it ringing away inside, yet no-one answered. They looked anxiously at one another, unsure what next to do, until Anna thought to try Elias on his mobile, which finally won a response.

'What?' he groaned.

'We're downstairs, outside the kitchen,' Anna told him. 'You couldn't come let us in, could you?'

He appeared a minute later, in a crumpled blue shirt, still zipping up his jeans. He raised an eyebrow as he unbolted and opened the utility room door for them. 'So where's the fire?' he asked.

'It's Hector,' said Greta. 'He's always up by now.'

'Come on. It was a big night last night. For him more than anyone.'

'I know. But still. When I say always I mean *always*. From when he was in the army.'

Elias caught the anxiety in her voice, and nodded. 'You think we should go check?'

'Could you, please? To put my mind at rest.'

'As long as you come with me. For when he bites my head off.'

They filed upstairs together. Elias called out and knocked gently on Brook's bedroom door, but got no answer. He did both again, more loudly. Still no response. He called out fair warning then went on in, motioning for Anna and Greta to stay behind. He looked around the door towards the bed then turned back to them and told them to wait where they were. Then, in an act that soothed their fears not one bit, he went all the way inside and closed the door quietly but firmly behind him.

SEVENTEEN

It was the smell that Elias noticed first, what with Brook's bedroom dark from the floor-length blackout curtains, and what little light there was coming through the half-open bathroom doorway. Not that the smell was particularly strong or even that ugly; more that it was so depressingly familiar from the squalid stairwells and underpasses he'd visited as a detective, so that he knew what to expect even before turning on the lights.

Brook was lying on his back on the far side of his king-sized bed, his thin white summer duvet half thrown back to expose his head, chest and arms, while still covering everything from his waist on down. His face was unnaturally pale, save for his lips, which were tinted the pale blue of a child sucking on a lolly; while his shoulders and arms looked unnaturally stiff, like a weightlifter bracing himself for a personal best.

Elias was well accustomed to overdose victims. He'd have recognised the signs here even without the syringe by Brook's right hand, or the trickle of dried blood upon the outside of his left arm. He stepped carefully over to the bed, making sure to avoid the robes and sandals that had been discarded in a crude line between door and bed, suggesting that Brook had been so tired last night that he'd simply stripped off while making his way from one to the other. He went around the far side to feel his forehead, in case this was some kind of grotesque prank he'd conjured up for the weekend. But his skin was several hours cold, which, when put together with the rigidity of his limbs, suggested he'd died shortly after they'd all split up last night.

Elias had lost count years before of how many bodies he'd seen. But he'd known only a few of those people personally before they'd died – and those had mostly been criminals of one kind or another, for whom he'd felt little sympathy. This was different. He'd known Brook for less than a day, but he'd already come to like him a great deal. More to the point, the man had hired him and given him the room next door at least in part because he'd believed there was a murderer in the house. That meant that this had happened on Elias's watch. It made it personal.

He pinched the edge of the duvet, lifted it to confirm what the smell of urine had already told him – that Brook had soiled himself and the bed, his bladder muscles likely relaxing at the moment of death. He pulled his phone from his pocket and was taking photographs when the door opened and Greta came in, fighting off Anna as she tried to hold her back. She must have been fearing the worst already from the way Elias had shut the door on her, yet she gave an anguished yelp anyway and started towards the bed, so that Elias had to hurry around to hold her back and stop her from touching anything.

'An overdose?' she said, bewildered, on seeing the syringe. 'But he never used those kind of drugs. *Never*. He hated them.'

'You can't be in here,' Elias told her gently. He wrapped his arms around her to walk her back to the door. 'Take her downstairs,' he told Anna, passing her across. 'Give her whatever she needs. Coffee, tea, brandy, anything.'

'And you?'

'I'm staying here. Until the police arrive.'

'The police?'

Elias nodded. 'This was no accident,' he told her flatly. 'This was murder.'

EIGHTEEN

Anna hugged Greta tight as she steered her sympathetically yet forcibly away from the bedroom door and to the main staircase, as though the pair of them were engaged in some macabre slow dance. 'It's okay,' she murmured, stroking the back of her hair, fully aware of the absurdity of her words, yet unable to think of anything better. 'It's going to be okay.'

A door opened back along the passage, and Anna heard footsteps; but she didn't even look around, too focused on making it all the way downstairs without a tumble, for Greta felt increasingly unsteady on her feet. They made it safely to the bottom, however, and were halfway along the passage to the kitchen when Greta put a hand on Anna's shoulder to beg a moment's rest. Her face was pale and her eyelids were fluttering. Her breath, already shallow, came faster and faster, and she began swaying so alarmingly that it became obvious she was about to faint. Then her legs simply folded beneath her, neat as an ironing board. She'd have crashed to the floor had Anna not grabbed her around her midriff in time, then lowered her gently with her back to the cellar door.

'I'm fine,' insisted Greta, trying to get back up, only for her legs to buckle once more. 'I'll be fine. Just give me a moment.'

Anna knelt beside her and took her hand. 'Can I get you anything?' she asked. 'A glass of water, maybe?'

'Oh. Yes. Water. Thank you.'

'Of course,' said Anna. It took her a few moments to find the glassware. She was squirting cold water into a tumbler when she heard a strangled cry and then a thud from out in the passage. She ran back out to find Greta lying face down on the carpet with Cameron Wolfe crouched over her. 'What the hell did you do?' demanded Anna.

'Not a damn thing,' he protested. But he wouldn't meet her eyes. He looked furtive, even guilty. 'She tried to stand up too quickly, is all. Her legs just went.'

Anna knelt down again beside Greta. She rolled her carefully onto her back then sprinkled water on her face and lifted up her head to tip a sip or two into her mouth as she began to recover – though that only meant remembering what she'd seen upstairs, and looking distraught once more.

'What's going on?' asked Wolfe. 'Has something happened?'

'Her brother,' said Anna.

'Hector? You don't mean…?'

'Yes.'

'But… Christ. How?' Anna looked up at him. He was saying the right words, yet his tone was somehow all wrong, tinged with gladness or even relief. 'Don't look at me like that,' he scowled. 'Why would I kill the man? He still owed me half my fee.'

'I never said he'd been killed.'

'Your face did.'

They helped Greta back to her feet and through to the kitchen, where they sat her at the table. Anna asked her what else she could get her, but all she wanted was more water and a pair of paracetamol. Anna took two for herself while she was at it, as did Wolfe. And the coincidence of them all having thumping headaches made Anna wonder exactly how big a punch last night's mead had really carried.

And why.

NINETEEN

Elias took a last few photographs before leaving Brook's bedroom, not wanting to contaminate the scene any further. He stood outside the door to call the emergency services, turning his back to the passage to make it harder for him to be overheard. He asked for the police. A woman answered. He told her of Brook's death and explained that he was a former detective inspector with Lincolnshire's Major Crimes Unit; and that although this looked superficially like an accidental overdose, he had good reason to believe it was more likely murder. She asked him to wait while she found the right person for him to speak to, then put him on hold.

He turned back around as he waited, only to discover he had an audience. Imogen and Raoul Flood were standing just a few paces away, she pale with shock or even alarm, while he tried to comfort her with an arm around her shoulders. An unwelcome arm, to judge by her expression. And Lucius Hyde-Smith was there too, standing half in and half out of his bedroom doorway. 'Hector murdered?' he said, a mix of disgust and disbelief on his face. 'Are you serious?'

Elias gazed at them, not entirely convinced by any of their expressions. 'Go back to your rooms,' he told them. 'Or have breakfast or whatever.'

'We're supposed to eat breakfast with our host lying dead upstairs?'

'Fine. Stay hungry then. Just keep away from here.'

'Who put you in charge?'

'I was a murder detective for ten years,' Elias told him. 'What's your qualification?'

'He's right,' said Imogen, making for the staircase, dragging her husband with her. 'He knows what he's doing. We shouldn't be here.'

They sloped off downstairs together, though not without a backward glance or two. He was still on hold, and beginning to fear he'd been forgotten, when a Detective Superintendent Trent of Suffolk Police came on, the background traffic noise suggesting strongly he was in his car. He listened patiently as Elias talked him through what he'd seen. 'There was a syringe by his hand?' said Trent, when Elias was done, though his tone was inquisitive rather than antagonistic.

'Yeah, I know how it sounds,' said Elias. 'But he didn't do drugs.'

'Sure. If you can't trust an addict, who can you trust?'

'I'm not going by what he told me. I've done the job long enough to know a junkie when I see one. There are no tracks on his arms and no paraphernalia in the room. More to the point, though, the injection was made in the outside of his right arm. Give me your number and I'll send you my photos. You can see for yourself how awkward it would have been to inject himself there.'

'So he was shooting up with a partner,' suggested Trent. 'They did a runner when they saw what had happened?'

'And left the syringe behind? Besides, there was no one like that in the house last night. What there were, instead, was half a dozen people Brook had invited for the weekend precisely because he suspected one of them of having killed his fiancée.'

'Bloody hell,' said Trent.

'Yeah,' agreed Elias. 'Any one of them could have sneaked into his room last night. And, if they did, I'm pretty sure they'd have found Brook lying on his front with his arms down by his side. They couldn't risk moving him without waking him, so they'd have had to inject him where they could, hoping that no-one would notice. Fentanyl would be my guess. A massive overdose would have killed him fast. But they couldn't leave him lying face down like that, not if they wanted you guys to buy it being an accident, because it wouldn't just have been awkward for him to inject himself that way, it would have been impossible. So they waited until he was dead then rolled him onto his back before they left. Only they didn't count on his bladder venting. The stains on his boxers don't map onto the ones on his sheet.'

'So he pissed the bed before they rolled him over?'

'That's how it looks to me. But give me your number. You can see for yourself.'

He texted his photographs across. There was the clacking of an indicator light as Trent pulled in to the side of the road. Half a minute passed, then Elias heard a grunt and Trent came back on. 'Okay,' he said. 'Point taken. Anyone else been inside the room?'

'Only the guy's sister and a friend of mine called Anna Warne. But neither of them touched anything. And I'm outside the door now, so that no-one else gets in.'

'Okay. Good. Thanks. Let me put together a team. You can tell me the rest when I get there.'

Elias fetched a chair from along the passage to sit guard. Anna brought up breakfast on a tray: coffee, a banana, two slices of buttered toast and a pot of honey, along with a glass of water and a pair of paracetamol. 'All the rest of us have headaches,' she told him. 'I figured maybe you did too.'

Elias caught her tone. 'You think we were drugged?'

'You'd know that better than me. But would you want to be caught in the small hours, sneaking into your host's bedroom with a syringe in your hand? Greta says they always ended their feasts with a toast of mead. If you wanted to make sure that everyone was fast asleep... And that bowl was easy enough to get at, off in a room by itself, and having to pass it to get to the loos.'

The first of the squad cars arrived with impressive speed. Four uniformed officers came upstairs to take over guard duty until Scene of Crime arrived. Unfortunately for Elias, they didn't stop at Brook's bedroom, but rather declared the whole of the upstairs out of bounds, including his own bedroom, meaning he had to go back down without his laptop or Brook's box-folder.

Detective Superintendent Trent himself arrived next, in a white BMW 4 Series convertible with its roof down and this year's plates. Elias went out to greet him. He liked to size people up when he first met them, filing the information away for future reference. Trent looked to be late thirties or early forties, well tanned and compensating for his slightly weak chin with a pointed goatee that was as jet black as his hair, though with the game rather given away by the grey flecking of his eyebrows and designer stubble. He was wearing a white cotton shirt and dark grey woollen suit trousers, with the jacket laid neatly across the back seat. He had a new model Fitbit on his left wrist and a plain gold band on his ring finger that he twisted this way and that, like a bad poker tell, whenever he was unconvinced by what he was being told. And there was enough wear and tear on his thin black leather belt to suggest struggles with his weight.

'I thought I recognised your name,' he said, noting Elias's yellow glove in good time to pat him on the arm rather than offer to shake hands. 'You're the one who took down that arsehole Trevor Wharton.'

'You knew him?'

'Played golf with him once, at an away day. Bastard took a tenner off me, even after I saw him kick his ball into a better lie. Couldn't make anything of it, though. His word against mine, and me well outranked. Laughed like a drain when I heard he'd been arrested, so I owe you one for that. But tell me about Hector Brook. What are you even doing here? Are you a friend?'

'Never met him before yesterday.' He relayed what Brook had told him up on Dragon Stone Hill, how he'd set up this whole weekend to smoke out Charlotte Ash's killer.

'The daft sod,' sighed Trent. 'Still wouldn't let it go, eh?'

'You know the case?'

He gave a reluctant nod. 'He kicked up such a stink about our original investigation that my boss had me review the file, just in case. But there was nothing there. The weird thing was that even he admitted it. Just a hunch, he said. What were we supposed to do with that?'

'He'd cobbled together some interesting footage from that summer, apparently. Motives for each of his guests disguised as a tribute to Charlotte. He hoped it would provoke a reaction. Not this one, I don't suppose.'

'You think this was about that, then?'

'A mighty coincidence, if not.'

Trent nodded and gave his wedding ring another twist. 'And the house was properly locked up, you said on the phone?'

'I did the rounds with him myself.'

'What about those cameras?' asked Trent, nodding up at the roof. 'Any footage for us to look at?'

'I'd imagine so, yes. But I'm not the person to ask. You should speak to Greta, Brook's sister.'

'Yeah,' said Trent dryly. 'Her I remember.'

They found her at the kitchen table, her eyes watery and bloodshot, but noticeably more composed. She nodded and rose to her feet when they asked about footage, glad of the chance to do something useful. 'I don't know how it all worked, exactly,' she told them, leading the way out of the kitchen, 'but I know where he managed it from.' She took them along a pair of dark passages to the Manor's modern wing and her brother's office: a large, plain room with a pair of grey filing cabinets, a heavy steel floor safe with a large blue-and-white porcelain bowl resting upon it, and fitted bookshelves bulging with ring-binders, box-folders and heavyweight texts on accountancy, farming, archaeology, military history and plenty else.

There was a long plain oak table beneath the double windows at its far end, set to catch the morning sunlight. An executive leather chair on castors sat in front of it, ready to be wheeled either to the neatly arranged paperwork on the left-hand end of the table, or to the computer equipment to the right, including a keyboard, mouse and an array of three monitors; with the server, router and printer tucked out of sight beneath.

Trent pulled on a pair of latex gloves to wake the computer from its slumber. It took a few moments for a lock-screen to appear. 'Seventy-three, seventy-three,' said Greta, looking over his shoulder, before hurriedly adding: 'We had no secrets from one another. We knew all each others' passwords.'

'Does that include the combination to his safe?' asked Trent.

'His birthday, reversed. At least it used to be. Though honestly that was years ago.' Trent went over to it, crouching to turn the dial this way and that as she called out the numbers. He pressed down its handle and the door opened with a weary sigh to reveal several fat bundles of high denomination euros, dollars and pound notes, a stack of deeds, contracts and other legal-looking papers, and the mahogany casket from last night. Trent took a look inside then turned it to show Greta and Elias. 'This would be the famous buckle, I assume?'

'Yes.'

'Not robbery, then.'

'Not of that.'

Trent replaced the casket, closed the door, scrambled the dials. A young Scene of Crime officer poked in her head, beckoned him outside. Elias could hear them talking, though too softly for him to catch more than the odd word. Trent looked troubled when he came back in. 'So my team agree with you,' he told Elias. 'He couldn't have injected himself like that. So it seems the daft sod really was...' But then he remembered that Greta was there too, and checked himself.

'Don't worry about my feelings, Detective,' she told him.

He nodded and went back over to the desk. 'All those cameras on the roof. He took his security seriously?'

'Yes,' said Greta, though hesitantly enough that she felt compelled to elaborate. 'You know how people are. There'd be some burglaries in town, or he'd run into some trespassers in the woods, and he'd—'

'You had trespassers in the woods?'

'Oh. I only gave that as an example. But yes, there are certain people around here who seem to consider the estate to be public property, however many signs we put up. Mostly, he tried to avoid them. But sometimes he'd be upon them before he realised it, and then there'd be a row. So up would go another camera, or he'd fit new locks, or he'd announce he'd be changing the code for both gates at least once a week from then on. But it never lasted.'

'*Both* gates?' frowned Trent. 'I only remember the one by the railway bridge.'

'No. He put in another a couple of years ago, at the foot of the stairs down from Dragon Stone Hill to the footpath beneath. But at least they both use the same code, so it's not that hard to remember.'

'What about staff? He can't have run a place this big all by himself.'

'He would have if he could have, believe me. But no. He had cleaners in for a few hours every Tuesday, and gardeners on Thursdays. He'd mostly camp in his office while they were here, or go visit one of his other properties. And he enjoyed a bit of DIY, so he handled most of that stuff himself, though he'd call in professionals if it was beyond him. I can get you all their details, though I don't suppose they'll tell you much. Like I say, he avoided them as much as he possibly could. He liked to be left alone.'

'To do what?'

'He read a great deal.' She gestured at the shelves. 'History, particularly military history. And the Anglo-Saxons, of course. Though he only really became interested in them because of poor Charlotte. But mostly he worked. He owned a lot of properties and businesses around here. They each have their own managers and staff, of course, but he kept a close eye on them even so. Heaven help them if he found discrepancies in their accounts! Not that he was a miser, or anything. He was incredibly generous to the right causes. He just hated being taken advantage of.'

'Don't we all,' said Trent. He settled himself at the computer, familiarised himself with its layout, then double-clicked the security app icon on the home screen. Live feed from eight different cameras appeared on the two side monitors, their screens quartered into four, while five second bursts played in rotation on the central one. It took Elias a few moments to work out where each of the cameras were placed. There were three on the Manor's roof, covering between them all the exterior doors. There was a fourth on the front door for dealing with visitors without having to meet them. The fifth, on the barn roof, covered the outbuildings and much of the back lawn. The sixth was on the automated gate by the railway bridge, and the seventh on the railway bridge itself, presumably to catch anyone who managed to slip by the sixth. And the eighth and last was at the foot of the staircase down from Dragon Stone Hill.

'What time did you pack up last night?' asked Trent.

'Eleven fifteen, eleven thirty,' said Elias. 'Something like that.'

Trent brought up the control panel, tapped in the earlier time. Last night's footage instantly came up. They were all still in the barn, so he skipped forwards until Brook emerged with his casket. He set it on fast forward, allowing them to follow along as the guests sped back to the house. Several of the catering staff headed off, as did the lyrist, the *Beowulf* performer and the Charlotte actress. Anna and Greta then left shortly afterwards in the Hyundai, while the rump of the catering staff stayed on to clear up the barn for another forty minutes or so, loading up their vans with black bags of rubbish before heading off in convoy. The intruder lights went out. Darkness fell. Trent sped the footage up as fast as it would go, but the lights never came back on and there was no further movement until well after sunrise, when Greta and Anna returned in the Hyundai.

'Can I have my guys take a closer look at this?' asked Trent.

'Of course,' said Greta. 'Whatever you need.'

'It's been suggested you were all drugged. How about you two? Fall asleep quickly?'

Elias nodded. 'I was out like the proverbial.'

'I don't even remember going to bed,' confessed Greta. 'And I always wake early in the summer, even without an alarm. Not this morning.'

The Crime Scene team had extended the area of search even further while they'd been looking through the footage. The whole of the Manor was now being sealed off, with the guests evicted to gather outside the front door. Lucius Hyde-Smith grabbed Trent by the arm as they went by, demanding to be let up to his bedroom so that he could pack up his belongings and leave. Trent smiled politely but otherwise ignored him. He went to stand on the front step instead, the better to address them all at once. 'You've no doubt heard by now the terrible news about Mr Brook,' he said. 'It's too early to know for sure exactly what happened, but you're all intelligent folk, so I expect you can work out for yourselves why we have so many officers here.' He paused a moment to let them get out their feigned professions of shock. 'We therefore have no choice but to seal off anywhere of potential interest, including this whole house, the back lawns, the barn and other outbuildings. Your vehicles, too, I'm afraid.' He held up his hands to shush their protests. 'I appreciate how inconvenient and intrusive this is, and I'm sorry, but we have no alternative. Anyway, I'm sure you're just as keen as we are to find out what happened to your friend and host as quickly as possible. To that end, we'll need to search your bedrooms, luggage and cars. If any of you have a problem with that, now would be a great time to let me know.' He paused and looked around, confident that none of them would speak up, aware of the extra scrutiny it would bring. 'Thank you,' he said. 'We appreciate your cooperation.'

'Cooperation!' muttered Hyde-Smith.

'There's also some reason to believe that you were drugged last night,' continued Trent, 'most likely via the mead. We'll therefore need urine samples. Fingerprints too. To exclude you from the scene.' Again he paused for objections. Again he received only gloomy acquiescence. 'Thank you. Please inform my officers when you next need to go. They'll show you what to do. We'll also be taking statements, of course, so I'd be grateful if you could make yourself available when asked.'

'How long will this all take?' asked Hyde-Smith.

'It's a big house,' said Trent. 'You can see that for yourselves. Then there are the cars and grounds and outbuildings. All on a bank holiday too.'

'That's not an answer.'

'This is a murder investigation. It'll take as long as it takes.'

'And in the meantime? I'm an old man. I can't stay out here all day.'

'Everyone's welcome to wait in my cottage,' murmured Greta. 'If that would help?'

'An excellent notion,' said Trent. 'Thank you.'

'And what if I don't want to?' said Hyde-Smith, who clearly preferred the complaint to the solution. 'What if I were to take the train home anyway? Would you try to stop me?'

'We'd be grateful if you didn't. As I say, we'll be needing your samples, prints and statements.'

'That's not what I asked. I asked whether you'd stop me.'

'For god's sake, Lucius!' said Bryony Mackay. 'Can't you think of anyone but yourself? Our friend was killed last night.'

'My point exactly,' retorted Hyde-Smith. 'He was *killed*. Almost certainly by one of us. Frankly, I have no desire to spend my day rubbing shoulders with a murderer. What if they're not done yet? What if they have a list, and I'm next on it? What if you are? Or any one of us?'

'There's no reason to think anything like that,' said Trent hurriedly, seeking to douse the flames before they could catch. 'My officers will be everywhere. You're in no danger, I assure you.'

'So you say.'

'Yes. So I say.'

'And tonight? What if your investigation takes all day? Where will we even sleep?' He gestured at the Manor. 'Because I'm not spending another night in there, I'll tell you that for free. Not in a room with no lock on the door and a murderer on the loose.'

'I'll find you somewhere,' promised Greta.

'In Woodbridge?' scoffed Hyde-Smith. 'At this short notice? On a bank holiday weekend?'

'My brother owned dozens of properties. There'll be something free, I assure you.'

'I don't want "something". I want to go home.'

'Enough!' cried Greta. 'You're staying. Everyone is staying. Or else.'

'Or else?'

'Yes. Or else. You saw that dragon buckle last night. You saw those barrels of rivets. My brother clearly found something extraordinary, either here or on one of his other properties. Don't ask me what or where or how. I don't know. He hid it from me, along with a great deal else, as it turns out. But if it's a new Sutton Hoo, as looks possible, excavating it would be the pinnacle of your career. Your name would live forever, alongside Howard Carter, Basil Brown and the rest. And don't try to tell me that's not what you crave. We all know it is.' She turned to Bryony Mackay and Philip Smallbone, to include them in her address. 'That goes for you both too. My brother meant to award it to one of you three, along with the funds to excavate and a six-figure donation to your organisation. I honestly have no idea what's going to happen to this place now, but I'll tell you this: if I have any say whatsoever in the matter, I will honour his intent. If any of you leave, however, or fail to give the police whatever help they ask for, then you'll immediately rule yourselves out of that excavation and the accompanying donation both now and forever. And I'll make damn sure the whole world knows why.'

'No need to be like that,' sniffed Hyde-Smith. 'I was merely asking.'

'And I was merely answering.'

'What about me and Imogen?' asked Raoul Flood, though his tone suggested curiosity more than any great desire to leave. 'We aren't archaeologists.'

'You were my brother's financial advisor,' replied Greta. 'I expect you've been earning a healthy commission from that. Stay and you can keep it. Leave and it's gone.'

'Of course we'll stay,' said Imogen, throwing her husband a filthy look. 'My god! Anything we can do. Anything at all.'

'Good. Thank you.' She turned to Cameron Wolfe. 'And you. I understand my brother was paying you to be here this weekend, yes? Do as the police ask and I'll double your fee, whatever it was. Leave, and you won't get another penny.'

Wolfe held up his hands in mock surrender. 'No need for the big guns. Never even occurred to me to bolt. Of course I'll tell the police everything I know, if that's what you really want.'

'It is, yes. Thank you.'

'I'm here for as long as I'm needed,' Elias assured her, when she looked his way.

'Me too,' said Anna.

She nodded gratefully at them both. Her point gained, the righteous fire inside her died away, leaving her self-conscious again, aware of all the eyes on her. She looked down at her feet then tugged her waistband a fraction to the left before tugging it back to the right again.

'That's settled then,' said Trent, well satisfied. 'Ms Brook's cottage it is. Give me a minute, and I'll have some of my people escort you.'

TWENTY

They set off for Gatehouse Cottage on foot a few minutes later, accompanied by the four police officers assigned by Trent to take their samples, fingerprints and statements. Anna plucked Elias by the sleeve to have him drop back with her a little way, the better to talk without being overheard. 'That thing you said last night,' she murmured. 'About who knows what the weekend will bring?'

'It was a joke,' he told her. 'It was supposed to be a joke.' But he recapped for her his conversation with Hector Brook on Dragon Stone Hill, how convinced he'd been that one of his guests had pushed Charlotte over the escarpment edge, how he'd designed the weekend to find out which.

'You think they killed him before he could expose them?' frowned Anna. 'But how would they even have known what he intended?'

'It was hardly a secret. He did everything he could to bully the police into an investigation. He flat out told the inquest that she'd been pushed. And then, for good measure, he hired two separate firms of private investigators to look into it. If it was you who'd pushed her, and you found out he'd invited the exact same guests for this weekend, wouldn't you be a little nervous?'

'Then why accept?'

'Because he twisted their arms so fiercely that refusing would have looked suspicious. Anyway, maybe it struck them as the perfect way to deal with the situation once and for all.

Because what better opportunity could a murderer ask for, than a houseful of other plausible suspects?'

'Have you told Detective Trent?'

'Sure, but Charlotte Ash isn't his focus right now. She died five years ago in what looked for all the world to have been an accident. Hector Brook died last night, in what was pretty clearly murder. He has a fresh crime scene to interrogate, a small pool of suspects, a ton of footage, witness statements, urine samples and all the rest. If you were him, where would you start? But that's *his* business, not *mine*. Brook hired me to find out the truth about Charlotte's death. I mean to do just that.'

'Good,' said Anna. 'How do I help?'

Elias hesitated, visibly reluctant to involve her in what could prove a hazardous investigation. She gave him a look to make it clear she wouldn't be putting up with that. 'There is one thing you could do,' he sighed.

'And? Am I supposed to guess?'

'If I'm right about all this, Brook was killed for refusing to let Charlotte's death go. But what if that's not it? Because there is another possibility. Those rivets. That buckle. Brook's mysterious new discovery, whatever it was. I can't see how it connects to his death, but that doesn't mean it doesn't. It's at least worth looking into. And it's far more your area than mine.'

'I wouldn't rule out a link too fast,' nodded Anna. 'My taxi driver yesterday hinted at a major new find. If he knew about it, anyone could have. And people have been killed for a lot less than a golden buckle, let alone for a new Sutton Hoo.'

They reached the cottage. Greta bid them make themselves at home. Anna went with her through to the kitchen, where she filled the kettle to its brim, took a fresh loaf of seeded bread from the fridge, and put out butter and jars of home-made jam. There weren't enough mugs to go around, so she rinsed out some old bone china teacups gathering dust on a high shelf. She was taking orders for tea and coffee when Greta suddenly froze up while decanting sugar into a bowl. Her back was to the room, but Anna could see her shoulders humping. She went over to her, took her in a hug, let her bury her face in her shoulder. 'He was my family,' said Greta. 'I don't know what I'm going to do.'

'Go upstairs. Rest.'

'What about breakfast?'

'We're adults,' Anna assured her. 'We can take care of ourselves.'

'You don't know where everything is.'

'We'll find it, don't worry. I'll come ask if we can't, I promise.'

'And my fingerprints? My statement?'

'We can do that now, if you like. Or later. I'm sure either will be fine.'

Greta dabbed her eyes on some kitchen towel. 'I'd rather get it over and done with,' she said. They found a kindly-looking young WPC with a sweet smile and hazel eyes. She took Greta's statement at the outside table while Anna sat alongside her for moral support. She gave her fingerprints and sample too, then Anna walked her upstairs to her room, assuring her again that she'd take care of everything. She drew her curtains for her, and was about to leave when Greta called for her to stay. 'Your detective friend,' she murmured. 'Do you trust him?'

'With my life. Yes. Why?'

'I thought of something just now, while I was giving my statement to that nice policewoman. But it's crazy. Crazy and horribly disloyal to my poor brother, which is why I didn't say anything. But what if it turns out to be true? I don't want everyone put through the grinder for nothing. So I thought maybe I could run it by your friend to see what he thinks. If he says I should tell the police, I will. But I'd much rather not.'

Anna nodded. 'I'll go get him.'

She found him outside, giving his own statement. She waited for him to finish then took him back inside, bumping into Cameron Wolfe as he came dancing down the stairs. 'Just checking if our good hostess needed anything,' he said.

'Yes,' said Anna. 'To be left alone.'

'Yeah,' said Wolfe, with a rueful smile. 'That much I gathered.'

Greta was hunched up on her side in bed, looking miserable. She turned on her bedside lamp and rose up on an elbow. 'Thanks for coming,' she told Elias.

'Anna says you have something to run by me.'

'Yes. Yes, I do.' But then she faltered again.

Elias fetched a chair so that he wouldn't loom over her quite so much. 'I won't pass it on without your say so,' he promised. 'You have my word.'

Still Greta hesitated. But finally she nodded. 'Okay. Thank you. It's just, I had the wildest thought earlier. Like I told Anna, it's not just that it sounds crazy, it's that it's so disloyal to my poor brother. But if there's anything to it...' She paused once more, then steeled herself and pressed on. 'It's about that syringe. Or more precisely about where it went into his arm. About how awkward it would have been for him to inject himself there, I mean. And what I suddenly wondered was, what if that was the point?'

'I don't follow.'

'I don't blame you. I barely do myself, to be honest. But what if Hector wanted people to think that it was murder when it fact it wasn't?' She grimaced at Elias's sceptical expression. 'I know, I know,' she said. 'But you never saw quite how broken he was by Charlotte's death, especially coming on top of his bomb-blast injuries, and the migraines and fits they'd left him with, none of which were getting any better. He was so depressed last winter that I started to worry he'd do something terrible. But then, around February or March, he suddenly improved. I won't say he became happy, exactly. He didn't really do happy. It was more that he found a purpose. And that was around the same time as he started making preparations for this weekend.'

'Ah,' said Elias. 'Go on.'

'He told you himself how he'd always believed that Charlotte had been pushed. What I don't think he made quite clear was how frustrated and angry he was with himself for failing to secure a proper investigation. He felt like he'd let her down. It consumed him. Hiring private investigators wasn't enough. He wanted it to be the police. So what occurred to me just now was this: What if last night was some dreadful twisted plan of his? Giving the police a second death to investigate, only this one undeniably murder. Filling the house with the exact same suspects, and making fear of being exposed as Charlotte's killer the most likely motive. Wouldn't that secure the investigation he'd so longed for, while also releasing him from a life that gave him more pain than pleasure?'

'You think he killed himself to get a proper investigation into Charlotte's death?'

'I know it sounds absurd. Why do you think I'm so hesitant? But honestly you should have seen him last Christmas, how low he was. Every day was a fight. And it wasn't my imagination, I assure you. He'd been on and off antidepressants for years, but his doctor seriously ramped up his prescription. She even hinted I should keep an eye on him. I used to dread going up to the Manor in the mornings, just in case. Then suddenly he improved, like night and day. You saw him yesterday, up on the hill and then at the feast. He was actually cheerful. He hadn't been in such good spirits for years. I thought he'd put it all behind him. But now I'm wondering if this wasn't the reason. That he'd finally found his path.'

'It's an interesting thought,' said Elias. 'And he certainly could have injected himself there, if he'd wanted to badly enough. Though...'

'Though...?'

Elias hesitated, for it was hardly a topic he'd have chosen to discuss with a bereaved sister. But he went ahead anyway. 'When people die, their muscles relax. Sometimes that leads to them evacuating their bladders, particularly if they've had a lot to drink. It seems to have happened with your brother. Theoretically, it should have stained the sheet and mattress directly beneath him.'

'And it didn't?'

'No. It looks as though he was rolled onto his back afterwards. But that doesn't prove your idea wrong. He could have set it up that way himself too. And it's certainly worth passing on. But I'll tell Trent it was my idea, if you'd prefer?'

'Thank you,' she said. 'I would.'

TWENTY-ONE

B ack down in the kitchen, Bryony Mackay had worked out how to operate the espresso maker, and had frothed up a large pan of milk too. Anna took a cappuccino outside, where she found Philip Smallbone giving his statement to the kindly young policewoman. She loitered nearby in order to bag her next, while trying not to seem intrusive. She could still hear him, though, as he insisted that he'd had not the slightest inkling of Brook's ulterior motive for the weekend, only for some kind of sixth sense to prompt him to look around and catch her gazing curiously at him. His expression flickered as he no doubt remembered accusing her last night of being here to play detective. So he turned back to the policewoman and smoothly added that he hadn't had any such inkling until he'd arrived here yesterday afternoon to find not only the exact same guests as before, but an ex-policeman too.

Anna took his place when he was done. He loitered in her eyeline, perhaps to see what she would say, or even to intimidate her into silence. But she had nothing to add to his account, so didn't mention it. Her statement given, she went hunting for Elias and found him in the sitting room, flipping through Greta's small collection of DVDs. 'Bit early for a movie, isn't it?' she teased.

'Not for this one,' he told her, holding up a plain white cardboard sleeve. 'Brook's tribute to Charlotte, with any luck.' He lowered his voice to a murmur. 'In which all our fellow guests supposedly make rather telling appearances.'

'You don't mean...?'

'I *do* mean...' He pinched the sleeve by its edges, tipped the DVD out into his hand then inserted it into the player and angled the pedestal TV away from the room so that they alone could watch. The screen flickered for several moments, then last night's *in memoriam* photograph of Charlotte Ash appeared to the soft strain of the same Bach cantata that Anna's mother had chosen for her own funeral, bringing tears briefly to her eyes.

The music and portrait both faded away. There came instead the excited hubbub of an expectant gathering. The screen remained dark for a few moments more, then Charlotte appeared on the Manor's front step, as DS Trent had done earlier that morning, as she prepared to address a group of maybe twenty-five students and volunteers. She looked in vibrant spirits, glowing with exhilaration and bouncing up and down on her toes, holding up her hands for silence and waiting for the chatter to die away before welcoming them to what she assured them would be a most memorable season.

Footage of that season duly followed. Charlotte was in every scene, at least to start, visiting the volunteers as they dug or sorted artefacts in the processing room, answering questions, offering tips, teasing and joking and otherwise geeing up whoever she was with. There was one short clip of her in particular, with her cheeks flushed and the sun making a halo of her hair, that could have come straight from a Christmas perfume ad. Another had her lying on her front on an improvised hammock above an excavation trench, brushing dirt and soil away from some buried artefact, while bantering with a handsome young Indian man who kept drifting in and out of shot, and to whom she kept turning and gesturing to leave her be, laughing despite herself, until finally she broke into a bewitching smile. And it was the easiest thing in the world to imagine men tumbling for her like ninepins.

It wasn't all of Charlotte, however. There were short clips of Bryony Mackay and then Lucius Hyde-Smith explaining finds and contexts to the camera. Volunteers milled around at lunch then shared beers at end of day. It began to feel less like a tribute, indeed, than a home movie, an effort to bottle the essence of some precious family holiday. Time and date stamps at the bottom of the screen made it clear that Brook hadn't assembled the clips in chronological order, but rather in service of the story he'd wanted told. Soon enough that story began in earnest, with Charlotte and Philip Smallbone kneeling together by an excavation trench, their shoulders almost touching, while he threw smitten sideways glances at her, punctuated by darker scowls as he tried in vain to break her hold over him. He appeared in the next few scenes too, stealing yet more clandestine looks. About the world's oldest story: An unprepossessing, undistinguished middle-aged man besotted by a beautiful young woman. Then came the most telling clip of all, with Raoul Flood mimicking Smallbone's mumbled Suffolk burr with wonderful precision and unexpected cruelty, mocking him for being lovestruck, while Charlotte laughed helplessly, neither of them realising that the man himself was on the other side of a protective canvas sheet, a look of such utter misery on his face that Anna couldn't help but feel sorry for him.

Cameron Wolfe sauntered over, chomping on an apple. 'So what are you guys watching?' he asked. Then he saw the screen and scowled. 'That's my bloody footage,' he said. 'The bastard might have asked.' He turned the screen around so that everyone else in the room could see. 'Hey Raoul,' he called out. 'You're on TV.'

Raoul and Imogen Flood were on the other side of the sitting room, talking urgently together in strained low voices, jabbing fingers this way and that. They both looked around as – on screen – Raoul and Charlotte passed through the latched gate at the top of the Manor's lawn, jostling each other as they walked, surreptitiously holding hands in the way of secret lovers. The camera was too far off to catch their voices, but sound was hardly necessary, even before Flood brought Charlotte's hand up to his lips to kiss.

Flood gestured frantically for Elias to turn off the TV. But too late. Imogen shook her head in dismay and disgust then stormed out of the room and the cottage both, slamming the front door so hard that she rattled the photographs on the sitting room walls. Without really thinking, Anna set off after her, to offer such consolation and support as she could. Imogen was nowhere to be seen, however, until Anna checked around the side of the cottage and spotted her vanishing into the woods behind along a thin footpath.

She hesitated a moment. The woods were old and dark, and she had good reason to be wary of such places. Besides, Imogen was entitled to be alone, if that was what she wanted. Yet she was entitled to sympathy too, a chance to pour her heart out. She carried on, therefore, hurrying to catch up, her feet crunching on the thick mat of dried leaves as she picked her path between creepers, branches and abandoned burrows. Imogen finally heard her coming and turned to face her, arms folded across her chest. 'What?' she asked, a dappled shaft of sunshine falling upon her face and making her squint. 'What do you want?'

'I'm so sorry,' said Anna, slowing as she neared her. 'That must have been brutal.'

Imogen tried to shrug it off. 'It's not as if I didn't know.'

'Even so.'

Imogen stayed silent a moment, but then she scowled and shook her head. 'I *worshipped* her,' she said. 'God knows I did. She always had *everything*. You'd think she could have left me Raoul.'

'Your sister, you mean?'

'Of course my sister. Who else?'

'I never knew her. What was she like?'

Imogen looked helplessly at her, uncertain where to start. Then she turned and strode onwards through the woods, while Anna tried her best to keep up, though having to fall back whenever the path grew too narrow. 'Our parents weren't very parenty,' she said, stamping down some thorny creeper as it snaked across her path. 'They were off to Gran Canaria the moment we'd both left home. But that was okay, because we had each other, like we'd always had. Charlotte was eighteen months older than me, but only one year ahead at school, thanks to the way our birthdays worked. I was a bit gawky as a kid. An easy target. But she always looked out for me. Then she went off to university, and I went to nursing college, so we didn't see each other as much as we'd have liked. As much as *I'd* have liked, perhaps I should say, because she was already so ridiculously popular by then. Everyone wanted their piece of her. No one wanted their piece of me.' Yet she said it with humour rather than resentment. 'Then she came here to run the excavation. She was still so young, but it didn't bother her one bit. She had such faith in herself. And not just because Mr Brook was crazy about her, but because this was her destiny. To find something amazing here, I mean.'

'How so?'

They emerged from the canopy of trees into sunshine so bright that it made Anna blink. A short distance ahead, on the summit of the hill, stood a large summerhouse in the last stages of construction – at least to judge from its unfinished exterior and the supplies and equipment half-hidden beneath a pair of dirty blue tarpaulins. They made their way around the front then started down the other side of the hill towards a timber rail fence overlooking the River Deben, sparkling blue in the late morning sunshine, crowded with dinghies, canoes and paddle-boards, all cutting foamy wakes that glittered like ice. But Imogen stopped before they reached it, by a huge grey boulder half buried in the ground. 'Have you seen this yet?' she asked. 'Our famous dragon stone?'

'Only in photographs.'

'The Angles dragged it up here, so they say, as some kind of marker or beacon. And of course you know Sutton Hoo across the river. Then there's Kyson Hill to our left, and Kingston Fields beyond that, whose names are each plausible corruptions of King's Tomb. Or so my granddad Tony always claimed. Plus there were the mounds on the back lawn, and traces of precious metals in the soil samples, and random Anglo-Saxon artefacts found here over the centuries, most of which are on display in the town's museum. Put it all together and you can see why all the local archaeologists considered this a hugely promising site. But that was never the real story. Not for Charlotte.'

'Then what was?'

'*Beowulf*,' said Imogen simply, sweeping her arm wide to embrace not just the landscape that lay beneath them, but all its centuries of history too. 'The real story was *Beowulf*.'

TWENTY-TWO

B
ack in the cottage, Raoul Flood marched across the room even as Imogen and then Anna left it, snatching the remote control from Elias's hand to skip the DVD ahead. Unfortunately, that only landed on more footage of him and Charlotte lying together on a picnic rug on Dragon Stone Hill, then out sailing on the river. Flood turned furiously on Cameron Wolfe. 'You were stalking us?'

'I hardly needed to,' said Wolfe, amused. 'You made it so easy.'

'You little shit. Spying on people's personal moments.'

'Personal moments!' scoffed Wolfe. 'You were screwing your fiancée's sister. Maybe it's not me you should be mad at. Maybe it's yourself.'

'And you think I'm not?' retorted Flood. He'd finally skipped beyond the clips of himself and Charlotte, so he tossed the remote down on the sofa then went outside to sit on one of the benches, muttering darkly and waving his hands this way and that, doing his best to convince some invisible jury.

'What was that about?' asked Bryony Mackay, from the doorway.

'Our host's tribute to Charlotte,' Wolfe told her. 'Seems it was a hit job.'

'What a surprise,' she said dryly, sauntering over. 'On who?'

'All of us, I'd guess.' He picked up the remote to set the DVD playing again and to turn up the volume. It showed twilit feed from an excavation trench camera as lively music boomed away in the background, along with the good-natured chatter of colleagues sharing a beer after their day's toil. Charlotte and Lucius Hyde-Smith then walked into shot, already engaged in a heated conversation, but now close enough for the microphone to pick up their words over the background hubbub. 'How many times?' sighed Charlotte. 'That's between me and the board. If it makes you feel any better, I told Bryony exactly the same. She thinks it's her I'm going to stab in the back, not you.'

'But I didn't *do* anything,' protested Hyde-Smith. 'Pretending to be offended like that. Lodging an official complaint. She's after my job, that's all.' His whine hardened into anger. 'And if she gets mine, no doubt you'll get hers.'

'That's enough,' said Charlotte.

'It's about that bloody article still, isn't it? I already told you how—'

A click and a burring noise. The screen went black. Elias looked across to see Lucius Hyde-Smith ejecting the DVD from the player. 'This is outrageous,' he said, trembling, when he saw them staring. 'This is slander.'

'Put that back,' said Elias.

'I will not.' He snapped the DVD in two, silver splinters flying in all directions.

'That's evidence you've just destroyed.'

'Not any more, it isn't.'

'We all saw it,' taunted Wolfe, thoroughly enjoying Hyde-Smith's discomfort. 'What was the article you were talking about?'

'There was no article,' said Hyde-Smith. 'It was a misunderstanding, that's all.'

'Bullshit,' said Mackay. 'Charlotte adapted a section of her thesis into a piece for the British Museum magazine. Grendel's mother as a Norse earth goddess, as I recall. She gave it to Lucius to review before submitting it. He kept putting her off and putting her off. Then she read a report of a talk he'd given in Oslo on that exact topic, copying all her ideas and evidence.'

'That's a grotesque distortion,' said Hyde-Smith. 'My talk was completely different. A little overlap, that's all.'

'A little overlap!' scoffed Mackay.

'So you're a plagiarist,' grinned Wolfe. 'Good to know.'

'I'll not take lectures from a child pornographer,' snapped Hyde-Smith, before turning back to Mackay. 'And I was cleared of all wrongdoing over that, as you well know.'

'Yes. By a committee of your mates. After Charlotte was no longer around to give evidence against you.' She gazed at him in disgust. 'You're such a fraud. The great man of Anglo-Saxon studies. Not an original idea in decades.'

'Be careful, young lady,' said Hyde-Smith, wagging a finger.

'Or what?' retorted Mackay, heading back out the door. 'You'll push me off the escarpment too?'

TWENTY-THREE

A rare cloud passed in front of the sun, offering a brief but welcome respite from the building heat of the day, while, on the far side of the river, a motorist queuing for Sutton Hoo's car park let out their frustration with a long blast of horn. 'Beowulf?' frowned Anna. 'I don't follow.'

'How could you?' said Imogen. 'I haven't explained. But it goes back to my granddad Tony. My mum's dad, an absolute Anglo-Saxon nut. He never went to university himself. In fact, he left school at sixteen and was pretty much completely self-taught. One of those eccentric characters who gets obsessed with a subject and manages to make a good living for themselves out of it, though you're never quite sure how. He spent years working out and then practising all kinds of Anglo-Saxon crafts. How they built their ships and homes, how they smelted iron and made tools and dyed their clothes. Academics tended to be a bit sniffy about him, but he was always being rung up by TV and movie people who wanted authenticity, only with a bit of added verve and colour. And by re-enactors, of course. Lots and lots of re-enactors.' She sat down upon the dragon stone, arranged her skirts rather primly over her knees. 'He absolutely loved *Beowulf*, as you can imagine. He'd babysit us whenever Mum and Dad were out, so we soon got hooked too. We made Anglo-Saxon jewellery together, and cooked Anglo-Saxon meals. If it was nice out, we'd dress up in the Anglo-Saxon costumes he made for us and hold mock battles or weddings or banquets or whatever in his back garden. Or he'd turn down the lights in his sitting room and we'd huddle around his fireplace while he did what that actor did last night, reciting passages in full-on Anglo-Saxon before giving us the translation. We loved those nights. They were magic.'

'Is that where your sister got the idea for her feasts?'

'Yes. Of course. He'd take us on long walks too. Not that we enjoyed those quite so much. It always seemed to start raining when we were furthest from home. That's Suffolk for you. We must have visited the fields around St Gregory's Church in Rendlesham thirty times, and god alone knows how many hours we spent hiking alongside the Deben. He'd tell us stories as we went. He never ran out of stories. Mostly they were based around an idea that captivated Charlotte so much that she wrote her thesis on it: that *Beowulf* wasn't really a poem about some heroic Scandinavian warrior who took on and defeated a series of terrifying monsters. It was actually a poem about how the Angles settled here in Suffolk and then made themselves masters of all England.'

Anna stared blankly at her. '*Beowulf*?'

'I know,' said Imogen. 'It sounds ridiculous, doesn't it? You'd never get that in a million years from reading the poem. But Granddad Tony believed it absolutely. And Charlotte came to too.'

'Go on, then. Convince me.'

'Oh god, no. I'm not the person for that. She posted a copy of her thesis on the excavation website, though. If it's still up, you should download a copy. Everything's in there, far better than I could explain it.'

'Just the nutshell, then.'

'Fine. Though don't blame me if I mess it up.' She took a moment to arrange her thoughts. 'So, as I'm sure you know, *Beowulf* is written in early Anglo-Saxon, which means it was composed in England, most likely somewhere very close to here. It's *by far* the longest Anglo-Saxon poem to survive, though it only did so by the purest chance, thanks to some random eleventh century cleric writing it down in a compendium of stories and poems about monsters. That was the only copy, and it almost got destroyed by a terrible fire back in the eighteenth century. Grandad Tony took us up to see it in the British Library one time. You can actually see the scorch marks around its edges showing how close it came, like it was meant to survive. That's what Grandad Tony thought anyway. And Charlotte too. She was always a lot more superstitious than academics are supposed to be. But the poem was composed long before it was written down. You can tell from the vocabulary and style, apparently. Which makes sense. I mean even I can spot the difference between Rowling and Dickens, or between Shakespeare and Chaucer. Plus there are more concrete clues. Christianity is very clearly the prevailing religion, for example, which means it can't have been composed before St Augustine arrived here in six hundred AD or whenever. Yet it probably wasn't that much later either, because it's dripping with such obvious nostalgia for the pagan past. Forget about humility, poverty, fasting and all those other tedious Christian virtues. *Beowulf* is a celebration of courage and glory, gold and feasting.'

'I can see that,' said Anna.

'Good. Okay. There's also reason to think it had a special resonance for the Angles here. Rædwald – the king buried at Sutton Hoo – believed himself descended from Wealhtheow, the woman played last night by the Charlotte actress. Wasn't she amazing, by the way? It gave me chills to see her. Anyway, Wealhtheow's family name was Helmingas, and Helmingham just up the road was likely named in her honour. Then there's Rendlesham itself. Like I say, Granddad Tony walked us around those fields countless times, hypothesising about the huge royal hall that would have been there, a place for Angle kings to hold their meetings and throw great feasts at which bards would have told their epic tales. They found it recently, almost exactly as he'd described. It was only a shame he wasn't around to see it. Though it would have riled him right up to hear them announcing it on the news, saying how it could have come straight out of *Beowulf*. Because they got it completely the wrong way around, at least according to him and Charlotte.'

'I'm sorry? How so?'

'You really need to read Charlotte's thesis. It's all in there, explained far better than I ever could. But imagine you need to write a poem set in a place you've never visited or even seen pictures of. Your ancestors came from there, sure, and you have some garbled folk-tales and poems to work with; but essentially you have to make up all the descriptions yourself using only your powers of invention. Try it sometime. It's really, really hard. Charlotte used a line from *Pilgrim's Progress* to illustrate it, when Bunyan talks about a field full of mountains. A *field* full of *mountains*. I mean it kind of makes sense, doesn't it, when you say it? But then you actually see a real live mountain, and it becomes absurd. No field could hope to encompass even one, let alone a whole number of them. So descriptions of practices and places are invariably shaped and coloured by the culture and landscapes you inhabit, whether you want them to be or not. By what you see around you every day. And if you take a second look at *Beowulf*, it becomes obvious how East Anglian it all is. Grendel is still the name for a Suffolk ditch, for example. And we tell our children stories about a terrifying dog called Black Shuck, which is what the monsters in *Beowulf* were called. Grendel's mother lived in a misty grey mere lit by strange fires. You couldn't wish for a better description of the Lantern Marshes around Iken, just a few miles north of here. A celebrated cleric set up a monastery there right around the time *Beowulf* was being composed. His name was actually Botwulf, would you believe? He and his monks famously had dreadful trouble with terrifying creatures who lurked like Grendel in the marshes all around them. The floor of Grendel's mother's mere was covered with discarded shields and swords, one of which Beowulf snatched up to cut off her head. They used to throw weapons into the rivers and lakes around here for some unknown ritual reason. When the water was still and clear enough, you could actually see them lying there. How spooky must that have been! And there's so much more that I've forgotten. But, once you start looking, you can see bits of the poem everywhere.'

'Including up here?'

'*Especially* up here. That's the point. Do you know what the Anglo-Saxons called burial mounds with treasure hidden inside them? They called them dragon hills. I mean, come on. What more could you ask for? Except there *is* more. Tons more. The poem pretty much starts with a ship burial, as I'm sure you know. It maps so closely onto the one at Sutton Hoo that it's almost journalistic, even down to the choice of grave goods that were found. But what got Granddad Tony and Charlotte so excited is that *Beowulf* doesn't just *start* with a burial. It *ends* with one too. Beowulf's own. A dragon was ravaging the kingdom in fury after a reckless servant stole a golden cup from its hoard. When no-one else dared take it on, Beowulf went after it himself, even though he was an old man by then. He tracked it to its lair and killed it, only to be mortally wounded himself. They buried him with a large part of the dragon's treasure in a huge barrow they built specially, so that travellers would see it from miles away as they approached. And, honestly, can you imagine anywhere else that fits that description anything like half as well as where we're standing right now?'

Anna laughed uncertainly. 'Are you suggesting Beowulf is buried here?'

'Not Beowulf himself, no. He's just a character from a poem. A name for storytellers to hang their heroic tales on, like King Arthur or Robin Hood. But a hero and a king, yes, absolutely. Granddad Tony was convinced of it – that there was a royal ship burial somewhere on these grounds, I mean. He was very matter-of-fact about it too, just as you might say there was a fine old oak up here, or a wonderful view. And, before you scoff too loudly, they said the same about Sutton Hoo, and look how that turned out. Now compare the two places, how much grander the setting here is than there. Doesn't that alone suggest that whoever was buried here was the greater of the two?'

'If anyone was buried here at all, you mean?'

'Yes. If.'

'And wasn't Rædwald the greatest of the Angle kings?' asked Anna. 'And don't we already know where he was buried? Or did your granddad think that was someone else?'

'No. The evidence for Rædwald is too strong.'

'Then...'

Imogen shrugged. 'I don't know. Though I think Charlotte did. Something happened towards the end of that summer. She'd been growing more and more despondent about how little her excavation was finding, though she tried not to show it to anyone else. She thought the whole season was going to be a frost. But then she came alive again. Electrified. I asked her why. She never told me, not in so many words. She'd learned the hard way to keep her ideas to herself. But I could read her better than most other people could, and I pressed her on it until she pretty much admitted to me the day before that she was on to something huge.'

'The day before?' asked Anna. 'The day before what?'

Imogen gave her a look. 'The day before she died, of course.'

TWENTY-FOUR

Elias was in the kitchen squirting tap water into a glass when Cameron Wolfe came in. 'So it was all bullshit, was it?' he asked, though without obvious rancour. 'That spiel Brook gave us last night, about you and your girlfriend being here to give a talk? You're actually his pet detectives?'

Elias shrugged. 'We were going to give a talk too.'

'And? What's the verdict? Was Charlotte pushed?'

'Let's just say I'm more open to the idea than I was yesterday. Aren't you?'

'I guess. Though to be honest I always suspected Brook was onto something.'

'You did?'

'Yeah. I mean you'll hear a lot about how everyone loved her. It's bollocks. The truth is that everyone *fancied* her. Us men, at least. Probably half the women too, if they're being honest. She had this way of gazing into your eyes. Ten seconds of that and you'd be sitting up like a puppy, begging for treats. She'd loop a string around your neck and take you anywhere she pleased. Not that I'm pretending I was any better, mind. She could have tugged my string anytime.'

'Nice.'

'It wasn't just her looks, to be fair. She was a blast to be around. Charismatic, too. There's something about people who know what they want from life, and who don't mind treading on a few toes to get it.'

'Did she tread on yours?'

'Woah. Spot the cunning questioning from the master detective. I pity the Lincolnshire filth having to do without those skills. Except I've had half the Met up my arse, mate. You're gonna have to do better.'

'Yes. I heard about that. Bullying teenage girls into making porn movies, wasn't it?'

'That's such bollocks. They knew the deal, believe me. An easy way to earn some extra wad without their parents knowing. Swear to god, never even had to advertise. Word of mouth brought me more business than I could handle. All that happened was some loser boyfriend got mad at this girl for dumping him, so he sent one of her vids to her parents. They were *not* happy, it's fair to say. Of course the little bitch span them a sob story about coming in for portfolio shots only for me to twist her arm into all the other stuff. Such bullshit. She signed up for the works, just like all the others. I've got the forms to prove it. But her parents had a mate in the tabloids, and it was the silly season, so suddenly I'm all over their front page as England's number one pervert monster. The bastards even used my photos for their damned story, putting those poxy little stars over the naughty bits. Should have seen the traffic to my site that day. Spiked through the fucking roof.'

'Two of the girls were underage.'

'Not according to their IDs.'

'IDs are easy to fake. You know that.'

'So what the fuck am I supposed to do? Cut off a leg and count the rings? Anyway, a few shots in their bras and knickers, it's hardly murder, is it?'

'Except it was more than a few shots, wasn't it?'

'Not with those two.'

'Yes. Funny that, isn't it? Almost like you knew.'

Wolfe only smiled. 'Like I say, I've had half the Met up my arse. You'll need to up your game.'

'Is that what you did?' asked Elias. 'Up your game, I mean. Because it occurs to me that bullying teenage girls into making pornographic films isn't a million miles away from taking compromising footage of a woman, then threatening to show it to their doting fiancé.'

'You think I blackmailed Charlotte?' scoffed Wolfe. 'You clearly didn't know her.'

'I think you *tried* to blackmail her,' said Elias. 'Except she wasn't the kind to take shit, was she? Like you just acknowledged. So she threatened you right back. Maybe with telling Mr Brook, maybe with going to the police. And you couldn't have that, could you? The tables turned on you, and by a woman too.'

'You couldn't be more wrong,' said Wolfe sourly. 'If I'd wanted to blackmail her, I could have filmed her and Raoul doing a lot worse than snuggling and holding hands, believe me. But I didn't. I liked her. I actually warned her to be careful. Brook was besotted, sure, but besotted people can be dangerous. Especially the ones with bits of shrapnel in their brains. He'd had a bunch of episodes, did you know? Blackouts. Fits. He'd lose himself for ten minutes at a time then come around not knowing what he'd just done. So I warned her to be careful. Because if I knew what she was up to, you can bet your arse he did.'

'And?'

He shook his head. 'She told me not to worry. She reckoned she could handle him. Like she reckoned she could handle pretty much any man.'

'Except you?' suggested Elias.

Wolfe laughed. 'God no. She could have had me clapping for fish along with the rest of her performing seals, if she'd put her mind to it. She did, in fact, right back when we first met. I was in the museum to film some artefacts for the doc I was working on. She chatted me up when we were on a break, made it clear she'd like a bit of screen time. I mean it wasn't really her area, but she was so ridiculously photogenic that I still found an excuse to put her in a couple of shots. Which is why she had Brook hire me, I think, because she knew I could make her look good. She had her future all mapped out, you see. She was going to find the next Sutton Hoo, and turn it into a documentary with herself as the star of the show. Then she'd leverage it to make herself the new face of TV archaeology. That meant always looking her very best on camera. Charlotte herself, I mean. She didn't give a toss how anyone else looked. The worse the better, as far as she was concerned. She'd come to see me in the evenings, make me dump any footage that wasn't up to snuff. I'd give her tips on her best colours and what makeup to use, because looking good on camera isn't the same as looking good in real life. I showed her how to manage her hair too, because it would fly all over the place in any kind of breeze. A bit of that is charming. Too much and it gets on your tits. She learned incredibly quickly. How to look as though she was listening intently, but without going over the top. How much dirt she could smudge on her hands and face to make it seem like she was working hard, yet still look hot. Knowing where all the cameras were, to get her best side. She could hit her marks as well as any actress, believe me. That DVD earlier, for example. Do you seriously believe that that camera caught her and Lucius by accident? Bollocks. She led him there because she wanted him compromised.'

'You think so?' asked Elias, who'd been wondering this himself.

'I *know* so. People behave differently on camera. Do my job long enough, you get to spot the tells. Charlotte always stood to the left, if she possibly could, in three-quarters profile. It was her best angle. Check out her other footage, if you don't believe me. The same pretty much every time. She'd also tilt her chin in a certain way; and, when there was a bit of breeze, she'd reach around the back of her head to pull her hair out the way, so that her hand wouldn't block her face. I'll bet Lucius realised it too. Not at once, obviously, or he wouldn't have mouthed off so stupidly. But afterwards, sure. And ask yourself this: if a man that pompous and self-regarding realised he'd been made a fool of by a little slip of a girl like Charlotte, and that she had his career and reputation at her mercy, do you honestly think he'd have taken that lying down?'

'Are you suggesting he killed her for it?'

'Hey, you're the investigator,' said Wolfe. 'I'm just being a good citizen, is all, telling you what I know.'

TWENTY-FIVE

I mogen and Anna arrived back at Gatehouse Cottage a minute or two before Greta emerged from her bedroom, having changed into an appropriately sombre plain black frock. She stood halfway up the stairs and made two announcements in a soft voice to all those who troubled to listen. First, she'd ordered pizzas, sides, salads and soft drinks for them all, which should be arriving within the next twenty minutes or so. Second, that her brother's Woodbridge hotel was currently undergoing a rolling refurbishment, meaning that its entire third floor had been sealed off to be redecorated and refurnished. Work had stopped for the long weekend, but enough rooms had already been finished to accommodate anyone who wanted one. She'd therefore asked for them to be aired and made ready.

It wasn't a perfect solution, as she herself acknowledged, but it was better than nothing. If the police agreed to it, she'd drive anyone who so wanted down there after lunch, to take care of the paperwork and make sure that everything was to their satisfaction. Then they could stay there in privacy, comfort and security until their belongings were released, whenever that might be. But it was clear from her tone and bearing that it wasn't their privacy and comfort that most concerned her. She simply wanted them all out of her cottage.

A car pulled up a few minutes later, a tower of pizza boxes belted in to its passenger seat. They took as much as they needed then sent the rest on to the Manor, for Greta had ordered enough for the investigating team too. The day was gorgeous still, if hot, so they flapped out a pair of tartan rugs in the shade of the oak and settled down to eat.

'Nothing stronger?' asked Cameron Wolfe, eyeing the soft drinks with obvious disfavour.

'There are some bottles of my brother's wine in the fridge and pantry,' Greta told him.

'Not much use in there, are they? How about we bring a few out here?'

Anna went inside with Greta to fetch bottles of her brother's Dragon Stone red and white, along with a corkscrew and some glasses. 'Would you like me to go to the hotel too?' she asked, when she had Greta alone. 'Or would you rather I stayed here? I'm happy either way.'

Greta put a hand on her wrist. 'Then stay,' she urged. 'Please. If you can bear it.'

'Of course.'

'Thank you. I don't think I can face being completely alone.' She glanced almost furtively back along the passage. 'It's just, there are so many of them. And I can't help but think that one of them...'

'I understand,' said Anna, to spare her having to finish the thought. 'I'll be glad to stay. Whatever you want. Just let me know.'

TWENTY-SIX

The pizza was delicious, if a little doughy, and swimming in so many salty, meaty juices that Elias soon had a mound of used napkins on the bench beside him. Lucius Hyde-Smith eyed them askance when he came to speak to him, nudging them aside with a fingertip before wiping the spot they'd been with his handkerchief and sitting down. 'So I saw you talking with that young policewoman,' he said. 'Did you tell her about the DVD?'

'Yes.'

'That I broke it, I mean.'

'Yes.'

Hyde-Smith sighed. 'I do wish you hadn't.'

'I'd imagine. But maybe in future you won't go around destroying evidence.'

'Evidence! It was from five years ago. Anyway, there are bound to be other copies.'

'There are,' Elias assured him. 'I told her where to find them too.'

'Ah. Good.' He didn't look terribly pleased, however. 'I have no objection to the police seeing it. But I don't see why it should be paraded in front of everyone else, allowing that... that... *girl* to continue her slanders, even after her death.'

Elias frowned. 'Is it because she was young or because she was female that you think her testimony should be discounted?'

'That's not what I meant at all,' said Hyde-Smith hurriedly.

'I only meant that she was a very ambitious young woman. And not above playing games herself, believe me. The way she had poor Hector Brook wrapped around her little finger! Making him give her the excavation to run. It wasn't right.'

'It should have been you, should it?'

He pursed his lips. 'Yes. Yes, it should. Or at least someone far more senior. For all anyone knew at the time, it could have proven to be one of the most significant excavations in decades. And it certainly shouldn't have been run by a... a...'

'By a mere slip of a girl?' suggested Elias.

'Stop putting words in my mouth. By a person of insufficient experience. Or do the police now entrust murder investigations to first-year recruits?'

'You've got me there,' said Elias. He finished his last mouthful of pizza, then wiped his hands and mouth and chin before anything dripped onto his shirt. Then he gathered up all his napkins and found a black bag to dump them in. 'So I read your statement to the police last night,' he told Hyde-Smith, on his return. 'I read everyone's, for that matter. And what I found interesting was that both Ms Mackay and Mr Smallbone said that you were off your head drunk the night Charlotte died. So drunk that you could barely keep your feet.'

'That's not true. I know my limits.'

'Then why do you think they said it?'

'Mischief makers, the pair of them,' said Hyde-Smith. But Elias had learned years before that silence was often the best interrogator, so he simply gazed at him until he cracked and gave in. 'I suppose it's not inconceivable that the glass or two I had mixed badly with my medication.'

'You were on medication? That wasn't in your statement.'

'Why would it be? It wasn't relevant.'

'What was it for?'

'A bad chest. I'd had it for a while. My wife kept nagging me to give up my pipe. I'd tried over the years, but tobacco is a beast. So in the end my doctor gave me some pills. They worked a treat. I haven't smoked since.'

'These pills? You remember their name?'

'It was five years ago. How would I?'

'Were they called Champix, by any chance?'

'I suppose they might have been. Why?'

'One of my first really nasty assault cases, it was a man on Champix. Champix and alcohol. He swore up and down he'd had nothing to do with it. He believed it too, I'm sure of it. Thing is, though, Champix can play havoc with the memory when mixed with alcohol. You should have seen this guy's face when we played him the CCTV of him kicking this poor kid as he lay there on the pavement. Just kicking him and kicking him.'

'I didn't kick anyone, I assure you. Or push them.'

'How can you be so confident? You claim you were fine, but we've got two independent witnesses saying you were not only drunk but belligerent too.'

'Independent!' scoffed Hyde-Smith. 'They're jealous, the pair of them. Of course they'd try to do me down.'

'Really? In a murder investigation? I mean isn't it at least possible that it's your memory that's screwed up, not theirs? And not just your memory of the meeting itself, but of what happened afterwards. You could have got up to anything that night, then woken the next morning with your mind a blank, except maybe for a troubling sense of unease once you'd learned what had happened to Charlotte, and remembered your fight with her.'

'This is absurd. It wasn't even a fight. A difference of opinion.'

'So you do remember it. How about that? Tell me: Do you ever dream about it? About finding yourself up on the hill with Ms Ash, I mean? A shouting match turning into a shoving match? Watching in horror as she tumbles over the edge?'

'Of course not. Why would I?'

'Because most normal people would, with memories as hazy as yours. They'd worry about it, even when they'd done nothing wrong, because that's how conscience works. It's only sociopaths who don't fret at all.' He reached for another slice of pizza, but it was so limp and cold that he put it back again. 'Did you know you got caught on camera leaving the house that night?'

'*What?*'

'Yeah. A couple of minutes after Charlotte set off, one of the excavation cameras catches you slipping out the boot-room door.'

Hyde-Smith glared at him. 'I don't believe you,' he said. But there was a catch in his voice. He wasn't sure. 'You're making it up.'

'If you say so,' said Elias. 'So how about this weekend? Did you know what Brook had planned? That it was all about finding Charlotte's killer, I mean?'

Again those pursed lips. Again Elias let silence work its magic. 'I wouldn't say that I knew, exactly,' sighed Hyde-Smith finally. 'But I can't claim that it was entirely a surprise either. The man was obsessed. He wouldn't let it go. And he obviously suspected one of us.'

'Then why come?'

'Because I didn't want him thinking that I had anything to hide or fear. Besides, there were those rivets he sent me and the others. He included a photograph of the three together and a cover note explaining that he intended to award the excavation and a large donation to one or other of us. Damned if I was going to let that Mackay woman win it without a fight. Or Smallbone either, for that matter.'

'Competitive lot, you academics?'

'What is it they say? Our politics are so vicious because the stakes are so small. Except not this time. It wasn't just the funding or the donation. Mr Brook also hinted strongly that he'd be giving the winner this entire estate, to be run for the benefit of the nation.'

'And you didn't think that that might be bait?'

'*Of course* it was bait,' scoffed Hyde-Smith. 'I'm not *that* big an idiot. But some worms are fat and juicy enough to risk a hook. Especially as Mr Brook copied our various bosses in on the offer, so that we'd have had some explaining to do if we refused. Then there were the rivets themselves. He was quite correct about them being larger than the ones from Sutton Hoo. It was the first thing I checked. Larger than those from Snape or Ashby or any other Anglo-Saxon ship burial.'

'And that's significant, is it?'

'Naturally. The bigger the ship, the wider the planks. The wider the planks, the longer and thicker the rivets need to be. Scale up the ship in proportion to those rivets and you're looking at by far the largest Anglo-Saxon ship burial ever found, which implies the most important, even though it's hard to see how it could be more important than Rædwald's. But that's half the point. We know so little about the early East Angles that anything is possible. His father Tytila. His grandfather Wuffa. Some other honoured forebear. Or someone we've never even heard of. Who can say? It could transform our understanding of that whole era. Think of the books that could be written! The tours! The documentaries! So, yes, I had the iron analysed, even though I suspected it a hoax. And not only did it have the same broad chemical signature as the rivets from Sutton Hoo, it was also forged in the exact same manner. So I had it radiocarbon dated too.'

Elias frowned at him. 'You can carbon date iron?'

'Not the iron itself, no,' acknowledged Hyde-Smith. 'Or not exactly. What you can do, though, is radiocarbon date the charcoal that was used to smelt it. It has to be charcoal, mind, and from freshly-cut trees. Fortunately, that was how the Anglo-Saxons went about it. They were outstanding smithies. Some of their workmanship wasn't matched until the Victorians came along. When I was still a young man, I found a short sword that... Not that you need to know that. Where was I?'

'Carbon dating iron,' said Elias.

'Ah, yes. Do you know how radiocarbon dating works?'

'One kind of carbon that decays into another kind?'

'Essentially, yes. More precisely, there's a radioactive isotope of carbon in the atmosphere known as carbon-14. Every living thing on the planet ingests it all the time, just as we're both doing right now, and all these trees around us too. But we stop doing so the moment we die, allowing the stock of carbon-14 we've built up in our system to decay very slowly but at a predictable rate into a different isotope called carbon-12 instead. Measure the ratio of these two isotopes in a sample and you can calculate roughly how long ago that organism died.'

'And it survives being turned into charcoal?'

'The ratio does, yes. And it gets transferred from the wood into the iron as it's being smelted too. You don't even need that large a sample. The rivet Mr Brook sent me was plenty. You simply sand away the outer coating of rust and remove any other possible contaminants until you get at the raw metal. Treat a few grams of it with nitric acid and blast it with oxygen until the iron has been turned to iron oxide, and the carbon to carbon dioxide, then run it through a couple more processes until you have your sample ready to test. A lot of work and expense to go to, I admit, for what I initially assumed had to be some kind of hoax. I'd never have done it, except that I have a good friend at University College London, where they not only have the necessary equipment, but also the students in need of practice.'

'And the rivet was old, I'm assuming? Or you wouldn't be here. How old?'

'Radiocarbon dating isn't precise, you understand. Or not as precise as some people would have it. There's always a fairly substantial margin of error, particularly in instances like this, what with all the charring and burning involved.'

'I get that. But roughly?'

'Fourteen hundred years before present,' said Hyde-Smith, with a rueful smile. 'That was the figure my friend gave me. Fourteen hundred years, plus or minus fifty. Which is to say, *almost exactly* the same age as the great burial at Sutton Hoo.'

TWENTY-SEVEN

A flare of light by an unused door was hardly proof that someone had followed Charlotte Ash up to Dragon Stone Hill on the night she'd died. But it was about the best lead Elias had, and plenty enough to give some trees a shake, to see what fell out. Lucius Hyde-Smith had seemed reasonably confident in his denial, Raoul Flood would still have been on his way back from the pub, and Imogen Flood and Cameron Wolfe had been watching the end of their movie together. That left only Philip Smallbone and Bryony Mackay. Of the two, Smallbone seemed the more likely prospect, motivated by some toxic mix of jealousy, lust and resentment. He was easier to get at, too, for while Mackay was on one of the rugs, talking to Imogen and Anna, he was standing all by himself in the narrow strip of shade offered by the cottage, gazing at the lunch party with a jaundiced eye.

Elias refilled his plastic cup with bitter lemon then went across to join him. 'So which is it?' he asked.

'Which is what?' replied Smallbone.

'Is it that you dislike everyone? Or just these particular people?'

Smallbone gave a snort. 'I don't see you talking to them.'

'I didn't spend a summer excavating with them.'

'Excavating is my job. My private life is separate.'

'Mine too,' acknowledged Elias. 'Mine too. Mind you, my job was mostly locking up murderers and rapists, so not quite the same. Weird thing, though. I'm with you when it comes to small talk. I can't see the point of it any more, not since the divorce. Or not since I stopped seeing the kids every day, to be more precise. You know all about that, right? You lose all your fun old mates when you become a dad. You find yourself hanging out instead with the parents of your kids' friends. You talk about the teams they're in, and who the good teachers are, and places to take them on rainy weekends. But then suddenly your kids aren't there any more, and you realise you've got nothing in common with these people except children of the same age. And so good riddance to them. At least, that's how it was for me. How about you?'

'Is that any of your business?'

'You're right, you're right. Of course it's not. It's just, divorce is such a bastard, isn't it? Not getting to see the kids every day. You don't realise how important it is to your mental health simply to know that they're okay. I worry all the time now that something bad's happened to one of them. Every phone call I get. Every phone call I *don't* get. You should see my pulse when the ex rings out of the blue. Sixty to a hundred and eighty in a time to turn Ferrari green.'

'You want to get that checked out. Sounds serious.'

'It used to take a pretty woman to set me off like that. Someone like Charlotte Ash, say. Though I have to ask: Was she really as special as everyone says?'

Smallbone gazed sourly at him. 'Yes,' he said. He looked about to say something further, but then thought better of it.

'Must have been galling. To find out she'd played you.'

'Played me?'

'Sure. That tribute film Hector Brook put together. Turns out it wasn't a tribute at all. Turns out it was a bit of a hit piece.'

'And it shows Charlotte playing me?'

'It shows you making a fool of yourself, mooning after her like a lovestruck teen.'

'I never mooned after her.'

'Yeah, you did. And that's okay. It happens. Would have been around the time your marriage fell apart too, so I'm going to guess the two were connected, right? And then to hear her and Raoul Flood making fun of you like that. No wonder it got you where it hurts. No wonder you looked like murder. No wonder you followed her out of the Manor that night.'

Smallbone turned to him in alarm. 'Followed her out? What are you talking about?' But his voice was a croak.

'You got caught by one of the excavation cameras,' Elias told him. 'It shows you plain as day, heading out the boot room door almost exactly two minutes after Charlotte.'

'Bullshit.'

'Perfectly true, I'm afraid,' he said. 'No one thought to check the footage at the time, but Mr Brook was going through it a month or two back, hoping for a last glimpse of Charlotte, and there you are, looking helpfully towards the camera. He showed it to me last night. He was planning to ambush you with it later today, to ask you why you followed her, and what happened when you caught up.'

'You're lying,' said Smallbone.

'Suit yourself,' shrugged Elias. 'But I've already told DS Trent about it, so I expect he'll be wanting a word in due course. And denial isn't going to wash with him, I assure you. Not once he's seen that footage. It'll only make you look even more guilty. Honestly, your best chance in a situation like this is to get out ahead of it. Explain to him why you were stalking Charlotte that night, and why—'

'I wasn't stalking her,' snapped Smallbone. 'It wasn't like that.'

'That's how it looks on the film,' said Elias.

'Then the film is wrong.'

'Go on, then. Tell me.'

He bit his teeth together, already regretting having admitted as much as he had. 'It was a dark night,' he said finally. 'That's all. I was worried for her, going out on her own like that.'

'Worried why?' But Smallbone only shook his head. 'She'd already told you flatly that she didn't want your company,' suggested Elias. 'So you started to suspect that she was off to meet someone else. Because jealousy's like that. It's a scab you can't help but pick at. Who did you think it was? Raoul?'

'Raoul was still at the pub.'

'Yeah. But you didn't know that then, did you? He could have come back specially to meet her. So you set off after her, because you had to know. What happened next?'

'Nothing happened next. I turned back.'

'Sure.'

'I did. I swear I did.' He gave a sigh. 'I heard a cracking noise. Like someone treading on a branch. I think in the woods, though I couldn't say for sure. Charlotte heard it too. She turned and shone her torch this way and that, like she was scared of being followed.'

'She *was* being followed.'

'By someone else, I mean. I was too far back for her to have heard or seen me. But it made me stop anyway. She was clearly on alert. Anyway, I'm not that kind of person.'

Sure you're not, thought Elias. 'Why didn't you tell anyone?'

'Tell them what, exactly? That I followed her out of the house up to the place from which she fell a few minutes later? Come on. How would that have made me look?'

'Guilty,' said Elias. 'It would have made you look guilty.'

TWENTY-EIGHT

Word arrived from the Manor that DS Trent was happy for everyone who so wished to relocate to Greta's Woodbridge hotel once they'd given their statements, prints and samples; and that he'd even be sending a pair of officers with them, supposedly for their protection, but no doubt in truth to make sure that no-one sneaked off unseen. He also promised to visit them there later that day, to update them on the investigation and let them know when they'd be able to reclaim their vehicles and belongings.

They squeezed into the Land Rover Defender and the squad car that Trent sent with them, taking the last two free spaces in the hotel's private car park. Its ground floor proved to be spacious, plush and deliberately old-fashioned in tone, with high ceilings, crystal chandeliers and large framed sepia-tinted photos of the Woodbridge waterfront from between the wars set against the purple and gold flock wallpaper. There were vases of fresh flowers everywhere, and two dozen or so black leather armchairs set in clusters around low glass coffee tables. There was no-one behind reception, but a harried middle-aged woman in a dark suit quickly appeared when the bell was pinged. Her face creased with sympathy when she saw Greta. She gave her a hug and murmured some words of condolence into her ear before returning back behind her side of the desk to check them in, and to book a conference room for when DS Trent came down later. There was a moment of awkwardness when it came to payment; but Greta handed over a credit card and insisted everything go on it, including any room charges that might be incurred.

'Mighty generous of you,' murmured Elias.

'Not really,' confessed Greta. 'It's on my brother's account. I did most of his shopping for him, you see, after he gave up driving. Easier than him having to reimburse me every time.'

'Your brother gave up driving?'

'One of his first ever blackouts happened when he was behind the wheel. He came around to find himself nose-down in a ditch. He never drove again. The thought of hitting someone terrified him. And it wasn't that big a sacrifice. Woodbridge isn't exactly shy of taxis, and I was always glad to drive him, if I was free. That's why he bought me that hulking great Land Rover outside. I'd never have chosen a beast like that just for myself, but it came in handy for when he was touring his farms.'

Room keys were handed out. They squeezed into a lift. The third floor smelled of paint, though not as pungently as it might have done, for the windows were all thrown wide open, and a thick sheet of translucent plastic had been hung like a stage curtain halfway along the corridor, sealing off the section where works were still underway. There was little smell to speak of in Elias's room either, what with the windows wide open; yet the walls had that almost liquid look of fresh paint. The bathroom was pristine too, well equipped and provisioned not only with the usual soaps and shampoos, but also – thoughtfully – with a brand new toothbrush, a small tube of toothpaste and a disposable razor. The bed was large and firm, and there was a presentation box of white and red bottles of Dragon Stone wine on the dresser, along with a corkscrew and a hotel compliments card.

His laptop was back at the Manor along with the rest of his belongings, and he disliked composing documents of any length on his phone's small screen. Fortunately, there was a plentiful supply of hotel stationery on the desk, along with a branded hotel pen. His right hand tended to cramp and ache when he wrote more than a few words with it, so he'd taught himself to use his left instead, albeit slowly and clumsily. But he sat down, all the same, to set down his thoughts and observations of the weekend so far, if only because doing so brought a perverse satisfaction. Advising large companies on their physical, intellectual and technological security was important and remunerative work; but Elias was a Major Crime detective at heart, and there was nothing to touch a murder.

TWENTY-NINE

Greta had over-ordered for lunch, as anxious people will. Anna packed the leftovers into a pair of pizza boxes and stowed them in the fridge, along with the unfinished sides, salads and sodas, and half a bottle of white wine that had somehow escaped Cameron's attention. She binned the rubbish, flapped out and folded away the tartan rugs, then filled the dishwasher and set it running.

That done, she found herself at a loose end. Her talk was clearly off, and she lacked the appetite for work. As much for a distraction as anything, she went in search of Charlotte's thesis instead, and found it – just as Imogen had suggested – in a subsection of the Suffolk Archaeological Service's website that had been set up five years before to document the excavation, and not yet taken down.

She took her laptop outside to read it. Yesterday's tabby prowled for a while before finally deciding she was safe, jumping up onto the bench beside her then snuggling into her lap, purring contentedly and digging claws into her whenever she tried to nudge it aside. In the end, she surrendered to its greater will and rested her hand upon its head instead, stroking it with her thumb, making its nearside eye briefly grow large before shrinking back down once more, which treatment made it visibly indignant, though not indignant enough to get up and leave.

Some kind of signal had clearly been given that she was safe, for two more cats now appeared: a black one with a white splash, and a mottled silver-grey. The former nestled against her other side, while the latter lay across her feet, all three purring happily while making it virtually impossible for her to move at all.

She wasn't sure what to expect from Charlotte's thesis – perhaps some kind of literary deconstruction of *Beowulf*, or an exploration of its historical value. It wasn't like that at all. It began instead with a rigorous, wide-ranging and heavily referenced analysis of what typically happened to indigenous populations after their lands were conquered – how they were variously slaughtered, enslaved, assimilated or displaced, with examples of the latter provided from the New World and elsewhere. She was only a few pages in when she guessed where it was going and checked ahead to make sure. Then she skimmed the rest of the thesis, twice laughing out loud at the cheek and ingenuity of Charlotte's ideas, and, to her surprise, being rather won over.

There were other fascinating materials on the website, including a large picture gallery. Mostly these were of the excavation team at work and play, but there were also a number of drone photographs of the back lawn, along with an aerial shot of the entire Dragon Stone Hill estate, which was substantially larger than Anna had realised, with acres upon acres of woodland running from behind the Manor's outbuildings around the back lawn all the way up to the railway bridge, then onwards over the drive. She zoomed in on the black slate roof of Gatehouse Cottage and the oak beneath which she was sitting now, then followed the footpath that she and Imogen had taken that morning up through the woods to the summit of Dragon Stone Hill – though of course there'd been no summerhouse there back when this photograph had been taken, only a pair of wooden benches facing out over the Deben towards Sutton Hoo.

The drone photos of the back lawn were even more intriguing. Knowing, as Anna did, that several burial mounds had been found upon them, the circles of slightly darker grass were easy enough to spot. What surprised her, though, was that they formed such a perfect arc that it was instantly apparent that they were merely a small section of a far larger circle that would have run on beneath the Manor at one end, and continued out into the woods on the other. Everyone on the dig must have realised this too, archaeologists and volunteers alike, though they'd also have been under strict instruction to keep quiet about it, for nothing drew the nighthawks with their metal detectors like loose talk of ancient burials.

Hector Brook would have known it too, of course. What's more, he'd had five years of uninterrupted access to search these woods since. Those rivets and that dragon buckle suggested he'd been successful. Maybe it was connected to his death. Maybe not. Either way, the source of those artefacts needed to be found and secured before the treasure hunters arrived, as they surely would, with whispers of their discovery already leaking. It should be easy enough. Three rivets were one thing. Three barrels of them were a completely different matter. However well Brook had covered his tracks, he was bound to have left some trace, most likely in these woods.

She snapped her laptop closed, pushed herself to her feet. Her cats hissed and clawed and glared at her as she propelled them from their berths, then stalked off with reproachful backward glances. She wrote a short note to Greta that she taped to the cottage's front door, then she locked up and crossed the drive into the trees on the other side, following the few thin paths and animal tracks that the dark old woods had to offer.

THIRTY

E lias was still working on his notes when there came a light knock upon his door. 'Yes?' he called out. But the only reply was another knock. With a sigh, he went to see who it was. To his surprise, it was Greta standing there, looking furtively back along the passage as if nervous of being seen. 'What?' he asked, more irritably than he'd intended.

She pulled an apologetic face. 'I'm so sorry to trouble you,' she said, in barely a whisper. 'May I come in a moment?'

'Of course. Of course.' He found a warmer smile then stepped aside to let her by, closing the door behind her and following her through to the main body of his room. She went straight over to his window where she stood with her back to the glass, the slanted afternoon sunshine laying buttery epaulettes upon her shoulders. 'Forgive me for barging in like this,' she said, still keeping her voice so low that he had to watch her lips. 'I really just wanted the chance to talk. To talk *privately*, I mean. To talk *freely*. Without worrying about who might overhear.'

'No problem,' Elias assured her. 'What about, exactly?'

'Last night, of course. It's driving me mad. I have to know what happened.'

'Trent strikes me as a good detective,' he told her. 'I'm sure he and his team will find out whatever there is to be found out. Be patient, that's all. Give them time.'

'I understand. I do. But still. I can't help but think they're missing half the picture. Because I was wrong and poor Hector

was right. Charlotte's death is at the bottom of this, I'm sure
of it. And what worries me is that Detective Trent may not
want to stir all that back up. Did you know he was on the
original investigating team? The one that concluded she wasn't
murdered?'

'He wasn't, actually. He only reviewed the file.'

'Okay. Fine. But even so. And I'm not having a go at him, I'm
really not. I mean I thought her death was an accident too, as
you know, so I can hardly hold that against him. But it's difficult
for people to admit they got it wrong. And I don't want that side
of it ignored just because it might prove uncomfortable for him
or his colleagues. My brother hired you to look into it, after all.
I'd understand completely if you didn't want to carry on, after
last night. But I'd be eternally grateful if you would anyway. I'll
gladly pay you extra.'

'Your brother paid me plenty,' Elias assured her. 'And I'm
already on it, as it happens.' He gestured towards the desk
and the notes he'd written up. 'Though I won't do anything to
interfere with the official investigation.'

'Of course not, no.'

'Good. And I was hoping to speak to you about it anyway, as
it happens.'

'You were?'

'Yes. About your brother's tribute to Charlotte. I watched
your DVD of it earlier. Or most of it. Mr Hyde-Smith took offence
at that clip of him and Charlotte going at it over her testimony to
some British Museum inquiry. He popped it out and snapped it in
two, I'm afraid. Which left me wondering how much I'd missed.'

Greta frowned. 'Not much, I don't think. That was close to
the end anyway.'

'I thought so. Though maybe I could check with you that I
caught everything of significance. About people's motives, such
as they are. Because you're right that they seem a little thin.
Though of course they don't actually need to be enough for
murder, only for people to have followed her up there that night.
Maybe they wanted a private chat, or to flirt a little, or to lobby

her to their cause. Only it became heated for whatever reason. A shouting match, a bit of jostling, a shoe slipping on the dewy grass.'

Greta looked doubtful. 'If it was an accident, wouldn't they have said?'

'Except how could they have proved it? Safer to pretend they'd never been there at all. But we're getting off the point, which is that they'd still have needed some reason to follow Charlotte that night. Your brother claimed he'd found one for each of them. I think I have them all, but if I could just run them by you...?'

'Of course.'

'Good. Thanks.' He fetched his notes, glanced briefly through them. 'Let's start with Hyde-Smith and that British Museum inquiry. Bryony Mackay had made some kind of allegation against him, as best I can tell, and Charlotte was due to give evidence. Do you know any more?'

'A little,' said Greta. 'Though it's all third hand, so don't rely on it too heavily. But apparently Lucius has quite a reputation around young women – particularly the ones he has some power over. Overly tactile, if you're being kind. A sex pest, if you're not.'

'And he tried it on with Bryony?'

'So she claimed, though whether it's true or not... I mean I did once overhear Charlotte warning a couple of our younger volunteers about him, so clearly there was something to it. On the other hand, he's always behaved like a gentleman to me. Maybe that's only because I've aged out of it, but then Bryony isn't exactly in her first flush either. And I also heard her grousing that summer about how he was past it and should retire. So maybe she really was after his job.'

'And Charlotte was to be the key witness,' said Elias. 'And both of them feared she was going to side with the other, giving them each some kind of motive.'

'Yes.'

'And Hyde-Smith was likely to have been particularly worried, because he'd filched some of Charlotte's ideas for a talk he'd given in Oslo, meaning that the inquiry might have been her chance to get her own back, and win promotion too?'

'Exactly, yes.'

'Okay. Good. That's those two. Now Raoul Flood. It's pretty clear he was smitten by Charlotte. He must have felt sick when she decided to marry your brother. So he's coming back from the pub with a few pints inside him, and in the knowledge that Charlotte likes to head up to Dragon Stone Hill at around that time of night. He could easily have set off up there along the footpath behind your cottage, maybe thinking to talk her out of it, or hoping for a farewell romp on the grass. Not hard to imagine *that* conversation turning ugly.'

'No.'

'Then there's his wife Imogen. She strikes me as pretty sharp – certainly sharp enough to have known what was going on. That gives her about the strongest motive of the lot.'

'Not Imogen, no,' said Greta flatly. 'I refuse to believe it. You should have seen her the next morning, when she heard the news. She was in bits. No one could have faked that.'

'She wouldn't necessarily have had to. Remorse can look an awful lot like grief. Anyway, I'm not trying to solve the case, just to get a handle on your brother's thinking. So, Philip Smallbone. He was besotted, too, at least until he heard Charlotte and Raoul Flood making fun of him. Honestly, if men could take a bit of that without losing their rag, it would cut violent crime in half. And he's admitted following Charlotte out of the house that night.'

'He has?' said Greta, stunned. 'But that's amazing.'

'He claims he turned back almost at once. But then he would, wouldn't he?'

'You think he's lying?'

'Well, it doesn't exactly look great, does it? Though to be honest I think he'd have denied it harder if he'd had a murder to hide. But who knows? Anyway, finally we've got Cameron Wolfe. He took some pretty compromising footage of Charlotte with Raoul. It wouldn't surprise me one bit if he'd threatened to show your brother unless she paid up. And she doesn't strike me as the kind to give in to blackmail.'

'No,' agreed Greta. 'She absolutely wasn't.' She looked as though she had more to say, only she wasn't sure how appropriate it was. Then she decided to tell him anyway. 'I hate speaking ill of people, but I'll gladly make an exception for *him*. Some of those poor young girls he bullied into doing his horrible movies were barely older than my own pupils.' She gave a shudder of pure disgust. 'Though there wasn't even a whiff of anything like that at the time. I want to make that clear. Hector would never have hired him if there had been, whatever Charlotte wanted. He was far too honourable.'

'Yet he invited him back this weekend.'

'He had to, for his wretched plan to work. Because he was the one Hector always suspected most, only he didn't tell you so yesterday, in case it prejudiced you. And he didn't suspect him just because of the possibility of blackmail. Cameron tries to play it cool, but he was every bit as smitten by Charlotte as the others. He never got over her dumping him.'

'They used to go out?'

'It was only a few times, and always far more serious on his side than on hers. She saw him as a bit of fun and a potentially useful contact. He saw her as the one. It started getting out of hand, with him demanding to know where she was all the time, so she stopped seeing him. He took it very badly, though. She even once hinted that he'd tried to do something stupid.'

Elias frowned. 'He tried to kill himself?'

'That's what I took from it, though Charlotte never said so explicitly. I assumed at the time that it was only his final bid for her attention, except that I heard the other day that he tried again after getting savaged by the tabloids. Which I must say surprised me. He hardly seems the type, does he?'

'I guess you can never tell,' said Elias.

There was an unintended hint of impatience in his voice, and Greta picked up on it at once, faint though it had been. 'Forgive me,' she said. 'I do rattle on.' She made her way to the door. 'And it's not as though I don't have things to do. My pantry looks as though it's been stripped bare by locusts. If I don't get out to the shops soon, poor Anna and I will starve.'

THIRTY-ONE

The woods were ancient, thick and parched from lack of rain, the carpet of dried twigs, leaves and branches crackling and crunching beneath Anna's every step. She had to take it slowly, for not only were the tracks thin and sparsely used, but the ground was pitted with old animal scrapes and burrows, and she had to keep stepping over thick tendrils of ivy and thorny creepers; while the few small glades created by fallen trees had been taken over by fat bramble bushes and tall clumps of nettles that tried their best to snag her or sting her as she passed. It was surprisingly dark, too, though pleasantly cool, for the heavy low canopy largely kept the sun at bay, except for in patches of filtered yellow shafts.

A squirrel scampered from her advance, taking refuge up a tree rich with birdlife, scattering them in their turn. She smiled as she watched, only for the ground in front of her to explode, a pheasant whirring up in panic from the leaf litter beneath her feet. Her heart began pounding. She felt a little sick. The nausea brought unwelcome memories with it too, for it had been through woods much like this that she'd once fled her abductor, after escaping the boot of his car. That had been at night, of course, and so dark that she'd had to run with her hands out in front of her, to spare her from crashing into trees or branches. Yet the smell of this place was the same. The smell and the woodland noises.

A clanking away to her right, like chains being rattled.

It grew louder and louder until she realised it was only the tracks of the East Suffolk railway line heralding the approach of another train – perhaps even the same one that had brought her here from Ipswich some twenty-four hours ago. It was shocking to her how much had happened in so short a time since.

The train passed by. Silence returned. But she'd rather lost her sense of direction, so she checked her location on her phone then plotted it against how her notional circle of burial mounds continued out into the woods. She pressed on until she'd reached the approximate perimeter of that circle, then wandered this way and that for a while, scouring the ground for signs of disturbance. It wasn't easy, covered as it was by a thick mat of leaf litter and other detritus, and with only the roughest idea of where to look. But at length she spotted a patch of earth that had clearly been dug up at some point, then replaced and stamped back down. And, once she'd found that first one, she quickly spotted a second and then a third, allowing her almost to predict where the fourth would be, for they formed a curved line that bent slowly back towards the Manor, while jiggling back and forth to avoid the trees and their roots. But while two of these pits were larger than the others, as though they'd offered some initial encouragement, none were much more than a yard across.

She found nine such pits this way before she drew so close to the edge of the woods that she could see the Manor's back lawn through the trees ahead. A pair of Scene of Crime officers in white protective suits were standing outside the barn and looking vaguely in her direction. The last thing she wanted was to have to explain herself to them, so she retreated the way she'd come until she'd arrived back at her first pit. Then she carried on in the other direction, looping around until she'd neared the edge of the woods once more, only this time looking out onto the Manor's gravelled forecourt, crowded with police vehicles and the marooned cars of Brook's weekend guests, cordoned off by police tape and with their doors, bonnets and boots wide open as they received the full treatment from Scene of Crime.

Anna retreated once more, paused to think. Ancient ships of any size had typically been built from shaped wooden planks known as strakes that had been joined together by one of three techniques. Early boatbuilders had lashed them with rope. Others had developed mortise and tenon joints. But the Anglo-Saxons had used a different technique again, overlapping the edges of their strakes then fixing them in place by hammering large, flat-headed pins through both strakes then through an iron ring on their other side known as a rove. They'd then sawn off much of the nail's protruding tip to leave a short stub that they'd hammered flat against the rove, creating rivets exactly like the ones Brook had produced last night. The clink clink clink from all that hammering had earned the technique the title of clinker built. Wind some wool around these rivets, coat them in tar to make them watertight, add ribbing for additional support, and you'd end up with a ship sturdy enough to survive even the wildest seas.

The passage of time, however, was another matter. The soil on this stretch of Suffolk coast was particularly acidic, so that it would soon have eaten away all the wood, leaving behind only neat rows of iron rivets to serve as markers of the ships that had once been there, allowing archaeologists to reconstruct them with remarkable precision. Brook had had well over a hundred of these rivets in his three barrels last night. That implied an excavation site several metres square at the absolute minimum, and probably a great deal larger. Nothing she'd seen so far had come even close.

So where was it?

It was only then that she realised the obvious solution. For if this was indeed a circle of funeral mounds, then it would have been a kind of sacrilege to bury a king or even a great lord upon its circumference, as though they were just another bead upon the necklace. They'd have been given pride of place instead. And pride of place in a circle was at its heart, with the other burials forming a ring around it.

She brought up the aerial photograph again to work out

roughly where that heart should be, then made her way towards it, having to fight through the thickest and thorniest undergrowth yet. But it too proved a disappointment, for while she found a number of the same small test pits as elsewhere, suggesting that she wasn't the first to have had this idea, there was nothing remotely large enough to—

A flash of colour out of the corner of her eye. A pair of dark trousers and a tennis shoe, both vanishing in an instant as he – Anna was sure it was a he, though she couldn't say exactly why – stepped out of sight behind a tree. And suddenly she was back in the forest of her nightmares, being stalked by a man who meant her ill.

THIRTY-TWO

Elias finished writing up his notes then photographed them on his phone and sent them to DS Trent along with a short cover note to explain what they were and to apologise for his bad handwriting. There was nothing else to keep him in his room, and, with all his luggage impounded at the Manor, he wanted to buy some clean clothes for the morning while the shops were still open. He duly took the lift down to the lobby and was making his way to the front door when one of Trent's two officers called out to him and waved him over to the table they'd taken, their chairs arranged to keep an eye on all the exits. 'Ms Brook was looking for you,' he said.

'She found me, thanks.'

'Where you off to, then?'

'Just for a walk. Too nice a day to waste indoors.'

'Want to leave us your number?' said his mate. 'In case we need to contact you.'

Elias grunted with amusement. 'In case I do a runner, you mean,' he said. They didn't so much as smile. He gave it to them then left the hotel and stood on its front step for a moment or two, wondering which way to turn. He'd not been to Woodbridge before, and had little idea of its layout. But he figured the shops were likely to be near the river so he set off downhill.

The pavement was narrow and increasingly crowded, mostly with elderly folk making stately progress, so that in his impatience he kept having to step out onto the road to get around them. Not that that was so much better, jammed as it was by cars filled with families who'd all conceived the same excellent notion of passing the afternoon sunbathing on some Suffolk beach, only to spend it sweltering in traffic instead.

He reached a charming pedestrianised centre where he killed a little time gazing through the windows of shops and cafés. An old-fashioned menswear store was open. He bought himself a double pack of plain white T-shirts, two pairs of black socks and a set of boxer shorts that they handed to him in a plastic bag with such tight handles that he could barely slip them over his wrist. A guitar-playing busker had gathered quite a crowd, only to be shooed on by a uniformed policewoman. He heard, instead, the come hither music of an ice-cream van. The afternoon was so baking that he decided to treat himself to a rare cone. Melted vanilla was soon dribbling all over his hand. He had to stop to lick it away. A siren blared as he approached the railway line, and the barriers lowered before he could make it through. A train came trundling slowly by. A young boy held up by his mother pointed excitedly at him through the window, his eyes wide and his mouth doubtless watering for an ice-cream of his own. It left him thinking of his own children, and as quickly as that his good mood turned dark.

The siren ended. The barriers lifted. He crossed the tracks and reached the River Deben, its calm grey surface jewelled by orange mooring buoys, its far bank crowded with trees whose branches stooped thirstily for water, as if they'd just made it across some unforgiving desert. Everyone in town seemed to be out enjoying themselves, scoffing down their fish and chips before the seagulls could snatch them, playing Frisbee and French cricket, sunbathing on rugs and deckchairs, sporting on boats or queuing for a river sightseeing trip.

Not so very long ago, he'd spent bank holidays like this with his own family, splashing around in the Mablethorpe shallows, building sandcastles and pigging out on his wife's picnics. They'd be doing that with a different man now. Elias had nothing against him personally. He seemed kind and decent and responsible enough, and the twins had certainly taken to him. It was the situation that he struggled to accept, evicted from the best bits of their lives, painfully aware that they were coming to look upon their occasional days together as disruptive and a chore, however hard he tried to make them fun.

The joyful shrieking of a young girl took on a darker tone. She sounded in real distress. He hurried up a bank to see if his help was needed, but she'd only fallen onto her backside while paddling in the shallows, and had got herself cold and wet and muddy. Her father had already picked her up in his arms and was telling her not to worry, that everything was going to be okay. And suddenly Elias was back at the cottage he'd been restoring, standing by the deep end of the derelict swimming pool he'd neglected to fence off, staring down in horror at his beloved son Marcus as he'd lain motionless in the foot of dirty water that had gathered at its bottom. And all the old grief and despair washed over him once more. Because there was a reason he no longer had a family, and why he didn't deserve one either.

THIRTY-THREE

Anna froze where she was crouched, nauseous and a little dizzy from the adrenaline pumping through her. But that brief moment of stillness at least gave her a chance to think. She'd assumed that all the test pits in these woods had been dug by Brook, but there was no real reason for that to be so. Any of the archaeologists or volunteers from five years ago might have realised the potential for more and richer burial mounds in these woods. Anyone, indeed, who'd simply checked out the Suffolk Archaeological Service's website, as she'd just done. A website, it now occurred to her, that had likely been set up and managed by Philip Smallbone.

The thought did little to comfort her. She tried not to judge people on their looks and manner, but it was hard not to judge Smallbone on his. His bitterness, particularly towards women, was too palpable. His general shabbiness as well, making it obvious that the collapse of his marriage had left him strapped. How tempting a cache of gold would have seemed. He'd have known exactly where to look too, and he'd had years to do it in. And he'd have had plenty of time to make it back up here from Woodbridge this afternoon. What was more, if it was him, he'd have every reason to want to cover his tracks, whatever that might take, or he'd be ending his career in dismissal and disgrace.

She turned her head slowly to the side, until she could see the tree behind which he was hiding out of the corner of her eye. She knew it was the right tree because she could see the phone he was holding out in his fingertips so that he could monitor her on its camera, suggesting he hadn't yet realised she'd spotted him. She brought up Google maps on her own phone, zoomed in on the woods around her to get a better fix on her location and orientation. The Manor was her closest point of safety, but the man was between her and it. The cottage, then, though it was considerably further away, and meant having to negotiate several hundred yards of woodland thick with nettles and brambles, with tripwire creepers, fallen tree trunks and abandoned burrows, any one of which could take her down if she put a foot wrong, which was all too likely in this confusing dappled light.

She turned around and took a few moments to pick out her best path. Then she set off along it, walking as casually as she dared, borrowing a trick from her stalker by holding her phone up high as if searching for a signal, while actually using its camera to see if he was following. There was no sign of him for the first few moments. Her spirits lifted. But then he slipped out from behind his tree to take cover behind another. It was too much for Anna's already frayed nerves. Something inside her snapped, she broke into a run. When he didn't immediately follow, she thought he was going to let her go. But then she heard noises behind and she glanced around to see him breaking cover and chasing hard.

She ran headlong, slaloming between trees, fighting her way through bramble bushes, hurdling clumps of nettles. Daylight ahead, far sooner than she'd expected. She veered towards it and burst out of the woods only to discover that she'd got her angles badly wrong, for she'd arrived not on the drive as she'd expected, but rather onto the narrow strip of gorse and heather above the railway cutting. Worse, she was moving so fast that she'd have gone plunging over the edge had she not managed to grab a branch and swing herself around, bringing herself to a sharp stop, teetering perilously on the old embankment's crumbling brickwork.

The man was still coming for her. She could hear him crashing through the undergrowth. With no time to backtrack, she turned right instead. She could see the railway bridge a hundred yards or so away, but the ground between her and it was so thickly covered by great bushes of gorse and heather that her only path was along the precarious tightrope of the embankment wall itself. She set off along it, forcing her way past the needles, treading down the bracken where it grew too thick for her to see, horribly aware that a single misstep would send her plummeting down to the tracks beneath. She told herself not to look. It didn't work. She kept catching sight of the rusted rails, the heavy concrete sleepers, the huge lumps of grey stone ballast. She couldn't help but remember how Charlotte had fallen down a drop very similar to this on the other side of the estate; and for a moment she wondered if she'd been running that night too; running for her life while being hunted by a man like this.

He burst out between the trees behind and almost went tumbling himself, only to catch hold of the exact same branch she herself had used. He yelled at her to stop, but all her concentration was on her footing. The bracken grew taller and thicker. She had to lift her feet as high as they'd go to tread it down. Needles of gorse and heather kept clawing at her trousers. She caught her foot on a thorny creeper, almost tugging her off-balance. But thankfully it finally thinned out enough for her to cut back through into the woods. She had her bearings now. There was the drive between the trees ahead, and then Gatehouse Cottage itself, its black slate roof and the honeysuckle that—

The man came out of nowhere to tackle her from behind. He took her down so hard that it punched the air clean out of her lungs. He span her onto her back before she could recover and pinned her shoulders beneath his knees, his cheeks bright red from the chase and his expression ugly with triumph.

'Got you,' he said.

THIRTY-FOUR

A footpath of ornately-patterned brick led Elias well out of Woodbridge before degrading into an earthen embankment that ran alongside the Deben as it meandered gently towards the sea, still some five miles or so to the east. It was fortified in places by protective barriers of granite rip-rap, and a few benches had been scattered here and there, for people to take a breather or admire the view, while occasional wooden staircases led all the way down into the water, their steps and handrails slick and green with algae.

He left behind the strangely rhythmic jangle of the sailboats outside the town's two yacht clubs. It grew so quiet that he could hear the screeching of birds from all the way across the river. A gull floated serenely by, content to let the current do the work. He fell in with the same leisurely pace as everyone else, nodding to them as he passed, crouching to chuck the friendlier dogs beneath their chins.

An archipelago of muddy mounds, each just a few paces across, made it hard to tell where the river ended and land began. He passed thick beds of seaweed and seagrasses, abandoned by the ebb and dried out by the sun, exuding a swampy, salty smell. Fields of reeds swayed gently in the light breeze, as if to some soft rock anthem. An old wooden sign declared the path ahead to be the private property of the Dragon Hill Estate. It was hardly the most forbidding of notices, yet – this being England – it was enough to divert most everyone else inland to Kyson Hill and the

National Trust car park. But he himself ignored it and pressed on.

He reached the concrete berm that had been laid to prevent further erosion of the hillside with its palisade of creosoted wooden planks and net of thick black steel mesh to hold in the exposed earth of the escarpment as it rose higher and higher beside him. A steel staircase appeared ahead, zigzagging up its face like a New York fire escape. There was a wrought iron gate at its foot, set in a short line of spiked railings, and with a dragon upon it, its wings spread wide and a great rock clasped between its claws. He tapped the code into the keypad to make sure he had it right. It clicked open. He waited until it had locked again then left it and carried on, passing the dock steps on which Charlotte Ash had been found, then continuing onwards for another hundred yards or so, until the path ended in a small seating area with a pair of weathered wooden benches facing out over the river, and only a strip of marshland beyond – though at least one person had mistaken the lush long grass for sturdy ground, for they'd left a deep boot-shaped hole in it where they'd planted their foot before realising their mistake.

He retraced his steps to the dock, gazed up the netted face of the escarpment to its top. He felt a little unsteady as he picked out the route down which Charlotte Ash must have plunged that tragic night. He crouched to run his hand over the rough bare concrete, though there was no trace of her impact, of course, nor any answer to the question of what had caused her fall. Yet it was easy to imagine her terror and her screams as she'd come tumbling, abruptly cut off as she'd hit the concrete before rolling unconscious over the edge of the dock to finish on the steps, face down in the water.

Again, the memory of his dead son came unwelcome to his mind. He forced himself to ignore it. The steps down into the water were wet and slick with reeds and algae, and smelled pungently of them too. The sun was high in the sky, so that its reflected dazzle made it hard for him to see how deep it was, though the silvery flash of a fair-sized fish suggested it was at least a few feet. He dipped his hand in to test the strength of the current. It was so weak he could barely feel it, yet apparently it had swept Charlotte's phone away, along with one of her shoes. A soft-soled shoe was easy enough to believe. But a phone? He made a mental note to find out what model it had been, and how heavy.

Footsteps on the path above. He looked up to see an elderly couple staring rather disgustedly at him as they went by. Word of Brook's death would be out by now. The locals would obviously make the connection to Charlotte, and these two clearly had him pegged as some kind of sensation seeker. He felt like telling them that he was police, except that he wasn't any more. And screw them anyway. He went over to the staircase gate, tapped in its code. The hinges were a little stiff, and gave with a teenage plaint. He pulled it firmly closed behind him, again listening for the lock to click back into place, then he set off up the metal steps to take a second look at the spot from which Charlotte must have plunged.

THIRTY-FIVE

I t wasn't Smallbone. That was something. It was a man Anna didn't recognise: young, burly, bearded and fit, far too strong and heavy for her, easily pinning her shoulders down with his knees despite her desperate efforts to throw him off. 'Easy now,' he said, breathing hard from the chase. He dipped his fingers into the inside pocket of his tan leather jacket to take out and show her his warrant card. Detective Sergeant Jack Pierce. At once she relaxed and just lay there, staring up at him in bewilderment. 'You're police?' she said.

'Yeah,' he said. 'That's my excuse. What's yours?'

'Christ, you gave me a fright,' she told him. 'I thought you were someone else. There was a murder.'

'I know,' he said dryly. 'Why do you think I'm here?'

'I don't know. I just saw you behind that tree and thought…'

'That I was the killer, come for a second scalp? It's a story, I suppose. What's your name?'

'Anna Warne. I'm a guest here for the weekend.'

'Try again, love. All the guests have gone into town.'

'All except me. Call Greta Brook. She'll tell you.'

'You got ID?'

'In the cottage, sure. The keys are in my pocket. Or there's my phone. I've got emails from her and her brother on it. Let me up and I'll show you.'

'In a minute, maybe. First, what were you doing in the woods?'

'Is Detective Trent around? I'd rather tell him.'

'Tell me first. Then we'll see.'

'Fine,' said Anna, hardly in a position to negotiate. 'At dinner last night, Mr Brook showed us some rivets and a buckle that he implied he'd found somewhere around here.'

'And you thought you'd grab yourself a nice souvenir?'

'No,' she said angrily. 'I wanted to find the site before anyone could loot it.'

'And I should believe you why?'

'Because I'm an archaeologist, that's why. Treasure hunters are my mortal enemy.'

He stared at her some more, but the righteousness of her indignation seemed to convince him, at least enough for him to take his knees off her shoulders. 'And you think this site is somewhere in these woods?'

'I did,' she said. 'It's what the pattern of burial mounds on the back lawn seemed to indicate. But there's no real trace of it.'

'Why not let us know before you went hunting?'

'It was only a hunch. I assumed you had more important matters to deal with. Anyway, it's not as though I kept it some great secret. I discussed it with Detective Elias.'

'Who?'

'Your boss knows who I mean. Ask him.'

He scratched his beard as he tried to make up his mind. Then he stood and took her by her arm to haul her to her feet. Gripping her unnecessarily tight, he marched her out of the woods onto the drive then turned right towards the Manor. A pair of heavy police barriers had been set up across the tarmac, a squad car with a dark blue bonnet parked sideways beyond them, the sun full upon it. A lanky uniformed constable climbed out as he saw them approach, sweat blotting through his black shirt and trickling down his forehead. 'Hey, Jack,' he said, taking in the dried twigs and leaves in Anna's clothes and hair. 'Amazing wildlife in these woods.'

'Tell me about it.'

There was a gap between the barriers. They had to turn

sideways to squeeze through. They carried on to where the drive opened up in front of the Manor. DS Trent was standing by the black Porsche, taking swigs from a small bottle of orange juice as he talked to a Scene of Crime officer kneeling on the ground beside its open driver door, checking beneath the seat. He heard their footsteps crunching on the gravel and turned with a frown. 'What the hell?' he asked, coming to meet them, gazing Anna up and down.

'Found her skulking in the woods,' Jack told him. 'Says she was after buried treasure.'

'That's not what I said at all,' scowled Anna, doing her best to act the injured party. 'I was looking for where those rivets came from. It could be a hugely important site. It needs to be found and secured before the looters get here. Because they'll be on their way, believe me.'

'And that gives you licence to wander around a murder scene, does it?' asked Trent, taking another swig of juice.

'It's not a murder scene,' retorted Anna. 'You told us specifically the house, the outbuildings and the lawns. You never said anything about the woods.'

'You didn't think to check first?'

'I figured you had more important matters to deal with.'

'That, and I might have said no.'

'Yes,' said Anna. 'That too.'

'She said she'd cleared it with a Detective Elias?' volunteered Jack.

'Ex-detective Elias,' corrected Trent. 'With no authority to clear anything.'

'I never said I'd cleared it with him,' said Anna, with a glare at Jack, who seemed to be doing his best to cause her grief. 'I said I'd discussed it with him. I'd hardly have done that if I'd meant to loot it, would I?'

'Discussed it how? Is he carrying on some kind of unofficial investigation?'

'Ask him, not me.'

'So that would be a yes, then. And he thinks the rivets and the buckle are material, does he?'

'Like I say: ask him. But it's hardly implausible. My taxi driver yesterday said there were rumours of a major discovery all over Woodbridge. And plenty of people would do crazy things for the next Sutton Hoo.'

He stared at her some more. But then he shrugged. 'Let her go,' he told Jack. 'It wasn't her. She wasn't even in the house last night.' He turned back to Anna. 'Be off with you, though. Before I change my mind and charge you with something petty and vindictive, just because I'm that kind of person.'

'Sure,' said Anna, rubbing her arm where Jack had squeezed it. Yet she made no move to leave.

'What now?' sighed Trent.

'That circle of burial mounds,' she told him. 'It doesn't just run across the back lawn and out into the woods.' She nodded at the house behind him. 'It runs under that too. And what if the place we should really be looking is beneath the Manor's cellar?'

THIRTY-SIX

Trent turned to look at the house behind him, then gazed coolly at Anna once more. 'Are you seriously telling me I might have an Anglo-Saxon burial ship beneath my murder scene?'

'I'm telling you that either Brook pulled off an incredibly elaborate hoax last night or he found those rivets somewhere. They didn't come from the woods, as best I could tell. Digging them up would have left far more extensive traces than anything I saw. Whereas the cellar is nicely hidden. Brook could have dug there to his heart's content, and no-one would ever have known. Isn't it worth at least a look?'

'Let's say it is. What should I be looking for? And what would I do next, if there's really something there?'

'This must be your lucky day,' Anna told him. 'Having an archaeologist right here.'

He snorted at that. 'How do I even know you're really an archaeologist?'

'Don't give me that. You've already had me properly checked out, along with everyone else here last night. Unless you're admitting you're rubbish at your job.'

Another snort, followed by a what-the-hell kind of shrug. 'Behave, though. I'll have my eye on you.' He led her inside and to the cellar door. It was still locked from last night, for Scene of Crime hadn't got around to it yet. The bolts slid easily but the lock proved more of a challenge, at least until they were directed to a cache of two dozen or so keys in a large blue-and-white porcelain bowl on top of the safe in Hector Brook's office, all helpfully tagged.

The lock was stiff. Trent had to lean his shoulder against the door before he could turn the key. There was a switch just inside. He flipped it and a string of unshaded bulbs came on below, dangling from bare flexes. Their light was rather feeble, leaving the place still gloomy after the bright sunshine outside. A set of rutted steps led down to an uneven floor laid with old red brick. Anna looked both ways. The cellar didn't run the full breadth or width of the house, yet it was still large enough to need rows of supporting pillars every few paces, the gaps between them mostly walled up with plasterboard to create a string of partitioned rooms connected by broad open doorways.

Ahead and to her right, a little daylight filtered through the gaps around a pair of wooden hatches, beneath which a trailer-load of logs had been dumped for the coming winter. Some had patches of mould and mildew on them, which helped explain the faint damp, musty smell. A silvery glint on the floor caught her eye. She stooped for a closer look, but it was only an old ten-penny piece, corroded and slightly bent, with smears of yellow and blue paint on it. Her eyes adjusted to the gloom. She spotted odd bits and pieces everywhere: green shards from a broken wine bottle; the white ceramic handle of a coffee mug; some bent and rusted nails; a pair of stubby screws with dabs of bright white filler on their tips; and an old blazer button with some navy blue threads still tied to it, as though it had got snagged on something, and been ripped off.

More pertinently, though, a cluster or two of bricks had been gouged up out of the floor in each of the rooms, then relaid afterwards with fresher mortar. Brook had indeed probed beneath them, though it seemed without reward. Like the test pits in the woods, none were remotely large enough to explain such an extraordinary number of rivets.

They wandered through the rooms anyway, looking for they knew not what. One was given over almost entirely to wine racks, their slots mostly filled with bottles from Brook's own vineyards, though with a fair few of champagne, sherry, port and spirits too, along with some top-end vintages for when the home brew wouldn't serve. Another chamber had been used for storage, with rolled up rugs and lengths of surplus carpeting stacked up against the wall, a number of rusting paint pots and other decorating supplies, and a pair of cardboard boxes that had largely fallen apart, the first filled with musty, yellowed paperbacks and the second with cast-off clothes, as though set aside for a charity shop some years before, and then forgotten.

They went back the other way, passing the stairs and the winter logs to the last chamber along. It was empty save for a pair of stained white dust-sheets covering some long, thin, low object set against the wall. Trent pulled off the dust-sheets to reveal a row of large brown storage boxes that turned out to be from the excavation five years ago, though with an intriguing gap in the middle from which a box had clearly been taken – perhaps the one containing all the footage used by Brook to piece together his tribute.

They started at either end and checked briskly through them, but the contents proved disappointing: mostly colour-coded ring-binders containing field notes, survey forms, site maps, personnel records, expense receipts, printouts of accounts and other administrative materials. Only the third box in from the right held anything of more likely interest: a set of journals penned by Charlotte herself, which had Anna briefly excited, until they proved to be devoted exclusively to the excavation, with little hint of the human dramas going on around it. She also found an artist's pencil case, a set of watercolours and half a dozen sketchbooks, mostly foolscap in size, but with two larger ones bound in sumptuous red leather, with thick leaves of well-sized paper, and C.A. embossed in gold leaf upon their fronts, suggesting they'd been a gift to Charlotte from Brook. Perhaps she'd thought them too precious to use, for she hadn't even started upon them yet, while the others were packed with pencil and charcoal studies of people, sites and artefacts. Archaeologists often developed a talent for drawing, for photography didn't always capture the character of a piece as well as a skilful sketch – and even a cursory look suggested that Charlotte had had a real gift.

'Anything good?' asked Trent, coming to look.

'Good, yes,' said Anna, flipping through some pages for him to see. 'Pertinent, not so much.'

'Okay. Put it back. We're out of here.'

'You never know, though,' she said, reluctant for some reason to let them go. 'I could give them a closer look, if you'd like? Let you know if anything jumps out.'

Trent squinted at her, wondering what she was trying to pull. But she passed him one of the journals and then a sketchbook so that he could see for himself that he and his team had far better things to do. 'Sure,' he said, though taking out his phone to photograph the box and its contents, to make sure he had a record. 'Why not?'

Anna replaced the books in the box then put its lid back on and picked it up. It was heavier than she'd expected, with plastic handles that bit into her fingers. She half expected Trent to offer to carry it, but either he was too enlightened, or not enlightened enough, for he simply turned his back on her and headed for the steps. So she adjusted her grip to make it more comfortable, then set off after him.

THIRTY-SEVEN

There was a second gate at the top of the zigzag staircase, though with neither lock nor keypad, only a simple latch. Elias passed through it then walked alongside the timber rail fence, pausing every few paces to lean out over it and look down at the footpath beneath, trying to work out from where Charlotte Ash had fallen. But again he learned nothing new.

The afternoon was pushing on. He felt the urgent need for a nice strong cup of tea. He climbed the hill to the summerhouse, then checked his watch before starting down the footpath through the woods on its other side, wanting to get an idea of how long it would have taken Raoul Flood to walk up here from the railway bridge on the night of Charlotte's death – though that, admittedly, had been uphill and in the dark.

He arrived at Gatehouse Cottage some nine and a half minutes later, only to find it locked and with a note from Anna to Greta taped to its door. He was about to text her for her whereabouts when he saw her approaching up the drive, struggling beneath the weight of a large brown storage box. He hurried to meet her then made a forklift of his arms to take it from her, while protecting his right hand. 'Been out burgling again?' he asked.

'They will leave their places wide open,' she told him, shaking out her fingers and arms. 'What am I supposed to do?'

'Anything juicy?'

'Charlotte's old journals and sketchbooks. From the cellar.'

Elias slid her a look. 'Does Trent know?'

'He was with me. After springing me from arrest. Speaking of which, I may have landed you in a spot of trouble.'

Elias laughed. 'Can't leave you alone for a minute, can I? How about a cuppa and you tell me all?'

They went through to the kitchen. Elias set the box down in a corner while Anna put on the kettle then found a clean mug in the dishwasher, still steaming from its cycle. She told him as she did so about finding a copy of Charlotte's thesis on the Suffolk website, along with the photographs of the Manor's back lawn that had prompted her to go searching in the woods, only to be pounced upon by Trent's detective. The kettle came to the boil. She popped a teabag into his mug, and the dab of sugar she knew he liked. For herself, though, she squeezed a quarter lemon into a tall glass filled with ice and sparkling water. It looked so good that Elias made one for himself too. Then they found a pack of digestives in the pantry and took it all out to the bench beneath the oak.

'So Charlotte's thesis,' he said. 'There's a bit in it about Grendel's mum and some Norse earth goddess, right?'

Anna raised an eyebrow. 'How did you know that?'

'We had a bit of a drama earlier, while you were off chasing Imogen. Apparently, Lucius Hyde-Smith nicked that bit for a talk he gave in Oslo. Without giving Charlotte any credit.'

'A department head nicking his assistant's work,' said Anna dryly. 'Will academia ever recover? Still, it was only one part of her argument.'

'Which was?'

'You honestly want to know?'

'Sure,' he said, taking a digestive from the pack. 'Why not?'

'Okay, then,' she said. 'You've asked for it. Essentially, her contention was that the three monsters in *Beowulf* weren't chosen at random, but rather because they each symbolised a real trauma suffered by the Angles. Suffered here in England, too, not back in Scandinavia.'

'Right,' said Elias, holding a hand over his mouth to avoid spraying her with crumbs. 'Because Suffolk was just teeming with ogres and dragons.'

'Do you know *The Tempest* at all?'

'Know it? I was in it once, back at school. Gonzalo, the old advisor. A seventy year old man, and me only twelve. Yet didn't even make a single shortlist.'

'It's a scandal.'

'I've put it behind me. No point being bitter. But why do you ask?'

'There's a monster in it called Caliban, as you'll recall. He's so like Grendel that some people claim he was based on him, even though it's hugely unlikely that Shakespeare had ever even heard of him.'

'And Charlotte's one of them?'

'No, actually. Her argument's more subtle. She claimed that the reason they're so similar is because they were both inspired by the same real world phenomenon. There's a line in *The Tempest* about how Caliban used to rule the island until Prospero stole it from him, just as Grendel used to rule the land in *Beowulf* until he got turfed out by the Danes. Yet instead of finding themselves somewhere else to live, they both chose to hang around instead, and cause trouble.'

'Ah,' said Elias. 'Go on.'

'Okay. So the New World was being settled right at the time Shakespeare was writing. Lurid stories kept coming back about scary indigenous people doing unspeakable things to god-fearing Europeans just for pushing them off their lands. As it happens, you often find the same dynamic following an invasion.'

'Including when the Angles arrived in Suffolk?' suggested Elias.

'Including when the Angles arrived in Suffolk,' agreed Anna. 'The good folk who'd been living here got pushed off the best land back into the forests and the fens, where they'd have scraped a miserable existence for a while, buoyed by the hope of eventually reclaiming what had once been theirs, and satisfying themselves by taking such vengeance as they could. Now put yourself in the shoes of those pioneer Anglo-Saxons. Wouldn't you have been terrified of such people? The shadows in the marshes. The whispers in the woods. The bogeymen who slipped into your villages at night to slit the throats of you and your loved ones while you slept? Particularly when you knew in your heart that they had justice on their side. In fact, their having justice on their side made it all the more necessary to turn them into monsters.'

'And that's where Grendel came from?'

'That's where Charlotte argued he came from,' amended Anna. 'A folk-memory of displaced natives taking revenge for their defeat.'

'Brook said something very like that to me yesterday afternoon,' said Elias. 'He also said that it would come up again over the weekend too. Then he said the same about some Icelandic volcanoes.'

'*Probably* Icelandic. There were some North American ones that went off at around the same time. It's even possible that it was both together. Not that it really matters. What matters is that the eruptions threw a heavy blanket of volcanic ash over pretty much all of Europe for a large part of the next ten years, East Anglia very much included. Harvests were dire. People starved. Then came a devastating outbreak of plague. The plague of Justinian, as it was known. The worst time ever to be alive, according to some historians. You might almost say a monstrous time.'

Elias squinted at her. 'The eruptions were Grendel's mum?'

'Not the eruptions themselves, no. No one here would even have known about them. But their effects, yes. Charlotte believed that Grendel's mother was a twisted version of Freya, the Norse fertility and earth goddess. She lived in a fenland lake, like Grendel's mother, and she too lost her beloved son – though Baldur was famously the most beautiful of all the gods, not an ogre. Freya was made so distraught by his death that she went into deep mourning, precipitating an endless winter called Fimbulvetr, during which the land was swept by disease and famine, causing war to break out everywhere, as people fought desperately over what little food remained. Sound familiar at all?'

'So Grendel represented the natives pushed out by the Angles?' said Elias, to make sure he had it straight. 'And the famines and plague that followed were punishment from his mum?'

'Or so Charlotte argued.'

'And the third monster? The dragon?'

'She was rather hazier on that. Which is unsurprising, to be fair. It's not just that dragons symbolised so many different things, it's that they were respected as well as feared. No army I know of ever put an ogre on its banners. But plenty of them used dragons, including the Roman cavalry units stationed here in Britain. They were also used as a kind of backhanded tribute for dreaded enemy generals. A Welsh warlord called Maelgwn Gwynedd got to be known as Insularis Draco, the Island Dragon. And Uther, King Arthur's dad, was given the title Pendragon, which literally means "chief dragon". Then, of course, there's the possibility that Beowulf's dragon really was a dragon.'

Elias laughed. 'Sure!' he said.

'It's not as implausible as it sounds,' Anna told him. 'There's a town called Bures on the other side of Ipswich that was famously terrorised by a wingless one for a while. It kept plundering sheep and scaring the life out of the villagers until the local lord put together a posse to hunt it down. They cornered it by the river and fired arrows that bounced uselessly off its scales, but they still managed to spook it enough that it slithered back into the water, never to be seen again.'

'I'll bet that's just how it happened too.'

'This was during the Crusades,' she told him. 'Knights were constantly coming back from the Holy Land with exotic relics and souvenirs. Saladin supposedly gave Richard Lionheart a Nile crocodile as a memento of his campaign. He kept it in London, as

I recall, but there was also a castle in a place called Clare, a couple of miles upstream from Bures, where they kept a menagerie of strange animals. Is it so hard to imagine that someone brought back a baby crocodile for their collection, and that it grew too large for them to cope with? That it got loose and made it to the river where it snatched a few sheep as they came to drink? And if you'd never seen a fully-grown Nile crocodile before...'

'Huh,' grinned Elias. 'A real live dragon here in Suffolk. How about that?'

THIRTY-EIGHT

ate afternoon arrived, but not yet Greta. Anna and Elias
were still chatting away in the shade of the oak when
a banged-up green Renault Clio arrived over the railway
bridge then trundled by, the sun so dazzling on its windscreen
that Anna couldn't see its driver until it drew level with her,
when she briefly glimpsed a woman with hennaed hair, a
colourful batik blouse and chunky metal earrings through its
lowered passenger-side window. She glanced their way as she
passed, but carried on up the drive towards the Manor, where
presumably she met the police barriers and was turned back, for
she reappeared a minute or two later and pulled up alongside
them. 'Is Greta not around?' she asked in a strained and brittle
voice.

They went over to talk to her. She looked to be in her mid-
thirties, with heavy eyeliner and scarlet lipstick that – along
with her clothes and abundance of costume jewellery – gave her
a distinctly Romany look. 'She's out at the shops,' Anna told her.
'Can we help?'

The woman gestured back up the drive. 'They just told me
about Mr Brook. I can't believe it. For it to happen again, I mean.'

'Again?' asked Elias.

'Poor Charlotte. I haven't seen either of them since. And now
this! My god. Why do the worst things keep happening to the
best people?'

'You haven't seen either of them in five years?' frowned Elias.

'What are you even doing here, then, if you don't mind me asking?'

The woman shook her head again, still struggling from the shock. 'Mr Brook called out of the blue a couple of months ago. He asked if I'd do a session. In Charlotte's memory, he said. She was about my oldest friend, so how could I say no? But I should have said no anyway. What was I even thinking?'

'How about some tea?' suggested Anna, for the woman looked too upset to drive safely. 'A glass of water or something?'

'Tea would be wonderful. If it's not too much trouble?'

'No trouble at all,' said Anna. They walked alongside her as she pulled in to the front of the cottage, then they went through to the kitchen together. 'I'm Anna, by the way. And this is Elias. Ben Elias.'

'Pleased to meet you both. I'm Patience. Patience Miller.'

'How do you take it?' asked Anna, putting the kettle back on and fetching another clean mug from the dishwasher.

'A nip of milk, please. Just enough not to scorch my mouth. But lots and lots of sugar. Three good teaspoons.' She came over to watch, to make sure Anna got it right. 'Don't worry about overdoing it. And as strong as you can make it. Two teabags, even, if you can spare them.' She went over to the kitchen table, shaking her head. 'I still can't believe it,' she said, slumping into a chair. 'What happened exactly? That policeman wouldn't say.'

'An overdose,' said Anna.

'They sealed off the house for an overdose?'

'They don't think it was an accident. Or that he did it to himself.'

'Oh lord,' said Patience.

Elias sat down across the table from her. 'You say Mr Brook hired you for a session,' he said, with his best friendly smile. 'Mind if I ask what kind?'

'Why do you want to know?' asked Patience. She gazed him briefly up and down. 'Oh. You're police too, aren't you?'

'Not any more, though yes, I used to be. Mr Brook hired me for the weekend, to help find out what really happened to

Charlotte.'

'Oh god. So *that's* what it was all for, was it? I might have guessed.'

'Your session,' he prompted again.

'Oh. Yes. Sorry. I'm all over the place, in case you couldn't tell. Okay. So I'm a spiritualist by trade. I do the Tarot for people, and read their palms, and sometimes I hold seances too. All that kind of thing.'

'You told fortunes for Mr Brook?' said Elias, surprised.

'Not exactly,' she said. 'Though yes, I suppose, in a sense.' Anna brought over her tea. She cupped the mug in both hands then took a sip and smiled appreciatively before taking a few moments more to organise her thoughts. 'My name's Patience Miller, like I said,' she began. 'I grew up in Melton, just a couple of doors down from the Ashes – from Charlotte and little Imogen and their parents. I'm a bit older than them, as I'm sure you can tell, though I overlapped with Charlotte at school for a year or so. But the point is, we've known each other forever. I babysat for them when there was no-one else around, and we baked birthday cakes together, and walked to school together, and brought over hot soup when anyone was ill. All the usual things that neighbours do for one another.'

'And you became Charlotte's spiritualist?' suggested Elias.

'Kind of, I suppose. I had this lovely little flat above the ironmonger's on Quay Street, if you know Woodbridge at all. I did readings in the sitting room, and Charlotte would sometimes pop in to say hi, when I didn't have anyone else with me. But only as a friend. I mean I'd never have dreamed of charging her. Though she'd take me out to lunch from time to time, or buy me a nice scarf or a bit of jewellery that she thought I'd like. So she kind of paid me that way, if you follow? Especially that summer. Because Mr Brook gave her a huge kitty to play with, supposedly for the excavation, but really just because he was besotted with her, and besotted people like to give presents to the people they love.'

'Yes,' said Elias.

'Okay. So where was I? Oh yes, readings. I didn't really do them for her, as I say. It was more that she liked having someone to talk to about what was going on in her life. Someone who wasn't a colleague, and who she could trust to keep it completely to themselves. And I'm a lot cheaper than a therapist, even when I do charge. But I wouldn't want to say I never read for her at all, either, because she did enjoy a bit of that. Especially the Tarot. My great grandad left me his deck, you see. It's old and beautiful and it has that look, you know; as if it should be magical, even if it's not. So she'd often ask me a question or two, particularly about where to dig. Because of Edith Pretty, of course.'

Elias frowned. 'The Sutton Hoo woman? What's she to do with it?'

'She was a spiritualist,' said Anna, glancing at Patience for confirmation. 'A fairly committed one, as I recall. Didn't she attend a spiritualist church in Woodbridge?'

'Not just any church,' said Patience. 'The one my great granddad belonged to. He always used to claim that he was the one who told her to dig up the mound where they found what's his name, that old king. But then he claimed a whole lot of unlikely things, so I wouldn't put too much store in that.'

'This is the family trade, then?'

'Except for my mum. She won't touch it. Freaks her out.' She contemplated this gloomily. 'Sometimes I think it's because she's the only one of us who truly does have some kind of gift. *She'd* have put the phone down on Mr Brook, no messing. Wouldn't even have picked it up, more like. Not like Muggins here. The rake hasn't been invented yet that I won't step on. And once I'd answered it, it was already too late. I found Mr Brook impossible to say no to. He had this terrible mix of kindness and authority, you see. If the one didn't get you, the other would. And I never could read him properly either, which didn't help. Except for how he felt about Charlotte. A blind man could have seen that from the other side of town, if only from the way she changed him.'

'So you knew him from before that summer, did you?'

'Not really, no.' She gave a sigh, frustrated with herself for explaining it all so poorly. 'I mean everyone in Woodbridge knew who he was. We used to see him around town quite a bit before that awful blast turned him into a hermit. I don't think I saw him at all after that, not until Charlotte went knocking on his door. That was it for him. He fell for her so hard, he wanted to spend all the time he could with her. She liked coming into Woodbridge, so he took to coming too. Then, one afternoon, she brought him to my place, mostly I think because he didn't believe her when she told him where she was going.' She paused and sat back as Anna tipped out the rest of the digestives onto a plate and set them on the table before her. 'He had a little bit of the green-eyed monster in him, did Mr Brook, at least when it came to her. And it amused her to tease him too, I think, because he was obviously such a total sceptic about my kind of stuff, so it gave him heartburn to find out that she gave it any credence at all. But he was too much in love to say anything, of course, so he just sat there like a beanbag in the corner, smiling politely and no doubt praying that he could get away without being seen.' She dunked a digestive into her tea for a moment too long, then had to cup her free hand beneath it as she rushed it to her mouth. 'Thing is, though, I deal with people like that a lot. Mostly it's the husbands, coming along to unmask me as a fraud. But it can be the wives or children too. I know how to handle them. You have to, in my trade. And while Mr Brook himself was hard to read, like I said, Charlotte had already told me a ton about him – including stuff that he'd never have suspected she could possibly have known. And I can put on quite a show when I set my mind to it. Cold reading, some people call it. Or paying attention, as I do. It's how I knew you for a policeman, for instance. And why I'd bet your girlfriend here is working on a PhD. History or archaeology would be my guess. And somewhere up north. York, maybe? Durham?'

'She's not my girlfriend.'

'Sure,' smiled Patience. 'Whatever you say.'

'You were telling us about Hector Brook.'

'Yes. I can put on quite a show, like I say, so I threw out some bits and pieces that took him by surprise. Enough to make him wonder, at least. But I still took it for granted that I'd never see him again, if only because he was so ridiculously embarrassed about it all. His horrible granddad had beaten into him the dignity of the Brook name, you see; and how he should never tarnish it or expose it to ridicule – by visiting Gypsy fortune tellers, to take just one example. But then, to my great surprise, he slipped in on his own one afternoon. I was dead chuffed. I thought I'd won a convert. But it quickly became clear that he was smarter than that. He knew that Charlotte came to see me maybe once a week or so, you see, and obviously he'd be one of the things we talked about. So when he crossed my palm with silver – which he did very generously, I must say – it wasn't my gift he was after, or even my goodwill, to lobby her on his behalf. It was my insider knowledge.'

'Ah. And did it work? Did you tell him what she was thinking?'

'Kind of, I suppose. I mean I never lied to him. I wouldn't do that, not to a paying customer, at least not one that paid as well as he did. But I fobbed him off that first time. I told him I had a client arriving in a minute, but if he'd care to come back in the morning... Then I texted Charlotte to let her know, and to ask her what to do. She thought it was a hoot. And useful too. Because he never quite believed her when she told him how much she liked him for himself, rather than for his status or his wealth. He thought she was far too beautiful for him, which of course she was. But beauty isn't everything, though, is it? I hardly need to tell you two that. And he never properly appreciated his other qualities. Which he most certainly had, once you got to know him. He was kind and gentle and strong and thoughtful and brave – and incredibly generous, too, at least to those he loved or trusted. So I suppose I acted like one of those diplomatic back-channels, if you know what I mean? A way for them to tell each other truths that might not otherwise be believed. That's how it started anyway. But I'm a good listener, though I say so myself, and Mr Brook soon came to value our sessions for their own sake. He had plenty bottled up, as I'm sure you can imagine, and no-one else to talk to; because he loved Charlotte and Greta too much to lumber them with his baggage. Whereas he didn't care two hoots for how much baggage he lumbered me with. So once he got started, it all came flooding out. He'd look up at my mantelpiece clock and three hours would have shot by. And he wasn't the kind of man you could tell that his time was up, so I took to making sure he was my last client for the day. Which suited him too. Fewer people around to notice him slipping in and out.'

'What kind of things did he talk about?'

'All sorts. His childhood came up a lot. To be fair to the poor man, it did sound pretty brutal. Some of the men his mum brought into their home did unforgivable things to him and even more so to Greta. He used to shred himself for not having had the strength or courage to stand up for her like she'd stood up for him. But he was only a boy. What could he possibly have done? He also talked about how he and Greta came home from school one day to find their mum unconscious on the kitchen floor; and how they managed to save her that first time, only to be too late when it happened again.'

'Christ.'

'Yes. Then there was his grandfather. He did wonderful things for him and Greta, but he was also incredibly stiff and demanding and unloving. Even after the old sod died, Mr Brook never managed to rid himself of the sense that he was watching him over his shoulder, and judging him too; and that he only had the Manor and all the rest on a kind of sufferance, and that it could still all be taken away from him, just like that. He also told me about some of the awful things he'd seen and done in the army, about getting injured by that IED, about being trapped for hours inside his vehicle with his dead crew until he could be rescued, about the fits and blackouts he'd suffered ever since. But mostly, of course, he talked about Charlotte, how badly in love with her he was. That was the actual word he used. Not deeply or passionately. Badly.'

'He didn't want to be in love?'

'He didn't want to be *hurt*. Not again. He'd had enough of that. He'd designed his life to make himself safe. But of course that all fell apart within five minutes of meeting her, let alone after finding out that she was pregnant with his child. Or what he hoped was his child, at least. Drove him wild, that did, thinking it might not be.'

'Didn't they do a test?'

'Did they? That must have been after I left.'

'Yes. And it was his.'

'Good. I'm so glad.'

'Did he suspect her of sleeping with anyone in particular?' asked Elias. 'And was she?'

'I don't know. I don't think so. She never told me so, and I think she probably would have. She wasn't at all coy that way. She did enjoy a good flirt, and then telling me all about it afterwards. And it wasn't just for fun. She was very young and inexperienced to be in charge of an important excavation like that, so she needed a different source of power. But flirtation can be dangerous. Not everyone understands the rules.'

'How do you mean?'

'She got worried she'd taken it too far with someone, though she never told me who. Not even that they were a man, though that's what I assumed. Apparently they got angry when they realised it was only a game to her. Angry enough that it put the spooks up her.'

'She told you that?' asked Anna. 'She told you she was scared?'

'In a jokey sort of way, but yes,' said Patience, shamefaced. 'She had me read the cards to see if they really were a threat. I mean it was kind of for a laugh, but also not, you know?'

'When was this?' asked Elias.

'The final time she came to see me. Two days before she fell.'

'Did you tell anyone?'

'Only Mr Brook. On his last visit.'

'Not the police?'

She shook her head, mortified. 'I was too embarrassed. I told her no, you see. I told her that they weren't any danger. Which was what the cards said, to be fair. And then, just two nights later...' She buried her head in her hands. 'I'm such a fraud. It's why I moved away. I couldn't bear living here any more. The thought of bumping into any of them.'

Anna and Elias shared a glance. Surely this was why Brook had been so convinced that Charlotte had been pushed, while his concern for the family name would also explain why he'd tried to bully the police into an investigation, rather than admit he'd been snooping on Charlotte behind her back, by seeing a spiritualist. 'You must have some idea who it was.'

'She never told me, I swear. Though I do know that Mr Brook was most worried about that rugby player with the funny name, the one as went on to marry little Imogen. Even Charlotte knew she'd gone too far there. She hated herself for it.'

'Then why do it?'

'People can't always stop themselves from doing the things they hate. You'd think a policeman would know that.'

Elias smiled. 'Did she tell you anything else?'

'About what?'

'About her pregnancy, for example? Was she surprised?'

'Telling me. She got into a terrible froth about it, insisting she'd taken all the right precautions, and wondering whether Mr Brook had somehow contrived it to trap her. But later she admitted she'd been getting a bit careless. They both had. Her first instinct was to get rid of it, before word got out and it disrupted her career. She came to ask me about it, because I'd been through it a couple of times myself, during one of my unhappier relationships, and she wanted to know how to go about it without any risk of Brook or anyone else finding out. But then she changed her mind. She'd always wanted to become a mum at some point, and I think to her surprise she realised she was ready. Not just to have a kid, you know, but to make the choice? About what she wanted from her life. And what she wanted was to marry Mr Brook and become a wife and mother and all the rest of those good things. She'd been brought up in a mid-terrace in our little housing estate, remember, with her folks in and out of work, and everything a bit hand-to-mouth. This was her chance to become the great lady of the area, never having to worry about money again. I mean, sure, she wasn't smitten in the same way Mr Brook was; but she liked him a lot, she respected him and enjoyed his company, and she was proud of him and what he'd sacrificed. She used to brag about the things he'd done in Iraq and Afghanistan, the citations he'd earned, the medals he'd won. And god help you if you made fun of his injuries or his epilepsy. Besides, that summer had been the best of her life, and he was the one who'd made it possible. Marriage would mean getting to repeat it, year after year, for the rest of her life. In a way, *not* finding anything was the best result she could have wished for. Better to travel than to arrive, and all that.' She gave a sheepish smile. 'Sorry. I'm rambling all over the place. They'll have me for trespass in a minute.' She gulped down the last swallows of her tea then looked hopefully at Anna for more. But there was a crunch of gravel outside before Anna could take her cup from her, a car pulling up in front of the cottage.

They went out together to investigate. It was Greta, popping the boot of the Defender to get at her shopping. 'My god!' she cried, the moment she saw Patience. 'It *is* you. I thought I recognised your car. But what are you doing here?'

'Your brother booked me for the evening. I only just heard the awful news. I can't believe it. I'm so sorry.'

'Thank you. Thank you. But... he *booked* you? For what?'

'He never said exactly. Just to bring my cards and shawl and all the rest of it, and that he'd explain after I got here.'

'Oh lord,' said Greta. 'Him and his surprises! But it's wonderful to see you. You vanished so suddenly. I've been worrying about you for years. Where are you living now? What are you up to? Come inside. You have to tell me everything!'

THIRTY-NINE

reta and Patience had five years of catching up to do, so Anna and Elias helped them bring in the shopping then left them to it, returning outside to enjoy the last knockings of the afternoon, the sun going down behind the trees, blazing orange on the underside of the few wisps of cloud that had finally appeared. 'So how do you think she knew?' asked Anna, settling back down on the bench, looking around wistfully for a cat to stroke.

'Knew what?'

'That you were a policeman and I was doing a history PhD at York? I didn't have any of my work out.'

Elias laughed. 'Come on, Anna,' he said. 'You were all over the media last year. We both were. Including all that speculation about us being an item. And that's if Brook hadn't told her we'd be here, which he probably had.'

'Oh. God. How stupid of me.'

'Don't beat yourself up. It's how people in her line make their living. Find out what they can in advance, then hold it back until they can deploy it to maximum effect. In fact, I'll bet that's what Brook was counting on. Charlotte will have told her lots of juicy nuggets about each of the other guests. Imagine her throwing some of them out as she read their cards, or turned the lights down for a séance. It would have put the rattle right up them.'

'Christ,' said Anna. 'He put some effort into it, didn't he? Her, us, his tribute film, those *Beowulf* performers. All that, and a ship burial too.'

'Yeah,' said Elias. 'Speaking of which. If it's not in the woods or beneath the Manor...?'

'I've been thinking about that a lot,' Anna told him. 'My best guess is one of his farms. All those fields getting ploughed up year after year. I mean this part of Suffolk is ground zero for ship burials, right? If even a single rivet ever got dug up, he'd have recognised it instantly for what it was, and he'd have known there was every chance of finding hundreds more.'

'You know they had a meeting the night Charlotte died?' said Elias. 'The last of the season. One of the items on the agenda was where to dig next year. Philip Smallbone wanted to try the woods. Bryony Mackay argued for the front lawns. But what was odd was that Charlotte didn't offer an opinion at all. Which seems very unlike her. So maybe she already knew.'

Anna nodded. 'Imogen told me how she'd grown more and more dispirited by their lack of finds. Then suddenly she came alive, like she was on to something big. She'd have known to keep quiet about it too. If word had got out, the treasure hunters would have had all winter to get busy.'

Elias leaned forward, elbows on his knees. 'What if she did tell somebody? Intentionally or otherwise.'

'You think that's why she was pushed? So that her killer could plunder the site in peace? But surely there'd have been traces.'

The front door opened before Elias could reply, and Patience and Greta came out. They went to wave Patience off, then the three of them wandered back to the shade of the oak where they sat in weary yet companionable silence for a while, drained by their already long days. A pair of squad cars drove by, then a Scene of Crime van. At least some of the police were packing up for the day. Trent appeared next, in his white BMW convertible, its roof now back up and his headlights on. He pulled in to the gravel where Patience had been, then got out and came across. He refused their offer of a drink and deflected their questions on the investigation, claiming, reasonably enough, that he'd prefer to tell them all together down at the hotel. Greta rang ahead to have them alert everyone to their arrival, then they locked up and set off, Trent inviting Elias to join him in his BMW while Anna and Greta went separately in the Defender.

'So?' asked Elias, belting himself in.

Trent waited for Greta to pull out, then followed close behind. 'You were right about the fentanyl. Enough still in that syringe to kill off the whole lot of you. Death would have been super quick. Two or three minutes max. Oh, and we got to the caterers before they could dump their rubbish, which was a result. Won't come as a surprise, I don't suppose, but the dregs of fruits and spices from the mead tested positive for flunitrazepam.'

'We were roofied?'

'You were roofied,' agreed Trent, slowing down as he crossed the railway bridge, wary of scratching his brand new paintwork on the narrow stone walls. 'Which of course explains your all being knocked sideways last night, and your headaches this morning. Sadly, that's about it for good news. Not a thing on any of the cameras. We really could have done with one inside, of course. And the urine samples were little help either. Markers for Rohypnol in every one, roughly in the amounts you'd expect from a horn of mead. I've ordered further tests in case someone took a blocker or a stimulant to counteract its effects, but that's more complicated and will take a while. Not that I'm too hopeful. Way I figure it, it would have been easy enough in the darkness to spill half your horn beneath the table then dribble the rest down your chin. That way, you'd remain awake after everyone else fell asleep. You sneak into Brook's room to do your worst then take another dose before going back to bed.'

'I trust the "you" is rhetorical.'

'Sadly, yes.' They followed the Defender out the automated gate before it could close again behind it. 'There's a camera on the barn roof and another covering the door where the mead was kept. Between them, it's clear you were the only guest never alone with it. Plus there's your lack of motive, of course.

Speaking of which, that obviously now includes Charlotte Ash. I know you've been thinking about that too, if only from the email you sent me earlier. Thing is, though, I've been kind of rushed off my feet. Not to mention your bloody handwriting.'

'Ah. You want the highlights?'

'If you wouldn't mind?'

'Sure. Of course. Okay, so let's start by assuming that Brook really was murdered, and that—'

'Assuming?' said Trent indignantly. 'You were the one who called us in.'

'And I still think he was. But there has to be a chance he set it up himself, doesn't there? In constant pain from his injuries and depressed from not only having lost Charlotte, but also from not getting her the full investigation he thought she deserved. So he brings all the chief suspects together for this weekend, then pisses his bed and injects himself in the outside of his arm to make it look like murder, forcing you to investigate at last.'

'Are you serious?'

'I'm not saying it's likely, just that it needs to be tossed into the pot along with everything else. But let's assume murder for the moment, and that Charlotte Ash's death was the motivating force. We know they brought roofies, fentanyl and a syringe with them, which is enough forward planning to suggest real fear of whatever Hector Brook had on them.'

'Which was?'

'I don't think he had anything, if I'm honest. He'd have taken it straight to you guys if he had, rather than bothering with this charade. His plan was to startle or unnerve Charlotte's killer into making a mistake. His tribute film was one element. I was another, as was that performance last night, and the spiritualist from earlier. God only knows what else he had up his sleeve.'

'Spiritualist?' frowned Trent. 'What spiritualist?'

'Patience Miller. Didn't your guy on the barriers tell you?'

'Only that some madwoman had turned up. Not that she was a spiritualist.'

'Okay. Then you need to know this. She stopped off on her

193

way out to commiserate with Greta. We got talking. Brook had hired her to put on a show this evening, though he hadn't yet told her what exactly, probably because she'd have said no if he had. She was an old friend of Charlotte's, you see. Charlotte used to pop into her place in Woodbridge once or twice a week that summer for a reading and a natter. Brook took to visiting her there too. It was his way of finding out what Charlotte really thought of him. My guess is that he invited her here today because he figured Charlotte would have told her a bunch of private stuff about each of his other guests – stuff that they'd have thought only Charlotte could possibly have known, which Patience could have used to startle them, and make them wonder.'

'Charlotte's ghost accusing them from beyond the grave?'

'I doubt it would have been that crude. But enough to catch out their lies, sure.'

'What lies?'

'Have you watched Brook's tribute to Charlotte yet? You really should. It offers motives for them all. Pretty weak, some of them, but enough to have got them up the hill that night. Like for example did you know that Bryony Mackay had accused Lucius Hyde-Smith of some kind of sexual impropriety? And that Charlotte was to be the key witness? I'll bet she told Patience exactly what she saw, which would have been plenty enough to freak one or other of them out. Oh, and Patience also said that one of Charlotte's flirtations had got so far out of hand that she grew frightened for her safety. That was just two days before she fell.'

Trent glanced across at him. 'Bloody hell. No one ever told us that.'

'I know. Patience was too ashamed because she'd assured Charlotte she wasn't in any danger. And Hector was embarrassed about seeing a spiritualist – especially as it was mostly to spy on Charlotte behind her back. He was the local bigwig, so I imagine he assumed he could simply bully you guys into an investigation. By the time he found out he was wrong, it was too late.'

'So that's why he was so convinced she was pushed. What an idiot.' He shook his head. 'Any idea who it was Charlotte got so spooked by?'

'Nothing concrete, though there are three obvious candidates: Philip Smallbone, Raoul Flood and Cameron Wolfe. All three fell for her hard, at one time or another. All three had motive and opportunity. Smallbone is the most likely, I think. Charlotte had led him on a bit, to the extent that it may have put his marriage into trouble. Then he found out what she really thought of him, and in a pretty cruel manner too. Plus he's admitted following Charlotte out of the house that night.'

'He has? Bloody hell.'

'Yeah. I bluffed him into it. He claims he turned back again pretty much straight away, which is possible. But still.'

'And Flood?'

'He'd been out at the pub all night, knocking back the pints. Easy to imagine him working up a grievance against Charlotte on his way back, or maybe a line of argument to convince her to dump Brook and choose him instead. He must have known she liked to visit Dragon Stone Hill at around that time. He may even have arranged to see her there. So he cuts up from the railway bridge, only for things to get out of hand. Then he hurries back down to the Manor and slips in a back way to avoid the cameras.'

'Didn't he have an alibi?'

'Only from his wife.'

'You think she'd have covered for her sister's murder?'

'Probably not. But then she never really believed it was murder, did she? No one did. They all thought Charlotte had slipped. And she was still very much in love with Raoul at the time, remember, so of course she'd have quashed any private doubts. But last night, when he was having a go at Brook after the toast, he flashed her a weird glance. A keep-your-mouth-shut kind of glance.'

'You never told us that.'

'It was only a flash, like I say. I could have misread it. Besides,

I had a head like a fenland fog this morning, thanks to those damn roofies. Which is another reason to think it might have been him. Spiking the mead made sense whoever it was, to cut their chances of being seen. But it would have been essential for Flood. He couldn't risk waking Imogen, and he wasn't just sharing a room with her, he was sharing a bed. Then there's the sheer bulk of the man. He could have drunk twice as much Rohypnol as anyone else, and still stayed clear-headed.'

'And Cameron Wolfe?'

'Yeah. He was watching the end of a movie with Imogen, but they went their own ways once it had finished. He could have made it up to the dragon stone by the time Charlotte fell. As for motive, apparently they went out a few times up in London, but he took it pretty hard when she broke it off. Maybe even tried to top himself.'

'Jesus.'

'Yeah. I guess she felt sorry for him, because she recommended him for the gig here. He repaid her by following her around, taking some pretty compromising footage of her and Raoul Flood. Wouldn't surprise me one bit if he threatened to show it to Brook. Or if Charlotte told him where to shove it. Pretty soon you've got a full-fledged fight on.'

Trent looked doubtful. 'That's all pretty speculative,' he said.

'Which is exactly what I said in my notes,' said Elias, 'if only you'd bothered to read the damn things.'

FORTY

They arrived in the hotel car park still in convoy, parked and went inside. Trent excused himself to go debrief his two officers in the lobby, but Anna, Greta and Elias went on ahead to the meeting room they'd reserved. Raoul and Imogen Flood were already there, murmuring quietly together in a corner, while Lucius Hyde-Smith had taken the chair at the head of the polished long table, looking his usual grumpy self. 'Well?' he asked, when Trent finally joined them. 'Will this take long?'

'Let's wait until everyone's here, eh?' said Trent.

Bryony Mackay arrived a minute later, then Philip Smallbone. Three more minutes passed, but still no Cameron Wolfe. Greta rang the front desk to have them call his room again. He wasn't answering, it turned out. Nor had he answered earlier. They'd left a message for him instead.

Trent beckoned for Elias to join him outside. 'What do you reckon?' he asked. 'Done a runner?'

Elias shrugged. 'He was drinking pretty heavily earlier. More likely out cold.'

'Yeah,' said Trent. 'More likely.' They went back to reception where Trent showed his warrant card to the woman on the desk. 'How do I get into Cameron Wolfe's room?' he asked.

'You'll need Mr Singh for that,' she said, reaching for the phone. He arrived just a minute later: short, slim and fussy with a twirly moustache and his beard trimmed to a point. They took the lift up together. Singh knocked and called out Wolfe's name. He gave it five seconds then did both again, more loudly. A final warning then he unlocked the door for them and stepped aside. They went in together. The curtains were drawn, meaning the room was dark, with only a single bedside lamp on. Wolfe was lying on his back on the double bed, his face tipped to the side and a little pinkish drool leaking from his mouth. His lips were tinted dark red, likely from the wine he'd drunk, as there were a pair of bottles on the carpet beside the bed, along with several miniatures from the minibar.

Trent pulled on latex gloves as he stepped over to the bed. He touched his throat and then his cheek. 'At least two hours,' he said, turning to Elias. 'Probably longer.'

'Bollocks,' said Elias.

A phone was lying on the duvet next to Wolfe's right hand, left there for them to find. Trent pinched it carefully to turn it on. Its lock had been deactivated. He got straight in. Its voice app was already open and cued up with a message. 'It was me,' he said, sounding muffled, slurred and strangely flat. 'I did it. I killed Charlotte five years ago and then last night I killed Hector too. I'm sorry.'

'Is that him?' asked Trent.

'Sounds like him,' said Elias, moving closer to the bed. 'Play it again.' Trent turned the volume all the way up before doing so. Elias nodded. 'Either it's him or they belong on Britain's Got Talent.'

'They can do amazing things with AI these days,' suggested Trent doubtfully.

Elias shook his head. 'AI would sound clearer. And more stilted.'

There was a waste paper basket by the bed. Trent plucked out and held up a pair of baggies, each containing a few flecks of powder. 'Leftovers from last night, I'd imagine.'

'Yeah.'

'Remorse, eh?' he said. 'Who'd have figured? Though you say he'd tried before?'

'Twice, from what I heard,' said Elias. 'Once after Charlotte dumped him, then again when the tabloids went after him.'

Trent gave a grunt. 'Self-pity. The only kind some people have.'

'Isn't that the truth.'

'Okay. So I guess this now becomes part of Hector Brook's murder scene. Charlotte Ash's too, come to that.' He took out his phone. 'I'm going to have to call my team back in. Won't they just love me? If you could send up my guys from downstairs then maybe tell the others?'

'Tell them what?'

'Tell them this. It'll get out soon enough anyway. They're welcome to stay here if they don't mind the corpse next door. Or they can look elsewhere, if they prefer, though good luck finding anything at this short notice.'

'What if they want their cars and luggage?'

'Sorry, no. We're not done with the Manor quite yet. Particularly not now. Tell them they can have them back in the morning.'

Elias took the lift back down. He sent up Trent's two officers then returned to the meeting room. 'So there's been a bit of a development,' he announced. 'Detective Superintendent Trent is sealing off Mr Wolfe's room right now.'

It took a moment to sink in. They stared at him in shock. 'What are you saying?' asked Hyde-Smith, half rising to his feet. 'Are you saying he's... *dead*?'

'Another overdose, it looks like. Self-administered this time. But no doubt you'll be relieved to hear that he left a message taking responsibility for both Hector and Charlotte.'

'He said he'd killed Charlotte?' said Imogen, bewildered. 'He really said that?'

'I just heard his confession myself,' Elias assured her. 'Oh, and Trent asked me to tell you that you're welcome to look for other accommodation if you don't fancy spending the night here. The Manor's still out of bounds, unfortunately, though you'll be able to collect your stuff some time in the morning.'

'But we can sleep here if we want?' asked Smallbone.

'As long as you don't mind the dead body next door.'

'I'm an archaeologist. Dead bodies are my job.'

'What about you others?' asked Greta. 'I could try to find you something else; but, honestly, at this time of night...' She looked so shattered, though, that it would have been cruel to take up her offer, and no one did. She nodded gratefully and beckoned to Anna so that the pair of them could get out of there before anyone changed their mind.

FORTY-ONE

G reta said barely a word to Anna on the drive back from the hotel. But she sagged in her seat as she pulled up outside her cottage and turned off her engine. 'What a day!' she said. 'What a wretched, wretched day.' She stirred herself finally to get out then fumbled her key in the front door. 'You're going to have to excuse me, I'm afraid. I'm absolutely done.'

'You must have something to eat first,' protested Anna.

'I suppose,' sighed Greta, though without enthusiasm. 'Is there any of that pizza left?'

'Only two boxes worth.'

'A slice of that, then. That will do me.'

'Good idea,' said Anna. 'I'll heat some up.'

'No need. Cold is fine. Honestly, I just want bed.'

Anna found her a plate. Greta took her choice then bid her goodnight and vanished upstairs. Anna popped two more slices into the oven for herself. Her brain was too frazzled for work, she'd left her earbuds behind in York and she could hardly listen to music or watch TV with Greta trying to sleep upstairs, so she took Charlotte's excavation journals from the storage box she'd brought back from the Manor's cellar and went through them in the hope of finding some explanation for Cameron Walsh's behaviour. But she found only a single mention of him, and that had been a good month before her death, when a student archaeologist had complained of him following her around too closely and filming her too much. Maybe Charlotte had had a word with him, and it had riled him up, but it was hard to see it as fuel for murder. She made a note of it all the same, to show DS Trent in the morning.

The sketchbooks next, packed with Charlotte's simple yet evocative pencil and charcoal drawings of broken pots and other artefacts. There was nothing much there either. She flipped through the first of the leather-bound A3 ones too, just in case, only to realise that she'd missed a trick earlier, for the pads were reversible and could be started from either end. She turned it around and opened it to reveal a watercolour of the Manor painted from its front lawn but angled to catch the River Deben in the background. It was meticulously detailed, even down to the leading in the windows and the brickwork in the chimneys. A true labour of love. A second landscape showed the Woodbridge waterfront from Dragon Stone Hill. Then came a series of charcoal and watercolour portraits, a few of people she recognised, but mostly not. The most striking by far was of Hector Brook. She'd painted him in three-quarter profile, meaning that she could have concealed his scarring, had she so wished. She'd put it centre-stage instead, then had given his chin a proud lift to make him look heroic rather than disfigured; and for the first time Anna truly believed that it hadn't just been his wealth and status that had persuaded her to say yes.

A whiff of something acrid. She remembered her pizza. With a curse, she turned off the oven and opened its door to see what could be salvaged. Her slices weren't as badly burned as she'd feared. In fact, once she'd scraped off the worst of the char, she rather enjoyed their new biscuit crunchiness. And they were so dry that they gave her the perfect excuse for a glass of nicely chilled Dragon Stone white.

There were more watercolours in the second leather-bound sketchbook, this time of scenes from *Beowulf*. Anna herself had always rather romanticised Beowulf in her mind, picturing him as a classical warrior hero, tall, handsome and kingly. Not Charlotte. She'd been truer to the poem, depicting him as broad shouldered and hugely muscled with shaggy long dark hair, and with scarred and rather battered features despite his youth; and, instead of armour or royal robes, she'd dressed him in thick brown animal pelts. In short, she'd made him look as much like a bear as it was possible for a man to get, no doubt inspired by his name – for Beowulf was a corruption of bee-wolf, which was to say a wolf partial to honey, or more simply a bear.

For all his size and power, though, Charlotte had made his opponent larger and more fearsome still: a grey-skinned ogre with a low brow, protruding ears, misshapen teeth and even more overdeveloped limbs. Yet Charlotte had allowed him a certain dignity, even so, for she hadn't given him an expression of malice or hatred, but rather of grim determination. This was *his* land. He meant to win it back.

Who else but Grendel?

She turned the page to a second watercolour. This one was set in an obscurely lit underwater cavern whose floor was littered with discarded armour and weaponry, with seaweed and seagrasses swaying this way and that in the gentle currents, and a pageant of exotic fish in the background. But Beowulf was centre stage again, this time stripped naked, save for a small strip of cloth around his loins, wrestling with a beautiful woman with long copper hair who might as well have been naked too, for her ripped and clinging white dress had been turned almost transparent by the water and concealed virtually nothing. One of her legs was wrapped around his, and she had her right hand on his shoulder. Ropes of her hair entwined them both like extra limbs, binding them even closer together, and it all looked so sensuous that they might have been making love rather than fighting to the death. But this was Grendel's mother, so fighting to the death they were.

A third watercolour now. No surprise to find Beowulf again, this time taking on the dragon in its lair. The beast was huge, and made huger still by the way it had spread its wings out wide, either to make itself as large and intimidating as possible, or perhaps to hide the hoard of goblets, coins, platters and other golden treasure that could be glimpsed behind it. Its mouth was wide open as it squirted a fiery jet at Beowulf, turning orange the ragged walls of its stony cavern. It was stretching out its right claw for him too, black talons digging deep into his chest. But Beowulf was fighting back hard, warding off the worst of the flames with his shield while thrusting his long sword upwards into the dragon's throat, dealing it its death blow even as he took his own.

She turned the page to the fourth and final watercolour, a nighttime scene of a burial pyre as it blazed lustily upon a hilltop, surrounded by grieving men, women and children in Anglo-Saxon dress, their stricken faces made all too apparent by the flames. She gazed at it for several minutes before putting it away. But something about it, or perhaps about one of the other pictures, tugged gently at her, like a shy child with something important to say. She took the book back out and flipped through the pictures once more, but she couldn't work out what. She put the book away again and went through to the sitting room, where she pulled her bodice-ripper back down from the shelf. But it couldn't hold her interest any more, for the watercolours kept nagging at her. She returned to the kitchen to check the sketchbook for a third and then for a fourth time, but it was no use. Her brain was too weary after her long day to find its hidden message, if indeed it even had one.

She went upstairs and got ready for bed. She lay there in the darkness, brooding still on what it was she'd seen, or more precisely on what it was she'd missed. Then suddenly she had it. In his third fight, when taking on the dragon, Charlotte hadn't depicted Beowulf as the scarred old king from the poem, but rather as the vigorous and still youthful warrior from the other watercolours, in the spring rather than in the winter of his life. She smiled when she realised this, knowing that sleep would come easily now that there was no more mystery to solve. For who could blame a young woman like Charlotte for preferring heroes of her own age to those already old?

FORTY-TWO

Anna woke early again, even though she'd taken the trouble to draw her curtains this time. It wasn't sunshine on her cheek, therefore, but rather an unusually vivid dream in which that third watercolour from Charlotte's book had come startlingly to life: of Beowulf as a strapping young man taking on a fearsome dragon in its lair, only to suffer mortal wounds himself as he slew it. And suddenly the true explanation for why Charlotte had depicted Beowulf that way was in her mind. It hadn't been personal preference after all, or even artistic licence. It had been because that was how she'd come to see him.

She sat up on the side of the bed, half expecting her idea to fall apart upon closer inspection, as such half awake dreams so often did. Not this one. She thought it through some more as she brushed her teeth, then in the shower, turning it this way and that in her mind to probe it for flaws and weaknesses. She tested it again while she dried herself off and then dressed for the day. But it only made it seem more solid.

She was first downstairs again. She made herself a cup of tea and two slices of buttered toast slathered with Greta's delicious home-made blackberry jam. She sat at the kitchen table and brought up Charlotte's thesis on her laptop, studying it more rigorously this time, searching for anything to back up or disprove her theory. She found nothing. No great surprise, though. If she had it right, Charlotte hadn't stumbled on this idea herself until long after her thesis had been completed; not, indeed, until the end of that excavation summer, perhaps on one of her moonlit walks up Dragon Stone Hill – walks that now struck Anna as in need of explanation, pregnant as Charlotte had been, with a baby she'd decided to keep. Surely she'd at least have tried to quit smoking. Yet, by all accounts, she'd continued without regret or interruption, including again that night. So what if it hadn't been nicotine that had kept drawing her back? What if it had been something else?

Greta finally arrived downstairs, dressed for the day yet yawning and still looking drained, though not as badly as last night. 'And I thought I was an early riser,' she said, putting on the kettle.

'I couldn't sleep,' admitted Anna. 'I kept thinking about your brother's rivets and golden buckle. About where they might have come from.'

Greta looked around at her, piqued by her tone. 'Do you know something?'

'Not exactly, though I have had an idea. It's pretty wild, but I think it's worth checking out, even so.'

'How very exciting. Tell me more.'

'I'd rather not, just yet. I haven't really got it clear enough in my head. But I was planning to go take a look, if only for the exercise. Would you like to come?'

'Goodness, yes. Of course. Though you must allow me a cup of tea first. I'm useless without my tea.'

It was cloudier out than yesterday, and with enough moisture on the grass and drive that it looked as though it might even have rained overnight. It was cooler too, and with such a brisk breeze that they both went back in for jackets. 'So this idea of yours,' prompted Greta, as she locked the cottage up behind them. 'You have to give me something.'

'Okay,' said Anna, as they set off on foot up the drive. 'Though please understand that this is all absurdly speculative. And it's not even my idea, I don't think. I'm pretty sure it's Charlotte's, that it's what she came to believe in the days before she died. And I wouldn't be putting much weight on it, even so, except for all those rivets your brother found, larger than the ones at Sutton Hoo, implying a burial for a king even greater than Rædwald himself. But that makes no sense, as you know, because no other Angle king came close. Not unless we've got our history completely wrong.'

'And have we?'

'No, I don't think so.' They reached and passed the police barriers, which had been set to the side of the drive, and with no squad car in attendance. The sun had risen enough by now to light up the tops of the trees on either side, their foliage exuberant with song. 'I think there's a different explanation. A slightly lateral one. Like I say, I'm pretty sure Charlotte was toying with it before she died, though she approached it from a different direction. Because she saw everything through the prism of *Beowulf*, of course. Did you ever read her thesis?'

'I skimmed it, yes. But that was at least five years ago. And, honestly, it was all a bit too technical for me. So many footnotes!'

'I know what you mean,' said Anna. 'But her argument was simple enough. She believed that each of the three monsters from the poem represented a real and terrifying threat that the Angles had had to face and overcome before they could make themselves masters of the land. Genuine threats are more resonant and visceral than imagined ones, you see. They imprint themselves deeper onto the psyche. Even an echo of them has the power to make you tremble.' The woods opened up, revealing the Manor ahead, stately and magnificent in the morning sunlight. 'So parents use them as stories to make their children behave, and those children grow into adulthood with them so much a part of their nature that they pass them on in their turn. And that's especially true for the ones who grow up to be bards, for they use them as the basis for the songs and tales they compose, until they've become so completely entrenched in the culture that people forget how they got there in the first place.'

'*Beowulf*,' said Greta.

'Exactly.' The gravel sparkled with moisture as they

crunched across it. It must indeed have rained. 'Beowulf's three monsters represent three genuine but separate threats that the Angles once faced. Grendel was the first, of course. He stood for the original inhabitants of this place, the ones they turfed out when they arrived. The menfolk whose homes and lands they stole, whose women they raped and took for slaves, whose children they raised as their own, but who survived to lurk in the woods and marshes around here, stealing into their villages at night to kill them as they slept.'

'I remember now,' said Greta. 'And wasn't Grendel's mother a volcano or something?'

'Kind of, yes. A series of eruptions in Iceland and maybe North America caused some terrible famines during the late 530s and early 540s, all made worse by a devastating outbreak of plague. But of course the people here wouldn't have been aware of the true reason behind those catastrophes, only of the catastrophes themselves, so they'd have looked elsewhere for explanations, attributing them instead to the wrath of the earth goddess for the injustice they'd done her children.'

'And the third monster?' asked Greta, as she unlocked the front door and let them in. 'The dragon?'

'That's just it,' said Anna, leading the way along the left-hand passage. 'In her thesis, Charlotte didn't give a specific explanation. She simply claimed that there must have been one, and threw out a bunch of suggestions inspired by what dragons represented. Because ancient mythology is packed with them, as I'm sure you know. They appear all over the place from the Golden Fleece onwards. The thing is, though, I'm pretty sure she came up with a concrete idea shortly before she died. Or so her sketchbook suggests.'

'And?'

'It'll sound dumb if I say it straight out. So let me answer it this way instead. Who gets to decide how grand a person's funeral will be?'

'I'm not sure I follow.'

'Think about it,' said Anna, as they passed the kitchen and

carried on. 'Didn't I see a copy of the *Iliad* on your shelves? And a biography of Alexander the Great? So tell me this. Which are probably the two most famous funeral pyres from Ancient Greece? One fictional, the other very real?'

'Oh. I suppose you mean Patroclus and Hephaestion.'

'Exactly. And was that because they were the greatest of the Greek kings?'

'Ah!' said Greta, as she saw where Anna was going. 'No. They were the *lovers* of the greatest kings. But surely you're not suggesting that Rædwald had a lover, are you? There's not a shred of evidence for that.'

'No. There isn't. But what he did have was a *son*. A beloved elder son called Rægenhere who he trusted to lead a third of his army at the Battle of the River Idle, even though he may still have been only a teenager at the time. A son, what's more, who was mistaken by Æthelfrith for Rædwald himself, causing him to charge straight at him with his whole army, thinking that, if he could kill him, the rest of the Angle army would break and flee, and he'd win himself a quick victory.' They reached Hector Brook's office, went inside. 'He succeeded, too, up to a point. He managed to kill Rægenhere and most of his men, only to provoke Rædwald into furious retribution, putting Æthelfrith himself and much of his army to the sword. And Æthelfrith wasn't merely the most powerful king in England at the time, as you know, he was a famously feared warlord who'd defeated every enemy he'd ever gone up against, and who'd earned himself a reputation for extreme cruelty too. In short, he was exactly the kind of man who'd have been dubbed a dragon by his foes, out of a mix of fear and admiration. The kind who'd proudly have flown a dragon on his banner. The kind that parents would have used to terrify their children into obedience.'

'Æthelfrith,' murmured Greta. 'Dragon of the North.'

'Yes,' said Anna, making her way over to the floor safe, taking the lid off the blue-and-white porcelain bowl resting upon it. 'We know for sure that even Rædwald was frightened of taking him on. He had to be shamed into it by his wife. His people would have been scared too. And rightly so. Losing wouldn't just have been the end for them personally, it would have seen their lands taken, their womenfolk raped and enslaved. But Rædwald took him on anyway. He defeated and killed him and won all his lands and treasure, only to lose his son in the process. Can you imagine how torn he would have felt? Victory transformed him from a minor king into the most powerful man in the land, with the wealth to match; yet it would have turned to ashes in his mouth on finding the body of his beloved son. And do you honestly believe he'd have left him there to rot upon the field, for his corpse to be scavenged by carrion and made food for worms? Or would he have brought him home with full honours instead, so that his mother could mourn him properly and they could bury him in a manner befitting his status and sacrifice? A sacrifice that would have demanded the greatest burial of all, greater even than Rædwald's own, when his time came a decade later?'

Greta let out a breath. 'You really think that's how it happened?'

'I don't know. But it's what Charlotte came to believe, I'm sure of that.'

'And? Do you know where?'

'I think so, yes,' said Anna, rummaging through the keys, checking each of their tags in turn. 'Partly because there's only one place fitting enough, partly because it's where Charlotte so loved to go at night, but mostly because it explains how come your brother found it.' And she held up the key for Greta to read its tag.

'The summerhouse?' said Greta, disappointed. 'But there's nothing there. It was the first place they tried. And they checked it thoroughly, believe me.'

'They checked it with the tools they had available,' said Anna, 'which is to say with aerial photography, with soil sampling and ground penetrating radar. None of which are a substitute for a proper test pit, like the one your brother dug.'

'What are you talking about?' protested Greta. 'He never dug a test pit.'

'Yes, he did. That's what I realised this morning. He had to, when he decided to put in a loo, plumbing and a septic tank.'

'Oh my,' said Greta, her eyes glittering. 'And you think he found something?'

'Well, we know he found something,' replied Anna. 'The only question is where. We've looked pretty much everywhere else, and once you've ruled out all the most likely places, as Sherlock Holmes might have put it... Besides, the dedication of the summerhouse was to be the highlight of your brother's weekend, remember? I'm guessing that the real highlight was meant to be him revealing what he'd found.'

'Goodness me!' said Greta. 'How very thrilling. Let's go take a look.'

FORTY-THREE

E lias's bathroom had been fitted with a deluxe new shower as part of the hotel refurbishment. It had nozzles on every side that were controlled by a combination of four dials that he couldn't for the life of him work out, so that it turned with baffling speed from cold to scalding hot and then back to cold again. He decided to leave it on cold and keep it brisk, for it needed more study than he was prepared to give it for a single use, what with his mind engaged elsewhere, still wrestling with the problem he'd taken to bed with him. Because Trent had been bang on in what he'd said about Cameron Wolfe not being the kind to do remorse.

Self-pity, sure. But not remorse.

Before turning in last night, Elias had taken a closer look at the trouble Wolfe had got himself into two years before. Tabloids were obviously prone to sensationalism, so it was telling that the police hadn't been able to charge him with any particular crime. Yet it was clear, all the same, that he'd been running a deeply sordid and unpleasant business, enticing attractive teenage girls to his studio with offers of free portfolio shots, then flattering, bribing or browbeating them into making unusually ugly and abusive pornographic movies that he'd put out through a Cypriot-based site. But what had struck Elias most was his reaction to being confronted by journalists outside his studio, shrugging it all off as legal, looking amused and defiant rather than frightened or ashamed.

Elias had met enough sociopaths in his time to know they could always find a tear or two should the situation warrant it. Put them in enough trouble and they'd throw themselves to their knees and plead for the mercy they'd never consider giving others. Maybe they'd even hint at suicide if they thought it would win them some breathing space. But none of that meant anything. Forgive them and they'd be straight back to their old ways, while also despising you for your weakness.

And Wolfe *hadn't* been caught. That was the point. Not for Charlotte's murder, nor for Brook's neither. He'd been in the spotlight, sure, but so too had several others. He'd still had every chance of getting away clean. How then to explain his suicide and confession? Perhaps it had been all that booze. People did stupid things when drunk – especially with lethal quantities of drugs so close to hand. Yet drink typically made people more self-justifying, not less. Besides, there'd been something off about the mumbled flat tone of his confession, as though he'd been admitting to no worse than nicking someone's lunch from the communal fridge. Most of all, why had he used the voice app on his phone, when surely it would have been second nature to him as a film-maker to talk to its camera instead?

He was drying himself off when there came a knock upon his door. It was still early enough for him to fear yet more bad news. He wrapped his towel around his waist and went to answer it, only to find Imogen Flood standing there, about the last person he'd expected. 'I'm sorry it's so early,' she whispered, looking nervously back at her own room's door, 'but I heard your shower running and then turning off. May I come in a minute?'

'Sure,' he said. He stood aside for her, closed the door. They went together through to the bedroom where he made a cursory effort to straighten his duvet before giving up, grabbing his trousers and the clothes he'd bought yesterday afternoon, then taking them into the bathroom to change. 'Well?' he asked.

'It was that thing you said last night,' Imogen told him, coming to stand outside the door, the better to keep her voice low. 'About Cameron confessing to killing my sister as well as Mr

Brook. Are you sure that's what he said?'

'Yes. Why?'

'If I tell you something in absolute confidence…' she began, only to trail off.

Elias zipped up his trousers as he came out of the bathroom. 'If you know something, you have to tell me. I don't care how uncomfortable it is. I promise you I'll treat it responsibly and with respect. But if it's material to a murder investigation…'

She sighed unhappily, but steeled herself anyway. 'Very well,' she said. 'I'll let you be the judge. The thing is, I don't really see how he could have.'

'Could have what? Could have killed your sister?'

'Yes.'

'Why not?'

She gave a grimace, as though her dentist had just selected some terrifying new implement from his tray. 'Because I was with him when she died.'

FORTY-FOUR

The grass was slick with moisture, so that, once they'd passed through the gate at the far end of the lawn, and reached the meadow and then the orchard beyond, it quickly soaked through Anna's shoes and socks to chill her feet. The smoked glass panes on the front of the summerhouse were covered with it too, little beads that kept gathering into larger drops to break and run like tears, as though they too were in mourning for the man who'd built this place.

The lock was stiff enough to suggest it hadn't had a lot of use. Anna had to give it a good jiggle before it turned. The double doors opened directly into a large main room that smelled so stale and musty that she left them open to air a little. The floor was laid with bare grey concrete, and contained just two pieces of furniture – the pair of weathered wooden benches that had once stood upon this spot, and on which Charlotte Ash had loved to sit and watch the river flowing by. Or so, at least, the brass plaques upon them claimed.

There was, however, plenty else in the room, stored here to keep it out of the rain. A spade, a pickaxe, a jackhammer and a power drill; a large unopened tub of sunlight yellow emulsion, some brushes and a roller set; several boxes of terracotta floor tiles; a petrol-driven generator and a plastic fuel can; a camping stove and a space heater with a spare cylinder of gas. She could see a toilet bowl and a cistern too, both unboxed but still in their plastic wrapping, ready to be installed, as were a pedestal washbasin and the plastic base and other components of an electric shower.

There were timber-framed plasterboard partitions on either side, with three open doorways that hadn't yet had their doors fitted. The one to their right led into what was intended as the kitchen, to judge by the boxed-up units and stainless steel sink waiting to be installed. The first of the two doorways to their left led into a small bedroom with a camp-bed, a rumpled blue sleeping bag and an indented pillow, suggesting that Hector Brook had already spent at least a night or two up here, in preference to the luxury of the Manor; while the second led into the bathroom, though again it hadn't yet been fitted, and was being used instead for surplus storage, its floor covered by empty cardboard boxes and black bags swollen with discarded packaging.

'How terribly disappointing,' said Greta, once they'd finished their short tour, though with a smile to take any sting out of her words. 'You had me all excited.'

Anna didn't reply, however. She remained standing in the bathroom doorway instead, for there was something off about the way the boxes and bags were spread out upon the bathroom floor, as if they'd been deliberately arranged that way to cover every square inch of it. She grabbed a pair of black bags and carried them through to the bedroom, then came back for more, followed by the boxes. It was quickly done, for while they were bulky, they were also light. Within a minute or so she'd exposed the floor beneath, or rather the large metal sheet that covered much of it, and which lay almost but not quite flat upon it. It was some four feet long by three feet wide, and maybe quarter of an inch thick, making it heavy enough that Greta had to help her with it, working their fingers beneath its nearside edge then lifting it up a foot or so until it was high enough for them to see beneath.

Anna gave a grunt. Brook had clearly laid the concrete before deciding to put in a bathroom. A bathroom required plumbing, so he'd broken up sections of the floor with his jackhammer, drilling a hole close to the side wall where presumably he'd meant to put the loo. But then he'd changed his mind once more – or, rather, he'd had it changed for him. For the hole was far larger than was needed for the job, and it plunged away into darkness, as though the ground beneath it had simply collapsed and fallen away. What was more, he'd hammered a fat steel peg into the concrete beside this hole, which explained why the steel sheet hadn't rested quite flush upon the floor. Then he'd knotted the top of a rope ladder to it, dropping the rest of it down the hole.

Anna grinned at Greta. Greta grinned back. Careful of their footing, they heaved the metal sheet all the way up until it was resting back against the wall. Then they stood there, breathing a little heavily, gazing down through the hole at a ragged, twisting shaft, and the wooden rungs of the rope ladder as it dangled away as far as they could see – though that wasn't very far, to be fair, for the only light they had was that coming in through the bathroom's frosted window and the two open doorways. Nor did the torches on their phones much help, not even when they knelt beside the hole and reached them down. The shaft and the ladder both continued beyond their range.

'My god,' murmured Greta. 'What do we do now? Do we tell people?'

Anna hesitated. There could surely be no doubt left any more as to where the rivets and the buckle had come from. Their duty was thus crystal clear. They needed to notify the appropriate authorities at once so that this place could be properly secured while an excavation plan was put in place. But the appropriate authority in this instance would be Suffolk's Finds Liaison Officer, whose first step would be to notify the county's archaeological society who in turn would appoint an officer to take charge and arrange next steps. Which all would have been fine, except that the officer in question was almost certain to be Philip Smallbone, seeing as he was already on site. And the thought of turning over a discovery like this to a man like that stuck in Anna's craw. Turning it over unseen, what was more.

Before Greta could say anything or otherwise stop her, she therefore sat down beside the shaft and fed her feet into it, feeling for a rung. She tucked her phone into her waistband with its torch pointed outwards, to give herself some light to work by. She grabbed the steel peg with both hands to hold herself steady and twisted around to commit herself to it. Then, with an admonition to Greta to stay where she was in case anything should go wrong, she set off down into the darkness.

FORTY-FIVE

Elias gazed at Imogen, unsure that he'd heard her quite correctly. 'You were with Cameron Wolfe when your sister died?' he said. 'But I thought your movie had ended well before then. I thought you'd both gone your own ways.'

'I know. I know. But it didn't happen quite like that.'

'Okay. So you need to tell me everything.'

Imogen nodded miserably, but said nothing further for a while, using the time to organise her thoughts, or perhaps simply putting off the moment. But she couldn't delay forever. 'I'm sure you already know that Raoul... my husband...' She closed her eyes and shook her head and decided to start over. 'Okay, so I really need to go all the way back. This is six or seven years ago now. Raoul's grandmother contracted a horrible degenerative disease. Her husband had run off to Australia with another woman ages before, so it was up to Raoul's parents to take her in and look after her. They both worked full-time, though, so the whole family had to step up, including Raoul. That wasn't a problem for him. He was very fond of her. Eventually, though, her end drew near. They brought her to our hospice. That was when we first met. I'd only been there a few weeks myself, and I couldn't believe how cold and indifferent some families were, so it really touched me to see him with her, because he was so kind and patient and concerned. He visited her pretty much every day, unless it was a game day, or he had unusually heavy training. And after she passed, he kept on visiting, only now it was to see me instead.'

'I'm with you,' said Elias.

'He was still young at the time. We both were. But we were earning just about enough between us to take a shoebox in Barnet that we could both commute from. His club saw him mostly as a prospect for the future rather than for right now, because you need to grow into these things, particularly as a forward, so he wasn't remotely confident he'd ever even become a first team regular, let alone turn it into a proper career. His head hadn't been turned yet by the fame and the razzle-dazzle is what I'm saying. But he loved it, and I loved him, so of course I backed him all the way. Then the club's star Number Eight got poached by one of their rivals and his backup did his shoulder really badly, and just like that Raoul found himself being chucked in at the deep end, way before he or anyone else had really expected. And he thrived. Some people just do. He did so well that journalists started asking him for interviews after the games, at which they'd press him more and more pointedly over which nation he'd choose to play for, because he was qualified for France too, thanks to his mum. But he was still gobsmacked when England called. It was a crazy time. It was wonderful. We were both buzzing. He asked me to marry him, and of course I said yes. Naturally, I wanted to show him off to people, particularly to Charlotte. I loved her, don't get me wrong, but it didn't happen very often that I got one-up on her. And here I had this handsome hunk doing wonders for his club and country, getting rave reviews on TV and even being touted as a future England captain. She was happy for me, at least on the surface. But underneath I guess she must have been jealous. Not of Raoul himself so much. She had all the men she could have wished for, and Hector too. But jealous of being nudged out of the spotlight for once, and maybe of what we had between us. So she set herself out to dazzle him. And it worked. He was hardly the first man to fall for her, but...'

'He was the first you were engaged to.'

'Yes. It was my fault too. Like an idiot, I saw what she was up to, but I thought he loved me too much to fall for it. I actually thought it would show her, would you believe? I didn't realise how wrong I was until it was too late. It put quite a strain on our engagement, as you can imagine. Anyway, Charlotte finally realised what she'd done. She felt sick about it. She never told me so explicitly, but her attitude to him suddenly did a complete one-eighty. She avoided being alone with him. She treated him coldly. He didn't take it well. He got angry. He got depressed. Which wasn't that much fun for me either, to be honest, because I still loved him, despite everything. I hated to see him in pain.'

'Was that what your fight was about that afternoon? Him and Charlotte?'

'Kind of. Superficially, it was about when and where we were going to get married, because we were both still pretending that everything was fine. And it was also about him wanting to go back to London early, while I wanted to stay on, because I'd made plans that required me being here. But obviously it was about Charlotte underneath, not least because her coldness to him and her engagement to Hector was why he wanted out of there. I should have let him go, but I wanted to punish him, I think. Who knows why we do stupid things? Anyway, he stalked off to the pub while I spent the evening in the kitchen with Cameron, streaming an episode of one of those wretched true crime series.'

'I thought it was a movie?'

'That's what we told the police, but actually it was a true crime series. You know the kind. They go on forever, but they're amazingly addictive, particularly the way each episode ends on some kind of bombshell, so that you have to know what happens next.'

'Ah,' said Elias.

'Yes,' said Imogen. 'Exactly. So the monthly meeting broke up. Philip and Bryony headed off upstairs while Charlotte popped in for a torch before setting off on her walk. Our episode ended a few minutes later, but we were both so hooked that we wanted to watch at least the start of the next one. It was a little after ten by then, though, which meant making no noise.

I mean no-one was going to shoot you for it, but we did our best to honour it. So Cameron suggested we go up to his room and stream it on his laptop, while listening on earbuds. Which is what we did. We went up to his room and we sat on the sofa with his laptop on our knees between us, and we watched the next episode. The first bit of it, at least.'

'How much?'

'I honestly can't remember. We got distracted. You have to understand, I knew Cameron was pretty much a creep, even before all that horrible stuff with the teenage girls came out. He was smug and sexist and mean, but he was also tall and fit and good-looking, and he kept gazing at me in that way men do, and pressing his thigh against mine. And I was miserable about how things were going with Raoul, and low on confidence, and it felt good to be fancied by a cocky, good-looking man. He put his arm around me. We kissed a little. We might have gone even further, except that Raoul came clomping up the back stairs at that point. Which brought me back to my senses in a hurry. Cameron too, to be fair. He's a big enough lad, but Raoul would have ripped his head off and used it for his tooth-glass. So I waited for him to go into our room, then I tiptoed into our shared bathroom and ran the taps for a bit, and flushed the loo, and pretended that that was where I'd been.'

Elias frowned. 'How long after Charlotte had gone for her walk was this?'

'I don't know,' said Imogen. 'I mean I didn't check the time. But a fair bit after. At least half an hour. Maybe more. Then I lay awake for a while longer, as you can imagine. And those old floorboards and back stairs creak pretty badly. I'd have heard it if Cameron left his room.'

'If you can't be certain what time this all happened,' said Elias, 'how could you possibly have given—'

'Don't,' begged Imogen. 'Please don't.'

'I have to. If you can't be certain what time this all happened, how could you possibly have given your husband his alibi?'

'It wasn't him,' she said. 'I swear to god it wasn't.'

'On what basis?'

'He's not like that. He truly isn't. You might not think it to look at him, but he's kind and thoughtful and gentle. You should have seen him with his grandmother. He spent hours with her, reading and talking and holding her hand. The only one of his family who did. He'd never intentionally have hurt anyone, let alone Charlotte.'

'He was a back-row forward. Hurting people was his job. And you just told me he'd have ripped Cameron's head off to use as his tooth-glass.'

'It was a figure of speech! A figure of speech!'

'Okay. Okay. Let's leave that for the moment and go back to what time it was. Your best guess. Even if it's just a range. A quarter to eleven? Eleven?'

'Not that late, no. It can't have been. And Raoul was downstairs in the kitchen for much of it, remember, toasting himself his sandwiches.'

'He'd had dinner in the pub.'

'Which would do most people, sure. But Raoul isn't most people. And if you think he's the kind who could kill a person then toast himself a sandwich or two... Honestly, I was in the car with him once when he hit a rabbit. He was a mess for hours. No. I'm sorry. The idea he'd have hurt Charlotte is ridiculous. So yes I gave him his alibi because I knew he hadn't done it, and it saved everyone from going off chasing wild geese. Anyway, I didn't come here to incriminate my husband. I came here to tell you that Cameron's confession makes no sense.'

Elias turned on his mobile. 'Okay. Thank you for that. For coming forward, I mean. It can't have been easy. But I'm calling Detective Superintendent Trent now.'

'No. You promised.'

'I promised to treat what you told me responsibly and with respect. That means calling Trent. I have no choice. As you already knew when you came to see me, which is why you found it so hard.'

'No!'

'Yes. And, when he gets here, you're going to tell him exactly what you just told me.'

FORTY-SIX

Anna took the descent slowly, uncertain how secure the rope ladder was, or what lay at the bottom. It twisted and yawed each time she changed her footing, so that her torch threw shifting patterns of light upon the fractured ground around her, which bellied out at first before closing in around her once more as she neared a second aperture, a kind of belted waist through which all this missing earth had evidently funnelled. She had no idea why it should have collapsed in this peculiar way until she reached that point herself and passed through a narrow hole in what appeared to be a vaulted ceiling of monumental limestone blocks covered by a layer of cracked and dessicated tar the best part of an inch thick, presumably to seal and protect whatever lay beneath from the rain that had fallen over the centuries since, diverting it instead to run harmlessly down its sides.

She was only halfway through this second aperture when she touched down on the floor beneath – or not the floor, exactly, but rather the mound of earth deposited there when the ground above had collapsed and fallen through. It left her with such little room that she had to get down onto her hands and knees to avoid banging her head against the surviving ceiling. Still hunkered down in this way, she took her torch from her waistband and turned it this way and that, its weak beam still powerful enough to reveal herself to be at one end of a substantial chamber with curved walls and a vaulted ceiling, whose floor still lay a good way beneath her, at the bottom of the earthen mound, down whose side she could see multiple sets of footprints, both coming and going, no doubt left by Hector Brook on his various explorations.

She took photographs on every side, hoping that the flash would capture more than her torch could. But it was impossible to make out much on her small screen. She told herself that that was enough for now, that it was time to head back up and alert the authorities, even if that meant handing the site over to Smallbone. Her feet, however, made a different decision, and she found herself scrambling down the side of the mound to the chamber floor instead, glad to be able to stand up to her full height again, and shining her torch around for a first proper look.

She was perched on a narrow strip between a wall of limestone blocks to her left and a pit to her right that was so wide and deep that it took her several seconds to recognise it for what it was, even though she'd been half expecting it. For a ship had been buried in the ground, a *huge* ship, a huge *funeral* ship, to be even more precise, presumably either dragged up here in the distant past by a small army of men, or possibly even constructed on the spot. This whole hilltop must have been sheared off and then hollowed out for the purpose, with the earth set aside for later. The ship would then have been filled with tinder and the body of Rægenhere before being set alight in a raging conflagration that would have turned the night sky red for miles around, visible even way out at sea, exactly as described in the great poem.

She could make out the charred remains of the ship's ribs and keel, while the scorched and even melted earth was punctuated by the neat rows of blackened rivets that had been left behind after the strakes had burned away. She could see, too, the row of pockmarks that Brook had created when he'd plucked away all the rivets within easiest reach to fill his barrels. Once the pyre had burned itself out, this limestone hall would have been built over it before being coated in tar then covered once more in all the excavated earth. And that was why there'd been no trace of it in the aerial photographs. There hadn't been a mound upon the hilltop for the simple reason that this entire hilltop was itself the mound.

The ship's carcass wasn't the only remarkable feature of this place. The stone structure above it, through whose ceiling she'd just arrived, was every bit as astonishing. It appeared to be the same shape as the ship beneath, only larger and upturned, as if a god had whittled it out of rock and slapped it down on top, creating a limestone carapace with sturdy ribs that mirrored the ribbing of the ship beneath, but whose extra size allowed for a narrow walkway around the ship's perimeter, much like the flagstones around a swimming pool, only laid instead with black and white pebbles arranged in circles, stars, spirals and other such geometric patterns.

Centuries of dust had accumulated upon this walkway, making it easy for her to read the footprints that Hector Brook had left on his exploration of this place – clearly the true reason he'd stopped work on his summerhouse, rather than the loss of heart he'd blamed it on. Yet instead of reporting the find, as he should have done, he'd built his twisted plan for this weekend around it, seeing it as his chance not only to reveal triumphantly how the woman he'd loved had been right about what lay here, but also to help him catch the person who'd killed her, and on the anniversary of her death too.

How sweet that must have seemed to him. How *fated*.

Anna set off around the walkway, pausing after a few paces to take more photographs of the ship beneath and the ceiling above. She'd barely started onwards again when she made another remarkable discovery: a pair of long wooden scaffolding planks that Brook had laid from one side of the ship to the other, creating a kind of makeshift bridge across it, from port to starboard. The planks were only a few inches longer than the ship was wide and looked so precarious that she couldn't for the life of her imagine why he'd taken such a risk – not, at least, until she'd passed beyond them and her torchlight fell upon a kind of shelf some two or three feet beneath this platform, and which also ran from one side of the ship to the other. Only this one dated back a further fourteen hundred years.

It looked at first glance a little like the kind of bench that crewmen might have sat on to pull their oars. But that was clearly not its purpose, in part because there was only one of them, in part because it was so untouched by fire that it must have been added after the pyre had burned itself out, but mostly because of the array of artefacts upon it, including a gorgeously wrought arm-ring, a large golden goblet, a jewel-encrusted torque, a gemstone necklace, a bowl filled with ancient coins, and finally, in a silver scabbard, one of the long knives or short swords known as seaxes that had been so popular among the Anglo-Saxons.

These treasures were arranged evenly upon the shelf, save for a telling gap between the necklace and the bowl of coins, where an outline in the dust of the exact right shape and size showed that this was where Hector Brook had found the dragon buckle from Friday night's feast.

In Sutton Hoo, Rædwald's mortal remains had been interred in a small chamber near the ship's keel, along with grave-goods to see him on his last great journey. But Rægenhere – assuming that this was indeed his pyre – would have left no mortal remains behind to inter. These artefacts, then, were his grave-goods.

She was crouching down to photograph them when she heard grunting and scraping from behind and she turned to see a flare of light as Greta arrived through the hole in the ceiling then came scrambling down the side of the mound. 'My god!' she said, standing up and looking around in wonder.

'You can't be down here,' Anna told her.

'Why not?' said Greta. 'You are.'

'I'm an archaeologist.'

'And I'm the owner,' retorted Greta. 'This belongs to me now.'

Anna shook her head, but she had little practical or moral authority, as neither of them should in truth be here, and she wasn't yet ready to turn back herself. Besides, the ceiling had survived fourteen hundred years until Brook had taken his jackhammer to the ground above it. It seemed unlikely to come down now. She snapped a final shot of the artefacts then carried on along the walkway until she reached the ship's prow and looked back along its length. The sight was so evocative of the wonderful black and white photographs from Sutton Hoo that it gave her a shiver and even brought a little moisture to her eyes. She made her way onwards around the prow to come back along the starboard side, trying her best to calculate just how big this funeral ship was. Rædwald's had been an astonishing ninety feet long and fourteen across. Yet, as best as she could figure, this was both longer and broader, though perhaps not by as much as the rivets would have—

'Oof!' cried Greta. 'That was close!'

It was the quaver in her voice as much as her words themselves that alarmed Anna. She hurried onwards until she was close enough to see. To her horror, Greta had crawled out onto the pair of scaffolding planks. Even worse, she was reaching down for the golden goblet beneath.

'Stop!' yelled Anna. 'Are you mad?'

Greta didn't even look up. 'Just this one,' she said, straining with her fingertips. 'To prove we've really found it.'

'What do you think our cameras are for?'

But Greta ignored her, shifting further across instead, to extend her reach. The left-hand plank tilted dangerously beneath her weight. Anna could see disaster coming. She rushed forwards to stamp upon the plank before it went. Too late, however. It flipped onto its side even as she put her foot on it, sending Greta crashing into and then through the shelf beneath, taking it and its precious cargo cascading down with her to land heavily upon the ship's charred keel. Worse still, the way the plank turned threw Anna off-balance too. She waved her arms and clawed the air in a forlorn attempt to save herself, but she reached and passed her tipping point a moment later, then went tumbling down the ship's steep side to its bottom, throwing up her arms to protect her head a moment before she thudded into Greta.

She lay there winded and stunned for several seconds, appalled at what had happened, yet relieved to find that they were both seemingly unhurt. She put a hand on the ship's charred keel for support as she sat up. That was when she heard an ominous creaking noise, as when the ice on a frozen lake starts to thaw. And then the ground beneath them, which Anna had assumed to be solid packed earth all the way down, suddenly broke apart under the double blow of their separate impacts, and they found themselves in free fall once again, plunging headlong into darkness.

FORTY-SEVEN

For the first time in weeks, Raoul Flood woke without the weight of impending doom upon his shoulders – a weight that had been bowing him down ever since Brook had invited him and Imogen for this weekend, then had refused even to listen to his various excuses. In truth, it had been bowing him down ever since the awful night of Charlotte's death. For years now, every unexpected knock or unrecognised phone number had provoked the same small pang of alarm. Was this it? Was this finally it? At long last, had justice arrived? He'd imagined the moment so many times that it had taken on almost the solidity of memory. That particular sound handcuffs made as they were being clapped on; the indignity of being bundled into the back of a squad car while the neighbours watched; the hours of interrogation before weariness and despair took hold, and confession was made; pleading guilty at trial in the forlorn hope of a lighter sentence; the lonely frightened years in jail before finally being released into the miserable rump of a life. But no longer. The case was neatly solved. The police were satisfied. The sun was up and it looked like turning into another fine day.

For once he meant to enjoy it.

He rolled over to share his happiness with Imogen, only to find her gone. She wasn't in the bathroom either. No worries. She'd always liked a hotel breakfast. It was one of her few indulgences. He took a shower and was getting dressed when there came a knock upon the door. He smiled to himself. Imogen was always forgetting her keys. He pulled on his trousers as he went to answer it, almost tripping over in his hurry. Only it wasn't Imogen standing there. It was DS Trent instead, along with four burly officers. He stared at them blankly for a moment, the grimness of their expressions. 'What?' he asked, his sudden dread all the more sickening because he'd thought it gone.

'A few questions, if we may,' said Trent.

'Questions?'

'Questions,' confirmed Trent. 'May we come in?'

'It's not...' He looked around, desperate for an excuse. But he couldn't think of one. 'Yes. I suppose.' He stood back to let them by. His mind was racing, his heart thumping. *What did they know? How did they know? Surely Imogen hadn't blabbed. Please god not that.* 'Well?' he asked.

'Maybe we could start with Charlotte Ash?' said Trent, opening the curtains all the way then leaning back against the windowsill so that the rising sun was just to one side of him, as though he were shining a lamp in Raoul's eyes. 'The night she died.'

'What about it?'

'Your best recollection, if you would?'

'I gave my best recollection five years ago,' he said, sounding, to his relief, far calmer and more composed than he felt. 'What makes you think I'll do any better now?'

'Please. Humour me.'

'Okay,' he said. He couldn't help but note how the policemen took up positions on every side, so that there was always at least one of them behind him that he couldn't see. They had their game faces on too, made wary by his physique, expecting him to try something. He felt trapped. He felt doomed. But he had to keep fighting. 'I stayed in the pub till about ten. I walked back to the Manor. Everyone was already in bed so I toasted myself a couple of sandwiches then headed up to my room. Immy was already in bed. That was maybe ten thirty or so. I can't be more precise, I'm afraid. It wasn't like we had any reason to check the time.'

'And your wife was already in bed? You're sure of that?'

'I just told you, didn't I?'

'Except it's not true, though, is it, sir?'

'What's not true?'

'That your wife was already in bed. She wasn't. She was in the bathroom.'

'I beg your pardon?'

'Your wife was in the bathroom when you went upstairs. Not in bed.'

'Did she tell you that?'

'Don't you worry about how we know. Just believe me that we do. She was in the bathroom, wasn't she? So why lie about it?'

'What is this?' But suddenly his voice was a croak. 'What's going on? Do I need a lawyer?'

'That's up to you, sir. But it wasn't ten thirty, either, was it? It was closer to eleven. Maybe even a few minutes past. So what did you do with all that missing time? Because it doesn't take forty minutes to get from the railway bridge to the Manor. Not unless you go via Dragon Stone Hill. Is that where you were? Taking one last shot at persuading Charlotte Ash not to marry Mr Brook?'

'No,' said Raoul. 'No. This is… No.'

'Is that what Charlotte said too? Did she say no? Did she tell you that she meant to marry Mr Brook and that it wasn't your business any more? Except that it *was* your business, wasn't it? You were the great Raoul Flood, next England captain. You wanted her, and that was that. She'd *made* you want her, what was more. And now she thought she could dump you for an old man with a ravaged face, just because he was rich. It wasn't right. It wasn't fair. You got angry. You shouted at her. You pushed her on her shoulder. But she wasn't having that, was she? She pushed you right back. She mocked you and told you that you meant nothing to her, so you shoved her again, only harder this time, so hard that she slipped and fell over the edge.'

Raoul swallowed. 'This is fantasy,' he protested. 'Absolute fantasy. You've no evidence at all.'

'Oh well. That's me convinced, that is.'

Raoul stared sickly at him. He didn't know how much Trent really knew, or what he was after, or how much he could prove. He didn't know what he needed to say. He lacked the mind for situations like this. He needed Imogen here, that was the truth of it. She was the one who'd always done the planning for them both. Their house, their wedding, their holidays, their finances. Back in their early days, she'd once tried to teach him chess, so that they could have a game together when he'd arrived at the hospice to find his gran asleep. He'd given it his best shot, he truly had, in his keenness to impress her; but the board had dissolved into a kind of shapeless fuzz whenever he'd tried to think more than a single move ahead, while she could plot her way through sequences and variations that left him baffled. 'I want my lawyer,' he said.

'You have a lawyer?' frowned Trent. 'Why do you have a lawyer?'

'I don't, actually,' he admitted sheepishly. 'But it's what people say, isn't it?'

'It's what guilty people say. Are you guilty?'

'No. No. Of course not.'

'Then why do you want a lawyer?'

Raoul stood there helplessly. 'I just do,' he said.

'As you wish,' said Trent. 'But tell me this one thing first, if you would. I've heard how well you looked after your grandma when she was ill. How you nursed her and washed her and changed her sheets. How you took charge of her medications and kept a record of what she needed to take, and when.'

'She was my gran. Why wouldn't I?'

'Did you give her her injections too? Did you order drugs for her over the internet? Painkillers that her doctors wouldn't prescribe, maybe?'

'Oh Christ,' said Raoul, only now realising where this was going. 'You've got it all wrong.'

'I wouldn't blame you one bit if you did. Doctors can be stingy, can't they? Even when their patients are terminal.

Whereas those Chinese suppliers, they don't care, they'll sell you anything. Heroin, opium, roofies, fentanyl, as long as you've got the money. All delivered swiftly and in a nice anonymous package. And it's not like someone your grandma's age would have had the first idea how to get it for herself. Your parents neither. It would have been a kindness.'

'No.'

'You'll be happy for us to take a look at your credit card history, then? So we can be sure in our own minds. And not just from when you were looking after your grandma. From more recently too. The last couple of months, say.'

Raoul felt sick. 'But Cameron confessed,' he said. 'He left you a confession.'

'So he did. But his voice is just a little bit muffled, you see. Muffled and drunken, which makes it hard to be absolutely certain. And why use his voice recorder when his camera's right there, not hidden away in some random folder on the third page, like his voice app was? But the voice app would make perfect sense for a skilled impersonator like they tell me you are. Apparently there's a clip of you absolutely nailing Mr Smallbone. I've got no great ear for such things myself, so I probably shouldn't say, but I'd imagine Mr Wolfe's voice would be much easier to imitate.' He turned to one of his colleagues. 'You're probably our best mimic, Jack. Which would you find easier? Mr Wolfe or Mr Smallbone?'

'Mr Wolfe,' said Jack. 'No question. He'd be a piece of piss.'

'Yeah. That's what I reckon too.' He turned back to Raoul. 'How about you? Do you think you could pull off a passable Mr Wolfe? Tell you what: Why don't you give it a go for us right now? Something along the lines of: "It was me. I did it. I killed Charlotte five years ago and then last night I killed Hector too. I'm sorry."'

FORTY-EIGHT

Anna's cry of alarm was cut mercifully short after barely a moment, for she thudded down onto the mound of rotted timbers and loose earth that had collapsed beneath her, rolling down its side to hit the harder floor beneath. She lay there for a few seconds, winded and stunned for the second time in less than half a minute, unable to believe the magnitude of this calamity – or indeed of Greta's greed and stupidity. 'What the hell were you thinking?' she said.

Greta didn't answer at once, but rather lay there whimpering, perhaps in hope of sympathy. 'My ankle,' she said. 'I think I've broken it.'

'Good,' said Anna.

She turned onto her back and sat up. Her left shoulder throbbed, as did her right knee, but she didn't think she'd done herself any serious damage, though tomorrow's bruises would be a sight to see. It was almost completely dark, save for the torchlight from her phone, half buried though it was in the fallen earth beside her left foot. She plucked it out and shone it around, revealing them to be in a chamber maybe twelve feet square, with open archways to her left and right, and built from the same monumental limestone blocks as above – though these ones were topped not by a vaulted stone ceiling but by a row of timbers instead, coated with protective tar yet still so rotted and weakened by the passage of time that three of them had splintered and given way beneath the double impact of them crashing down upon the keel above.

But what even was this place?

Her first thought was that it must be a burial chamber, like the one in which Rædwald had been interred. Except that there were no grave goods in view, only a pair of benches on either side, and numerous small niches in the walls for clay oil lamps, and a series of panels skilfully sculpted into dramatic scenes of hunting and feasting, of men on horseback and in boats. An antechamber, perhaps, in which Rædwald and his wife had come to bid their final farewell to their beloved son. Except that, if Anna was right about what had happened here, their son had gone up in a massive blaze, leaving no remains to mourn. Yet perhaps the great poem gave the explanation once again – for after describing how Beowulf's body had been consigned to the flames, it spoke of his grief-stricken people gathering his ashes together to bury beneath a great mound, along with much of the golden treasure recovered from the dragon's lair.

From earth it had come, the poem went, *and to earth it was returned*.

She shone her torch upwards. The ceiling was maybe ten feet above the chamber floor – though less than that from atop the mound of earth and rotted wood they'd brought down with them. The surviving timbers looked frail, but they hadn't yet collapsed, so perhaps they had some strength left. With a leg up from Greta, she could probably grab the lip of the hole and haul herself out – assuming that she didn't simply bring down more of the ship, and hurt herself in the process too.

She rose gingerly to her feet then went over to the nearer of the two archways, if only to get away from Greta's plaintive mewling. A winding passage led into darkness as far as her torchlight reached, which admittedly wasn't very far. But it was still spooky enough to send her back across the chamber to the other archway. And this one stopped her dead.

The great treasures of Sutton Hoo had mostly been reduced to fragments by the time of their discovery, first shattered by the collapse of the burial chamber, then corroded by the acidity of the surrounding soil. But there'd been no such collapse here, nor any such corrosion, what with this place almost hermetically sealed. Everything here, then, had been preserved almost as perfectly as in Tutankhamun's tomb.

She played her torch over it from the doorway, not daring to go inside. It was round with a domed ceiling, some ten feet across and tall; and everything inside proclaimed it to be a royal burial chamber. Its walls were built from the same limestone blocks as elsewhere, inset at shoulder height with niches for oil-lamps of copper or bronze, but its floor was laid with slabs of white marble. A slender silver pedestal stood at its heart, with a gorgeously-wrought golden casket resting upon it, presumably containing such ashes of Rægenhere as his people had been able to recover. Against the wall to her left stood a small armoury: swords both long and short, some battle-used, others ceremonial. There were axes and daggers and shields of cracked wood and blackened leather. She could see three different helmets, including a gorgeous one wrought from bronze and iron, decorated with ram's horns on either side and with a dagger for its nosepiece. There were spears of different hefts and lengths, a pair of greaves and a suit of chain-mail whose links still glittered like silver beneath the dust.

Against the right-hand wall, a number of wooden barrels, presumably of food and drink, were stashed beneath a high table on which stood bowls of coins and brooches, of rings and bracelets, of combs and necklaces. There were four tall golden goblets too, backed by a set of silver platters that worked like mirrors to enhance her torchlight. A pair of dessicated leather satchels on the floor beyond had split apart, offering a glimpse of the ivory scroll holders within. And who could even guess at the treasures they contained? Historic records to fill the gaping holes in their knowledge about the early Angles. More bardic masterpieces to rank alongside *Beowulf*. Correspondence with other kings, perhaps even from other lands. Early Christian texts, so recently brought back into the country by St Augustine on the orders of Pope Gregory the Great. Beyond those, a number of wooden chests and lidded caskets were stacked higgledy-piggledy on one another. Then came a lyre for making music, and the kind of golden circlet that a prince might wear, along with a sceptre like a blunted sword, topped by a bull standing upon a hoop. There was the harness, saddle and other tack of a horse, whose decapitated head was also there, its shrunken skin pulled back over its mouth to give it a ghastly grin. And that was only part of what the chamber contained, for she could make out a treasury of other artefacts half hidden behind these – much of it doubtless plundered from the Dragon of the North, again as hinted at by *Beowulf's* final few lines.

'Am I supposed to just sit here?' whined Greta.

Anna turned reluctantly back around. Greta had propped herself up against the far wall and had taken off her shoe and sock to inspect her ankle. To be fair, it did already look bruised and swollen, though at least no bone had punctured or distended the skin. 'What would you have me do?' Anna asked her.

'I need help.'

'Telling me.' But she looked around for ideas, even so. She found one too, for Greta hadn't just brought down with her the goblet, short sword and other treasures from the shelf, she'd brought down the scaffolding plank too. It had to be at least twelve or thirteen feet long, plenty enough to use as a ramp to climb out on. It was partly buried in the fallen earth, so Anna tucked her phone back into her waistband then went to wrest it free. She raised its far end like a caber to feed up through the hole in the ceiling before resting it as gently as she could against the ship's broken keel, careful not to do it any further damage. She leaned it at an angle that she could climb then worked its base into the bed of fallen earth beneath her, stamping it down until it was secure. She tested it to make sure that it would hold, then went to help Greta to her feet. But Greta shook her head. 'I can't climb that,' she said. 'And what am I supposed to do about the rope ladder?'

'Okay,' said Anna. 'Then stay here. I'll get help.'

'You're going to leave me?'

'It's one or the other, isn't it?'

'Fine,' said Greta, making to stand up. 'I suppose I can give it a go.' She grimaced as she put weight upon her ankle, let out a yelp of pain. Then she turned back to Anna with a pitiful expression. 'What will we tell people?'

'The truth.'

Greta's keys had fallen from her pocket during her fall, and were lying on the floor where she'd been sitting. Anna stooped to pick them up for her, along with a lacy handkerchief, a two pound coin and a short steel screw with a dab of bright white filler on its tip. Anna frowned. She'd seen two others just like it recently, she was sure of it. Yes. On the floor of the Manor's cellar yesterday afternoon. And, though she didn't yet know quite why, the realisation sent a shudder straight through her, like the first small tremor beneath ones feet that announces the quake about to strike.

FORTY-NINE

E lias watched as Trent and his officers marched Raoul to the lifts, uncomfortably aware of Imogen standing beside him, appalled at what she'd wrought. She held her tongue somehow until the doors had closed upon her husband, and the lift was on its way down. Then she turned on him with her fists bunched. 'You bastard!' she said. 'I trusted you. I'd never have come to you if I'd known you'd do this.'

'Yeah, you would,' he told her. 'Don't kid yourself.'

'*What?*'

'Five years you've been worrying it was him. How exhausting must that be, going to bed every night with the man you think murdered your sister?'

'No!'

'Yes.' He nodded towards the lift. 'This way, at least, you'll get to know the truth, one way or the other. Isn't that what you're really after?' He didn't wait for her to respond, or even for the lift to return, but rather set off down the stairs instead, if only to walk off the tension jangling through him.

He made his way out the front doors, glad to leave the hotel behind. But now what? He felt a powerful hankering to see Anna, to share this latest development with her and Greta as soon as possible. His Leaf was still up at the Manor, and he was too impatient to walk, so he headed down to the railway station and its taxi rank. There was no answer to his knock at Gatehouse Cottage, even though the Defender was parked outside. He tried Anna's phone but got kicked straight into voicemail. He'd already paid off his taxi so he set off for the Manor on foot, walking along the side of the drive to get some morning sunshine on his face.

Greta's Hyundai was still parked on the forecourt, along with his Leaf and all the other cars. Yet there was no sign of Anna or Greta or indeed anyone. He made a full circuit of the house, trying all the doors and windows, but the place was locked up tight. Anna still wasn't answering her phone, so he left her a message to call him and followed it up with a text. Then he checked around the back of the barns and outhouses and even went into the woods for a bit, shouting for her and Greta, but without result.

Two people had already died this weekend. Little wonder that he felt uneasy. He told himself not to worry, that the police had their man, that Anna could look after herself. It didn't help. Even the slight possibility that she might be in danger was so disturbing to him that it took him back to the worst day of his life, and how it had started when he'd looked around for his young son Marcus, only to discover that he wasn't there. He tried to push the memory aside but it wouldn't go. He hurried back to the Manor, banged uselessly on its doors and windows. He stood on the front step and gazed out over the lawns to the Deben as it wound sedately to the sea. The cooler, stiffer breeze had brought more craft out upon the river, their colourful sails swollen taut by the wind; while, on the far bank, the rising sun struck sparks of light off the windscreens in line for Sutton Hoo. It made him wonder whether there'd be similar queues here one day, should a funeral ship ever be found. Hector Brook had meant to give this whole estate to the nation, but Elias wondered whether Greta would really follow through. This was her home too, after all, and what a wrench to give it up for an ancient site that had surely never meant as much to her as it had to...

Elias frowned. Brook had twice seriously contemplated donating this place to the nation, first in his eagerness to please Charlotte, then again as part of his plan to unmask her killer. A man that rich would doubtless have left himself plenty for a life of great comfort, yet his grand gesture would likely have evicted Greta from her cottage, and maybe even meant she'd have to survive upon her salary too. But that threat was gone forever now, thanks to his death. She was set to become one of the wealthiest women in the county instead.

'Give us a chance,' sighed Trent, when Elias called. 'I'm letting him sweat for an hour or so. Then I'll crack him like an egg, believe me.'

'I doubt it,' said Elias. 'I don't think it was him any more.'

'But you're the one who gave him to us,' protested Trent.

'I know,' said Elias. 'My bad. But there's something I didn't tell you yesterday. Though only because I didn't pick up on it myself until about a minute ago.'

'And?'

'That spiritualist woman who came by yesterday afternoon. Patience Miller. Remember how Charlotte told her she was scared of one of the people she'd been flirting with?'

'Yeah. Exactly. Raoul Flood.'

'Could be. I don't know. But the point isn't *who*. The point is *when*. Because she said Charlotte told her this just a couple of nights before she died. And here's the point. Patience also said that she'd told Hector Brook about it. Yet she never saw him again after Charlotte fell.'

'So?'

'So when did she tell him? He could go on for hours once he'd started talking, apparently, so Patience made sure he was her last appointment of the day. He also hated anyone knowing that he was seeing her at all, so he's bound to have used a cover story. The night Charlotte died, he claimed he'd been off playing bridge with friends on the other side of Ipswich. No one ever followed up on that, because why would they? He was the only person pushing for an investigation, and he'd hardly have done that if he'd had anything to hide. But I don't think he was playing bridge at all that night. I think he was in Woodbridge instead, having his final session with Patience.'

'I don't get it,' said Trent. 'What difference does it make where he was?'

'It makes no difference where *he* was. It makes a huge difference where *Greta* was. Brook insisted on having his sessions with Patience alone. Greta was his driver. I don't know how it worked exactly, but I'm guessing she'd drop him off then kill time in a bar or grabbing something to eat or whatever. Which means she was alone in Woodbridge with an alibi and a car at the exact time that Charlotte set off on her nightly walk. She could easily have driven over to Kyson Hill, left her car in the car park there, and made it up the staircase to the top of Dragon Stone Hill before Charlotte arrived. And she'd have been back in town in plenty of time to pick her brother up again.'

'*Greta?*' said Trent incredulously. 'That bag of nerves? You can't be serious.'

'Forget about how she comes across. That's simply how she chooses to present herself. Put yourself in her shoes instead. Five years ago, her brother wasn't just about to marry, he was about to become a father too, crushing any hopes she might have had of ever inheriting big. Plus he was talking about giving the estate to the nation, without even discussing it with her, even though it was her home too. Would you really blame her for feeling upset?'

'Feeling upset is one thing,' countered Trent. 'Murder is another. Anyway, you've still got her brother's death to explain. The Manor was locked up tight. You told us so yourself.'

'It was locked up tight because she was the one who insisted on it. And a clever woman like her, given the run of the house for months, with easy access to all the cameras and the security app on her brother's computer... She could have found any number of ways around his defences. We'll find out how she did it when we look, believe me. Her bigger problem by far was that her motive was so obvious. Who's the first person you look at when the local plutocrat gets topped? The beneficiary, right? Yet she slipped right by us, even though I'll bet she scoops the lot.'

'Yes,' said Trent grudgingly. 'She does.'

'There you go, then. She'd have been your number one suspect, except that the place was locked up tight and filled with likely alternatives. She couldn't have asked for a better opportunity.'

'And Cameron Wolfe? She forced him to confess, did she? Or is she some kind of freakish mimic?'

'This is a guess, okay,' said Elias, 'but it's not a crazy one. After Greta went back to bed yesterday morning, Wolfe went up to see her. He claimed it was to ask if she needed anything. But come on. He was the last kind of person to give a toss about that. What if he knew something instead? What if he'd seen her during the night, say, or he'd figured out what she'd done in some other way? The detail doesn't matter. What matters is that he had Greta over a barrel just as she was about to inherit huge. It was Christmas come early for a man like him. He had a problem, though. He had no *proof*. If he told you guys straight away what he knew, you'd likely be able to nail her. But in a few months time? In a year or two? His assertions would be useless. So what he needed was a way to turn his temporary hold over her into a permanent one. Specifically, he needed to get her to confess on camera. That way, he'd own her forever. And that's why he went upstairs. But she put him off until the afternoon, when we all moved down to Woodbridge. It gave her time to come up with a plan. So picture this. She goes to see him in his hotel room and asks him to tell her exactly what it is he wants her to say. She has her own phone on to record him while he does so. Maybe she does this more than once, to make sure she's got one that will work. Then she spikes his drink with fentanyl and waits until he's comatose or dead before copying it over to his phone instead. Which is why it's on his voice app rather than his camera, of course, and why the quality was so poor.'

'And he just let her kill her, did he? Even though he knew how dangerous she was?'

'You met the guy. Way too cocky for his own good. Too cocky and too drunk. I think it went like this. She had complimentary bottles of wine sent up to all our rooms, no doubt to get him as drunk as possible. Then she told your two men in the lobby that she needed to speak to me about something, to give herself an excuse for being on the third floor at all. She goes to see Wolfe first, ostensibly to discuss the situation with him, but in truth to record him telling her what he wants her to say, and to dose his wine with fentanyl. Then she flaps her hands and tells him she needs more time to think about it, but that she'll be straight back. She leaves his room unlocked and comes to see me, partly to kill time and partly to justify her having come up to the third floor at all; but also to plant the idea that Wolfe had tried to kill himself twice before, to make us think it was in his character. Then she returns to his room, by which time he's drunk his fentanyl and is comatose or dead. She unlocks his phone with his fingerprint, transfers her recording and plants her baggies in his waste paper basket for good measure. Then it's back downstairs again and off to the shops to give herself an excuse for being away so long.'

There was silence as Trent digested this. 'Bloody hell,' he said finally. 'Where is she now?'

'That's the thing,' said Elias. 'She's not at home or up at the Manor. And I'm very much afraid she has Anna with her.'

FIFTY

It wasn't only the screw with a dab of bright white filler on its tip that pointed Anna at the truth. It was also the fleeting look of panic on Greta's face as she made to snatch it back, so that Anna's mind leapt straight to the answer without touching any of the steps between. But knowing the answer made figuring out those steps infinitely easier. Greta looked so alarmed because she was guilty. And what else could she be guilty of, except her brother's murder? A murder, after all, that left her sole owner of his entire estate, as she'd bragged just a few minutes ago, despite having claimed yesterday not to know what was in his will. And the stubby little screw with the dab of bright white filler on its tip was part of how she'd pulled it off.

The screw was identical to the two from the cellar floor. Those had surely fallen from her pocket too. But why had they been there at all? Again, it was knowing the larger answer that helped her find the smaller. Greta hadn't been suspected of her brother's murder because the Manor had been sealed up tight and there'd been no trace of intrusion. But it would have been easy enough for Greta to move the intruder sensors so as to create a safe path between them, perhaps even practising at night until she knew she could reach the house unseen. And while the cameras covered all its exterior doors, she'd no doubt redirected them away from the wood-hatch, secured only by a padlock whose key it would have been simple for her to borrow or have copied. Her real challenge, then, would have been to get from the cellar into the main body of the house through a locked and bolted door. But that was the whole point, Anna now saw.

The door had been locked as well as bolted.

The housing loops for the bolts had been larger than the bolts themselves, which was why Trent had found them so easy to draw yesterday afternoon. The lock, on the other hand, had been so stubborn that he'd had to lean his shoulder against the door. When Greta had rattled the handle on Friday night, it had therefore been the lock rather than the bolts that had held the door in place. But she could have unlocked that herself from the cellar side, leaving the door secured only by its bolts. And that was where the screws came in. She'd have replaced the originals with the shorter, thinner ones, kept in place only by dabs of filler – bright white, of course, because it was still so fresh. Then all she'd have had to do was give the door a good hard shove with her shoulder and out they'd have popped, falling silently to the passage carpet along with the housing loops. Fix those back in place with their original screws, while pocketing the others, and she'd be almost home dry.

But she'd have still had one remaining problem: to bolt the cellar door behind her after she left. That was why she'd feigned her fainting fit the following morning, sending Anna off for a glass of water to buy herself the time to do it. Only Cameron Wolfe had caught her at it. 'Never even occurred to me to bolt,' he'd said when they'd gathered outside the Manor yesterday morning. 'Of course I'll tell the police everything I know, if that's what you really want.' A subtle threat of blackmail that had meant he'd had to die too.

As Greta's look of alarm had betrayed her thoughts, so now did Anna's one of horror. Greta must have realised instantly that she'd been discovered, for her expression twisted with such savage hatred that Anna didn't hesitate. She set off up the scaffolding plank in hopes of getting away before Greta could stop her. But Greta was too fast. She pulled the plank away from its bed of fallen earth, bringing Anna crashing back down along with bits of broken ceiling, stirring up clouds of dust that caught in her eyes and throat, blinding her and racking her with coughs. She staggered back to her feet all the same, stumbled over a fallen timber and went crashing into a wall. She wiped a sleeve across her eyes but everything was still such a blur that it was only from the wicked snakelike hiss it made that she realised Greta had drawn the short sword from its silver scabbard. But now her sight was back, in time to see Greta come hobbling over the mound, the sword raised high to bring it down upon her head. Anna threw up both arms to protect herself. The blade was blunt with age, but it still crashed into her left wrist and right forearm with such shattering force that it sent her tumbling to the floor. She twisted onto her back even as Greta reversed her grip upon her sword to stab it down at her chest. Anna tried to slither aside, yet it still caught her in the ribs with enough force that it tore through her shirt and she heard as much as felt the crack of bone. She turned onto her hands and knees and scrambled away across the chamber floor, everything happening too fast to take in.

She struggled to her feet, made it through the nearer of the two archways, staggering along the dark narrow passage. Her forearm and wrist both hurt, but they were as nothing compared to the jabbing from her fractured ribs, as though a spear was being stabbed deeper into her chest with every step. She was bleeding too, she realised, though she wasn't sure from where. She could feel it blotting onto her shirt and trickling wetly down her arm. And still Greta came after her, giving metronomic little cries of pain each time she put weight upon her bad ankle, yet with an expression of grim resolve on her face, as though fate had handed her an unpleasant and exacting task, but one she meant to see through to its bitter end.

FIFTY-ONE

Elias finished his call with Trent then paced back and forth across the Manor's gravelled forecourt, impatient for him to arrive with the keys. But the man had been in Martlesham, a good fifteen minutes drive away, even if he put his siren on. Fifteen minutes that Elias now decided he wasn't prepared to wait.

Either Anna and Greta were still on the estate, or they'd already left. The only ways out were across the railway bridge or down the staircase from Dragon Stone Hill to the footpath beneath. Both of those were covered by cameras, meaning that their footage should tell him which. The old Tudor windows were small with leaded panes. He therefore went over to the modern extension, where they were large and sashed instead. The Manor's whole frontage was lined with grey stone flowerpots planted with geraniums, chrysanthemums and other colourful flowers. He grunted with surprise at the weight of one of these when he picked it up. There was a great crash as he heaved it through the nearest window before reaching in to release the catch and lift up the empty frame. He brushed the shards from the sill then climbed on through, his shoes crunching on all the broken glass.

Brook's office was a little way down the passage. He ran to it and turned on the computer, cursing its slowness as it chuntered into life. He tapped in the passcode to get past its lock-screen then opened the security app. Footage from each of

Brook's cameras popped up on the array of monitors. He scanned them briskly but could see no sign of Anna, Greta or anyone else. He set it on fast rewind, therefore, his eyes flickering from feed to feed. Suddenly there they were, speeding backwards across the front lawn from Dragon Stone Hill. To his immense relief, they seemed to be on good terms still. He paused the footage as they reached the Manor. The resolution on the front door camera was so sharp that he could see a tagged key in Anna's hand. Surely that was what they'd come to the house for. His first thought was that it was for the staircase down to the dock, except that that was opened with a code rather than a key, and didn't even need that from this side.

Only then did he remember Brook's summerhouse – Brook's *unfinished* summerhouse, its septic tank and other supplies half-hidden beneath those blue tarpaulins. 'Bollocks,' he muttered, as he realised how blind he'd been. He took out his phone as he made his way out of Brook's office and back along the passage, calling Trent even as he clambered out of the broken window, to let him know where Anna and Greta had gone, and why. Then he set off sprinting across the gravel forecourt to the lawn.

FIFTY-TWO

Anna's injured forearm and wrist made it too painful for her to hold her phone, so she tucked it back into her waistband instead, its torch flashing this way and that as she lurched along the winding vaulted passage, illuminating almost at random the walls on either side. These were pocked by a multitude of recesses of all shapes and sizes, the smallest mostly housing oil lamps of clay or bronze, but the larger each containing a single urn or burial casket; and in such numbers that it was immediately obvious that this place hadn't been built for Rægenhere alone, but rather for all the Angles who'd lost their lives at the River Idle, brought home by their comrades to be buried with the honours their dread sacrifice had earned.

Some of the caskets were adorned with crosses, fish or other early Christian symbols, while others bore pagan images and tokens. No surprise there, for although Rædwald himself had been baptised by St Augustine, he'd notoriously allowed the continued worship of the old gods alongside the new, for which act of tolerance he'd earned himself the withering contempt of early Christian writers such as Bede. Inscriptions had been cut into the stone beneath many of the niches too, some in the Latin script reintroduced by Augustine alongside his new religion, but others in the Anglo-Saxon runes known as *futhorc*.

Left and right the passage kinked, sometimes almost turning back on itself, at others splitting off before converging once more, while also throwing in random short flights of steps both up and down, so that Anna soon lost all sense of direction. Onwards she stumbled even so, blood congealing cold and sticky on her shirt and trickling down her forearm to drip from her fingertips, leaving what would have been a treacherous trail had it not been so easy for Greta to follow her anyway, what with her shuffling footsteps dragging a line through the dust.

Her ribs thrust into her side with every step. She wanted to cry out from the pain of it, but she bit down instead, unwilling to give Greta anything. Lack of breath finally got to her, however. She dared not sit down, lest she never got back up again, so she leaned against the wall instead, allowing herself a few moments to recover. Her torch lit up some caskets across the way, and the crudely carved names inscribed beneath them. There rested Ecgheard, for example. There Cwichelm and Ælfgar. She couldn't help but wonder what kind of men they'd been. She couldn't help but wonder how soon she'd be joining them.

Greta was drawing closer, letting out yelps of pain every time she put weight upon her ankle. Anna forced herself to start moving again, now hobbling past a set of chamber tombs, presumably for those nobles and commanders who'd lost their lives that day. These were handsomely furnished with grave goods of their own, with brooches and caskets and silver bowls, even with swords and spears. But Anna let these be, for she lacked the grip to hold them, let alone the strength to wield them. And the chambers were too small for her to hide in, even without the telltale trail she was leaving.

Her breath ran out once more, her strength with it. She leaned again against the wall. Her beam fell this time upon a humble clay urn set low down across the way, upon whose flat lid rested a comb delicately fashioned from antler or some other kind of bone, too dainty and feminine to Anna's eye to have belonged to a warrior, more likely a token of love from some grieving sweetheart. His name had been Oswine, according to the inscription hacked into the stone beneath, the lettering even cruder here than elsewhere, yet somehow all the more evocative for that. Another footsoldier in Rædwald's army. Another life lost in the forging of this country's history. She felt a sudden flare of anger on his behalf, on behalf of all these men, their lives cut short in service of other people's greed and ambition. And somewhere in that anger she found defiance; and, in that defiance, strength.

A flicker of torchlight behind her, then Greta came shuffling into view, her rhythmic cries beginning to sound almost anguished as her ankle became ever more swollen and painful. Yet she was too far down her path to turn back now, though Anna couldn't imagine how she hoped to get away with it. Perhaps she'd seal up the summerhouse and hope no one ever looked. Or perhaps she'd simply grab her passport and all the cash she could get her hands on, and flee. More likely, though, she hadn't thought that far ahead, and was acting out of rage and hatred rather than any particular strategy.

A short flight of steps led Anna down into a large atrium with a domed ceiling, its walls sculpted in high relief to portray the last moments before a great battle, as two opposing forces faced one another across a floor laid with slabs of some bluish stone. What else but the River Idle? The mass of forces to her right had been made to look large and cruel and ogrish as they waved their dragon banners; while, to her left, a grossly outnumbered detachment was led by a handsome, bare-headed young man upon a rearing horse, given – as everyone else in the tableau – new life and motion by her own uncertain torchlight.

There were more steps directly across the atrium from her. She lurched over to them. A staircase led upwards into the darkness, far longer than any of the shorter flights she'd negotiated so far. Her spirits sank. No way could she manage it head on. She turned around instead and sat down upon her backside, then set off up it that way, one step at a time, pressing her arm in tight against her side in an effort to staunch the bleeding and manage the pain. Being closer to the ground, however, meant that the dust that she herself was stirring up soon caught in her throat and made her cough, each one like being struck in the side with an iron bar, leaving her drained and on the verge of despair. Yet still she carried on.

The dust grew thicker and thicker the higher she climbed, turning the steps almost into a ramp. Except it wasn't actually dust any more, she noticed, but rather earth. *Damp* earth, at that. She felt its cool wetness first with her palms and then seeping through the seat of her trousers. A flicker of hope kindled inside her, for the dampness and the earth both suggested that this place had an imperfect seal, and thus that escape might still be possible.

She continued upwards with renewed vigour, only for the staircase to end in a landing shortly afterwards. She looked around. It was several feet square and had a low perimeter wall upon which rested the rounded underside of a vast grey rock, as though some monstrous egg had been laid upon a cup, so low above the floor that she had to duck her head not to bang it. She reached up to run her hand over it. It was cold and rough as well as huge, the size if not the shape of a Stonehenge megalith. Her mind was so fuzzy that it took her a few moments to realise that it wasn't some random unknown boulder, but rather the dragon stone as seen from beneath. Which meant, of course, that the Angles hadn't set it upon the hillside as some kind of beacon or monument, as everyone had always assumed. No. Its real purpose had been to serve as a kind of portal into this necropolis, massive enough to thwart any aspiring grave robbers while still affording access to Rædwald himself, with a whole army at his disposal. She could picture him now, having it heaved aside on each anniversary of the River Idle, so that he, his queen and the families of all these others could come to mourn their lost beloveds. Which meant there was open air on its other side. Open air and open ground and just the possibility of survival.

Defying the pain in her wrist, she took her torch from her waistband and shone it this way and that. The perimeter wall was built not from limestone but rather from large blocks of white marble, chosen presumably for their strength as much as their beauty. Even so, several of these blocks had cracked under the remorseless weight of the great stone, shedding chips and larger fragments to lie among the earth and dust, while the wall itself had warped and buckled over the centuries, bulging out so far in places that it looked on the verge of collapse.

The perimeter wall was of necessity shaped like a horseshoe, in order to accommodate the staircase up which Anna had just arrived. A pair of timbers had been laid like joists across the top of the open end, to offer the stone some additional support. These were mostly black from the thick coating of tar they'd been given; but that coating had fallen away in places to expose the wood beneath, enabling Anna to see that the rain and worms had been to work on their innards, giving them the aerated texture of a termite mound. The nearer one, in particular, was so bowed in its middle from its long labour that she was surprised it still held. She struggled to her knees and reached up for it. More patches of tar fell away simply by being touched, exposing the soft wood beneath. She clawed weakly at it, yet it still came away in clumps until she'd reached the harder core within.

A flash of light at the foot of the staircase. Greta finally appeared, her torch in one hand, her short sword in the other. She stood there for several seconds, as daunted by the climb as Anna had been. But then she steeled herself and set off, putting her good foot up first before bringing her bad one up to join it, still letting out her strangled howls each time. She paused halfway to shine up her torch and gave a grunt of satisfaction when she saw her quarry cornered.

Anna looked around for inspiration. One of the chunks of broken marble not only had an edge to it but looked to fit snugly in her hand. It hurt to grip it, yet she did so anyway. She rose up onto her knees and used it like an axe upon the timber joist. Her blows were feeble, yet even the harder interior wood was so rotten that it fell away in lumps. The timber creaked and groaned beneath her assault, indignant at being so rudely woken from its long slumber. It bowed a little further in its middle too, releasing a flurry of flakes that fell upon her hair and shoulders, allowing the great stone to lurch ever so slightly above her head.

Greta was almost upon her, however. Anna retreated back

beneath the dragon stone to the landing's far wall, where she turned and sat with her back to it, still holding her marble fragment, though as a weapon rather than a tool. Now Greta arrived, her lips clamped and her expression ugly not just with malign purpose, but with bitterness too. Bitterness at Anna, sure, for working out the truth and so upending her plans; but also bitterness at the world in general for bringing her to this point. At the deprivations and cruelties of her childhood, and how she'd only been rescued from them by someone else's grandfather. At having had to bow and scrape to her younger brother for all these years, and at having had to settle for Gatehouse Cottage rather than the Manor. Bitterness at being unloved and unmarried and childless. Bitterness that all her scheming had come to nothing, after all.

They gazed at each other across the landing, each lit by the other's beam. Neither spoke. There was nothing to be said. Greta got down onto her hands and knees then ducked her head beneath the dragon stone, advancing warily until she had Anna almost within reach of her sword. There wasn't enough room to swing it over her head or even from either side. She'd need to spit her with it instead. Anna watched her eyes as she sought out her points of greatest vulnerability, finally settling on her throat. She drew it back in both hands then stabbed it forwards. But her assault was so well telegraphed that Anna parried it easily, deflecting it past her cheek to ping the wall behind.

Greta scowled. She took a moment to recover her balance then tried once more, aiming for the larger target of Anna's chest. But again Anna swept the blade aside and even managed a counterattack of her own, swinging her marble fragment at Greta's face. Her effort was even more laboured than Greta's, and easily evaded, yet it still carried enough menace that Greta retreated beneath the dragon stone to think again.

Anna rested back against the wall. The coughs kept coming, she couldn't stop them. Her mouth and throat filled with the ugly warm taste of blood, while fat droplets spattered her hand and trousers and the ground around her. Exhaustion turned to resignation. There was only one way this could end. But she could still make Greta work for it. Inflict some proper damage on her face, and Elias would see it. He'd see it and know the truth and then he wouldn't rest until he'd found this place, and her with it. Then he'd make Greta pay, by god he would. That certainty gave her heart. The certainty that he cared for her and would do right by her. Yet at the same time it dismayed her terribly to know how grieved he'd be. She wished there was some way to tell him it was alright.

Greta began another slow advance, determined to finish it. Her knees came shuffling across the dusty stone floor. But then she stopped and looked anxiously up and around. Now Anna heard it too, a low creaking as the nearer of the two timbers finally buckled beneath its burden. It happened slowly at first, scattering gentle flakes as it bowed further and further in its middle. But then, with a thunderous splintering noise, it burst like a breadstick being snapped in two, the separate pieces falling onto the landing behind Greta before clattering down the staircase and coming to a stop.

Its first line of support now gone, the great stone lurched in its cup before coming to rest a moment later upon the second joist. For a moment or two, it looked as though that second joist was going to hold. But it was being asked too much. With a terrible unearthly groan, it too split and fell away, releasing the dragon stone to tip forwards, like a drawbridge being lowered over a moat, using the wall behind Anna as its fulcrum or pivot point, and pressing the marble blocks on either side ever further outwards as it came.

Greta stared up in horror as it descended slowly upon her. She had only a moment or two to make her escape, but she wasted those two moments in indecision, torn between hatred for Anna and her urge to save herself. And then it was too late, for the dragon stone completed its collapse in a rush, catching her still beneath it as she finally turned to flee, bringing its full weight down upon her back. There was a horrible brief crunching of bone and a last truncated scream as the air was squeezed from her lungs and her face was crushed into the landing floor. Then there was only silence.

As for Anna, she twisted around to lie on her side against the end wall, which had mercifully stayed somewhat intact, creating a small hollow between it, the dragon stone and the floor, sparing her Greta's awful fate. But perhaps that fate would have been kinder, or at least quicker, for her small refuge now began to fill with dislodged soil, diminishing her already scarce supply of air. *At least this way we'll be found for sure*, she thought. *At least people will know. Elias will know.* She thought of him now, she couldn't help herself. The pain he'd feel. She could almost hear, indeed, the anguish that would be in his voice when he realised what had happened. *Anna!* he'd cry. *Anna!* Then she realised, to her bewilderment, that it wasn't her imagination at work, but rather that he was actually nearby and shouting out her name. He was shouting out her name and calling for help and for an ambulance. *You idiot*, she thought, with fond amusement, *they'll never be able to hear you, not from all the way up here.* Then she realised he was probably on his phone. Yes. That made more sense. He was on his phone, calling for help.

Pleased with herself for working it out, she closed her eyes for what she thought was a moment, only to open them again to find that she'd been dragged somehow out of her stone tomb, and that Elias was kneeling bare-chested beside her, his face and torso drenched with sweat and covered in dirt. The spade from the summerhouse was lying discarded on the ground beside him, and he was pressing a folded white T-shirt against her side in an effort to staunch her bleeding, while pleading with her to fight. He looked so panicky and distressed that she felt an intense hot pang of tenderness for him. *It's okay*, she tried to tell him. *Everything's going to work out fine.* But she was too spent to find the words, so she reached out to touch his hand instead, to cover it weakly with her own. Then, resting her cheek against the dewy cool grass, she closed her eyes and let herself slip back into the comfort of her sleep.

EPILOGUE

R aoul Flood waited until they'd left Martlesham police station and were halfway across the car park before breaking his silence. 'Bastards,' he scowled. 'Absolute bloody bastards. They've known for hours it wasn't me.'

'I'm sure it wasn't personal,' said Imogen. 'They have procedures to follow, that's all.'

'Procedures!'

'Yes. Procedures.' They reached the car. He held out his hand for the keys, but it was trembling so violently that Imogen shook her head. 'Not while you're this angry,' she told him.

'Don't I have a right to be?'

'Yes, you do. But you're still too angry to drive.'

He shook his head but maybe he realised she was right, for he went around the passenger side without further protest, then sat there with his arms folded, glaring sulkily out of the window, as if the landscape too had disappointed him. Imogen let him stew while she navigated the Ipswich bypass, but they had too much to talk about to let it go on forever; so, once they'd reached their roundabout, and had taken the London road, she reached over to tap him on his arm. 'You thought it was me, didn't you?' she said, as mildly as she could. 'All this time, you thought it was me who'd pushed Charlotte off that cliff.'

'No.'

'It's okay. Just tell me.'

He gave a grimace. 'What was I supposed to think? I come

back from the pub and you're not downstairs or in our room. Then you come in five minutes later looking guilty as sin and saying you'd been in the bathroom. For fuck's sake! I'd just walked past that bathroom. Its door had been wide open and its lights were off. How was I to know that you were in that arsehole's room, doing god knows what. I thought you despised him.'

'I did despise him. We watched a show together, that was all.'

'Then why not tell me?'

'Because you get jealous, you know you do. I didn't want you doing anything stupid.' He folded his arms again. He glared back out the window. She reached across once more, this time to give his arm a squeeze. 'That nice policewoman said that you didn't tell them about me not being there, not even after they accused you of killing Charlotte yourself. You could have pointed them at me, but you didn't.'

'Of course not,' he said grudgingly. 'You're my wife. Even though *you* pointed them at *me*.'

'That's not true. I told Elias categorically that it wasn't you. But I also told him it couldn't have been Cameron either. Which it couldn't have been. And if it wasn't Cameron, then his confession was bullshit and it wasn't suicide. And how could I keep *that* to myself?'

'Even so,' he said, not ready to give up his resentment quite yet.

She gave it another minute before speaking again. 'All this time,' she said, with a rueful shake of her head. 'Each of us thinking it might have been the other. No wonder, eh?'

'No wonder what?'

'Don't give me that. You know exactly what I mean. No wonder our marriage is so shit. How is any relationship supposed to survive that?'

He gave a snort of laughter. 'Sure! That was the problem.'

'What else do you think it was?'

'Me not being the man you thought I was.'

'What?' She turned to him in genuine bafflement. 'What are

you talking about?'

'Come on, Immy. It's okay. You married a rugby international who couldn't play rugby any more. I mean I don't blame you...'

'I married the man I fell in love with,' she told him, with genuine anger. 'If you think that had anything to do with rugby... I mean I knew you played a bit when we started going out, but I honestly never believed you'd make a career out of it. You were twenty-two years old, and still playing for the seconds.'

'It takes time,' he protested.

'I know that now. But I didn't then.'

'It's not like football or cricket,' he persisted, though his point was already won. 'Especially in the forwards. You've got to grow into your body.'

'I know! I'm just saying, I fell for you long before you even got a regular start for your club, let alone got called up by England. I'd have been just as happy if you never had.'

'You didn't want me to succeed?'

'Stop twisting everything, Raoul. Of course I did. I was so proud when England called you up. So proud and so happy. But that was because I knew it was what you wanted. I wanted it *for* you. But it was never what I wanted *from* you.'

'Then what did you want from me?'

'You, of course. For better or for worse. For richer or for poorer.'

He gave a grunt. 'It'll be for poorer now, that's for sure. They only ever kept me on because of the Brook account. I'm certain to lose that now. They'll dump me the moment it's gone.'

'Good,' she said.

'Good?'

'That job makes you miserable. This will be your chance to find something else. Something you'll be good at. Something you'll enjoy. How about teaching? You came alive last year when you were coaching those kids. Everyone said how great at it you were.'

'It was kind of fun,' he admitted.

'That's it, then. Become a teacher. A sport's coach. A physio.

Whatever.'

'What if I'm no good?'

'You will be. Trust me. You'll be terrific.'

'And you wouldn't mind? Not having the same money coming in?'

That made her laugh out loud. 'I'm a hospice nurse, for god's sake! Which do you think I'd prefer? A happy modest home or a wealthy unhappy one?'

He fell silent again, this time in thought. 'Are you serious about this?'

'I'd be drinking champagne for a month.' Then she frowned and added: 'Or perhaps Prosecco, all things considered.'

He grinned and sat up, looking happier already. Younger, even. 'Okay, then. I'll do it. I'll hand in my notice in the morning.'

'No,' she said firmly. 'Tell them you've lost the Brook account and make the bastards fire you. The least they owe you for all the years of misery is a half-decent pay-off.'

THREE DAYS LATER

Anna woke to find Elias sitting beside her, clasping her hand between both his own. For a moment, in her confusion, she thought that only a few seconds had passed since his rescue of her on Dragon Stone Hill, but then she realised she was outside no longer, but rather in bed – a hospital bed at that – no, an ICU bed – with curtains around her to screen her from her neighbours, and attached to tubes and drips and monitors and other strange devices.

She allowed herself a few moments to study him. He was wearing a plain white T-shirt, making her wonder if it was the same one he'd pressed against her side to staunch her loss of blood. He'd taken off his glove, so that she could see the livid scarring on his hand. And his face was drawn and bowed, while his eyes were closed, in weariness or in prayer. 'You're here,' she said finally, her voice barely a whisper.

He lifted his head and gave a smile of such brilliant happiness that she found herself taken aback. She hadn't realised that she had it in her to provoke quite so intense a reaction. 'Of course,' he said, keeping his own voice low too. 'Though I had to tell them you were my fiancée before they'd let me in.'

'And they believed you?'

'That awful piece of costume jewellery on your ring finger,' he told her ruefully. 'Now they all think I'm the cheapest sod on god's earth.'

She laughed at that, though not for long. The pain in her side was too sharp. But at least it helped stir her. 'I guess you'll just have to get me a better one, then, won't you?' she joked.

'I guess I will,' he said.

She looked to her left and right then down at the foot of her hospital bed, before raising an eyebrow to ask the question – for though she had some dim memory of being talked at by a doctor, she couldn't for the life of her remember what he'd said.

'You're going to be fine,' Elias assured her, getting straight to the nub, pressing her hand between his own for extra comfort. 'You lost consciousness and a very great deal of blood. But the air ambulance got to you in time, thank god. They were good. They were very, very good.' He closed his eyes as he relived it. 'You were barely breathing by then. I couldn't find your pulse. I was doing everything I could, but... Anyway, they had to intubate you and give you plasma and god knows what else. They loaded you onto their helicopter and brought you here. They had a team already waiting. They took you straight into theatre and opened you up to take a look inside and repair what needed repairing. No major organs damaged, thank the gods, except for a nick on your small bowel which had them worried about sepsis for a while. But they've been pumping you full of antibiotics and they're monitoring you very closely, as you can see, and they seem confident you're clear of that too, though they're going to keep you here a little bit longer, just in case. Other than that, you had fractures to your seventh and eighth ribs, which they say should heal by themselves in another fortnight or two, as well as to your left forearm and right wrist. Those are in plaster, in case you couldn't tell, and will take a bit longer to set. You'll also be doing some rehab for a fair while after that, but then they say you'll be as good as new, save for a nice bit of scar tissue.'

'See,' she murmured. 'I told you it would be alright.'

'You did?'

'Maybe not out loud. But I thought it.'

She closed her eyes for a moment then opened them again to find that more time had passed, for her curtains had been drawn back and Elias was no longer sitting beside her but rather was standing outside the ICU door instead, talking urgently but in a low voice to a middle-aged woman in a white coat who was blocking his re-entry. The woman noticed she was awake. She shut the door firmly on Elias then came over to the bed.

'Elias,' Anna told her.

'You're not to—'

'Elias,' she said.

He sat back down beside her. She could see him wondering whether he was allowed to take her hand again or not. It was different when she was asleep from when she was already awake. But she waggled her fingers until he smiled and took her hand between his own once more. 'Tell me everything,' she said.

'Everything?'

'The important stuff.'

'Okay. Then I guess you'll have gathered by now that Greta was the baddie. Her stabbing you with that sword was probably the giveaway, if you hadn't got there already. We're still piecing it together, but they've found Charlotte's phone beneath Greta's floorboards, which she either kept as a trophy or because she was unsure how to dispose of it safely, in case there was anything incriminating on it. That puts it beyond doubt that she really did kill her, likely out of fear for her home or her inheritance. Then she murdered poor Hector for the same reason, before he could donate the place to the nation. They found keys to the Manor's wood-hatch and cellar door along with Charlotte's phone, so it looks like that's how she got in. We reckon Cameron Wolfe realised this somehow and tried to blackmail her. So he had to go too.'

'Yes,' said Anna.

'That's pretty much it. All the others have already left. They scattered the first moment they could. Though, to be fair, Imogen has called several times to ask after you. She and Raoul want to come say hi.'

'They want to come here?' said Anna bleakly.

'I've put them off, don't worry. But they feel indebted to you,

I think. Five years they've been married, each of them fearing that the other had murdered Charlotte. Can you imagine? Now all that weight is gone, thanks to you. They sound happy. Happy and in love.'

'I'm glad. But don't let them come.'

'I won't. Bryony Mackay called too. She sends her best wishes, but she said nothing about coming to visit.'

'Good.'

'And not a peep of any kind from either Hyde-Smith or Smallbone.'

'Even better.'

'Yeah, but still.' He shook his head. 'Why are we men all such dicks?'

'You're not *all* dicks,' Anna assured him. 'Hector Brook was what a man should be. And I'm sure there's another one somewhere. It'll come to me in a moment.' She gave his hand a squeeze, to make quite sure he knew she was joking. 'What about the site? That's what matters.'

'Yeah. The story's gone national, as you'd expect. They've sealed it up and assigned some serious manpower to guard it, which is good. But now the British Museum and the National Trust and all the other usual suspects are trying to plant their flags in it. Heaven alone knows who'll win.'

'And you?'

'Me?'

'Don't you have a job to get back to?'

'Oh, god. Don't worry about that. My boss is Colin Vaughn, remember? The one you helped spring from jail during that King John business. He says I'm to take as long as I like. My clients have all been great too. They've been calling up to wish us both well. Though I suspect that's because one of the nurses here must have blabbed, as the journos are all reporting that bit about us being engaged. And I can't exactly correct them, can I, or they'll kick me out.'

'You poor thing,' said Anna, giving his hand another squeeze. 'Trapped by your own big mouth. It's like the perfect set up for a romcom, isn't it? Just as well for you I don't have a crazy dad with a shotgun to make you see it through.'

'Yeah,' said Elias, with a wry smile. 'Just as well.'

AUTHOR'S NOTE

One of the more enjoyable yet challenging parts of my job is coming up with new ideas for books. There just aren't enough lost treasures with genuine historic mysteries attached to them to go around. And many of those that initially seem promising fall apart on closer inspection, for I sincerely try to hew as closely as possible to real history, so that – even if my readers don't much enjoy my books – they'll at least feel that they've learned something along the way.

When the idea behind this book was first suggested to me, I confess I was pretty sceptical. It seemed far too unlikely, what with Beowulf being a fictional hero; and, anyway, wouldn't he be somewhere in Scandinavia, not Suffolk? But the more I looked into it, the more plausible and intriguing I found it.

The parallels between Grendel and Caliban have long been known, as too the possibility that they were each separately inspired by tales of indigenous populations displaced by invading forces. Equally well known are the similarities between Grendel's mother and Germanic earth and fertility goddesses, particularly Freya. Some academics even believe that the legends of Fimbulvetr and Ragnarök were originally inspired by the long volcanic winter and plague that followed eruptions in Iceland or North America from 536 CE onwards, and which hit Scandinavia more brutally than elsewhere. As far as I know, however, the association between Beowulf's dragon and Æthelfrith is my own.

For avoidance of any doubt, there is no dragon stone, nor any Dragon Stone Hill. The Dragon Stone Hill Estate is very, very loosely based on Kyson Hill, which does exist – as too do Kingston Fields. Both are almost directly across the River Deben from Sutton Hoo. And there have been rumours for a while of a great new Anglo-Saxon funeral ship buried somewhere in their vicinity.

But then, as I say in the book, there are always rumours.

ABOUT THE AUTHOR

Will Adams

Will Adams pursued multiple careers over the years before deciding to concentrate on his lifelong dream of writing fiction. His books have been translated into over twenty languages and have appeared on bestseller lists around the world.

Printed in Dunstable, United Kingdom